DANA SCHWARTZ is a television writer and the creator of the number-one-charting history podcast *Noble Blood*. As a journalist and critic, Schwartz has written for *Entertainment Weekly*, *Marie Claire*, *Glamour*, *GQ*, *Cosmopolitan*, *Vanity Fair*, and other publications. She lives in Los Angeles with her fiancé and their cats, Eddie and Beetlejuice. Her books include *Choose Your Own Disaster* and *The White Man's Guide to White Male Writers of the Western Canon*.

also by
dana schwartz

*The White Man's Guide to
White Male Writers of the Western Canon*

Choose Your Own Disaster

And We're Off

anatomy

a love story

dana schwartz

PIATKUS

PIATKUS

First published in the US in 2022 by Wednesday Books,
an imprint of St. Martin's Publishing Group
First published in Great Britain in 2022 by Piatkus
This paperback edition published in 2022 by Piatkus

1 3 5 7 9 10 8 6 4 2

A CIP catalogue record for this book
is available from the British Library.

ISBN 978-0-349-43337-0

Printed and bound in Great Britain by
Clays Ltd, Elcograf S.p.A.

Papers used by Piatkus are from well-managed forests
and other responsible sources.

Piatkus
An imprint of
Little, Brown Book Group
Carmelite House
50 Victoria Embankment
London EC4Y 0DZ

An Hachette UK Company
www.hachette.co.uk

www.littlebrown.co.uk

To Jan,
who has my heart

To examine the causes of life,
we must first have recourse to death.

—MARY WOLLSTONECRAFT SHELLEY,
FRANKENSTEIN

anatomy

a love story

prologue

HURRY UP!"

"I'm digging as fast as I can, Davey."

"Well, dig faster."

The night was nearly moonless, so Davey, standing on the damp grass, wasn't able to see Munro roll his eyes down in the grave he was in the process of digging up. It was taking longer than normal—the wooden spade Munro had managed to steal from behind the inn down on Farbanks was smaller than the metal one he'd started off with tonight. But it was also quieter, that was the important thing. Ever since Thornhill Kirkyard had hired a guard to watch over the graves, keeping quiet was essential. Already, three of their friends had been picked up by the guard and were unable to pay their fines. Davey hadn't seen them on the streets since.

Something was wrong. Davey couldn't quite put his finger on it, but something seemed strange tonight. Maybe it was the air. The grease smoke hovering low in Edinburgh's Old

Town was always dense, heavy with the smell of cooking oil and tobacco and the noxious combination of human waste and filth that had sent the well-to-do into the fine new buildings down the hill and on the other side of Princes Street Gardens. Tonight was windless.

Davey didn't mention it to Munro, the strange feeling he had. Munro would only have laughed at him. *You're supposed to be a lookout for night men, not strange feelings,* Munro would say.

In the distance, Davey could make out a candle burning in the window of the rectory behind the church. The priest was awake. Could he see movement this far into the kirkyard in the darkness? Most likely not, but what if he decided to come out for an evening stroll?

"Can't you go *any* faster?" Davey whispered.

In answer came the unmistakable sound of wood hitting wood. Munro had reached the coffin. Both boys held their breath for the next part: Munro lifted the spade high as he could and brought it down hard. Davey winced at the crack of the lid breaking. They waited—for a shout, for dogs barking—but nothing stirred.

"Throw me the rope," Munro called up. Davey did as he was told, and within a few moments, Munro had expertly tied the rope around the dead body's neck. "Now pull."

While Davey tugged the rope, Munro, still in the grave, helped to guide the body out of the small hole in the coffin and back toward the surface world, a strange reverse birth for a body past death. Munro successfully removed the body's shoes as it left its coffin, but it was up to Davey to strip off the rest of its clothes and throw them back in the grave. Stealing a body was against the law, but if they actually took any property from the grave, that would make it a felony.

The body was a she, just as Jeanette had told them. Jeanette worked as a spy for whichever resurrection man paid her the best that week, sneaking around funerals, standing just close enough to make sure that whoever was being buried hadn't been given an expensive stone slab atop the coffin to prevent the very crime they were currently committing.

"No mortsafe and no family," Jeanette had said when she showed up at the door to Munro's flat in Fleshmarket Close, scratching her neck and grinning up at him from beneath her curtain of copper hair. Jeanette couldn't be more than fourteen, but she was already missing more than a few teeth. "Or 'tleast not much family, anyways. Coffin looked cheap too. Pine or sum'thing like it."

"Weren't pregnant, were she?" Munro had asked hopefully, raising his eyebrows. Doctors were so keen to dissect the bodies of pregnant women that they were willing to pay double. Jeanette shook her head and extended her hand for payment. As soon as darkness fell, Munro and Davey set out with their wheelbarrow and spades and rope.

Davey averted his eyes as he peeled off the body's flimsy gray dress. Even in the darkness, he could feel himself blushing. He had never undressed a live woman before, but he'd lost count of the number of times he'd taken the clothing off a woman the day after she was put in the ground. He looked down at the stone half-hidden by dirt and darkness: PENELOPE HARKNESS. *Thank you for the eight guineas, Penelope Harkness,* he thought.

"Throw it here," Munro said from below. Davey tossed him the dress. As soon as the woman's clothes were back in her empty coffin, Munro pulled himself out of the hole and onto the wet grass. "A'ight," he said, clapping the dirt from his hands. "Let's fill it back in and be done with it now." Munro didn't say it, but he felt something strange, too, an odd thinness in the still air that made it harder to catch his breath. The candle in the rectory window had gone out.

"You don't believe she died of the fever, do you?" Davey whispered. The woman's skin wasn't pocked or bloody, but the rumors these days were impossible to ignore. If the Roman fever really was back in Edinburgh . . .

"Course not," Munro said with certainty. "Don't be daft."

Davey exhaled and smiled weakly in the dark. Munro always knew how to make him feel better, to cast away the fears that crept into his brain like rodents in the walls.

Silently, the boys finished their task. The grave was as well covered with soil and weeds as it had been that morning, and the body, stiff with rigor mortis, was in their wheelbarrow, covered by a gray cloak.

Something was moving at the edge of the cemetery, along the low stone wall that ran the kirkyard's entire east side. Davey and Munro both saw it, and they whipped their heads around to follow its motion, but as soon as their eyes adjusted in the darkness, it was gone.

"Just a dog," Munro said more confidently than he felt. "Come on. The doctor likes us out back before dawn."

Davey pushed the cart, and Munro walked alongside him, gripping the handle of his spade tighter than usual. They had almost made it out of the cemetery when three men in cloaks stepped in their path.

"Hello," the first man said. He was the tallest of the three, and looked even taller because he wore a stovepipe hat.

"Lovely evening," said the second, a bald man, shorter than the others.

"Perfect for a stroll," said the third, whose yellow grin was visible behind his mustache even in the darkness.

They weren't night watchmen, Davey saw. Maybe they were fellow resurrection men.

Munro clearly had the same idea. "Out of our way. She's ours, get yer own doornail," he said, stepping in front of Davey and their wheelbarrow. His voice shook only a little.

Davey looked down and saw the gentlemen were all wearing fine leather shoes. No resurrection man wore shoes like that.

The three men laughed together in near unison. "You're quite right," said the short man. "And, of course, we wouldn't dream of calling the night watchmen." He took a step closer, and Davey saw a length of rope under the sleeve of his cloak.

The next moment was impossibly quick: the three men advanced, and Munro leapt around them and ran at full tilt up the path and toward the city. "Davey!" he shouted, "Davey, run!"

But Davey was frozen, still behind the wheelbarrow, forced to hesitate at that moment by the choice of whether to abandon Penelope Harkness while he watched Munro sprint into a close and disappear. By the time his feet allowed him to follow his friend, it was too late.

"Gotcha," said the tall man in the hat as he wrapped his meaty hand around Davey's wrist. "Now, this won't hurt a bit." The man took a blade from his pocket.

Davey struggled against his grip, but no matter how he tugged or twisted, he was unable to pull away.

The man with the blade ran it delicately along Davey's

forearm, revealing a trail of crimson blood that looked almost black in the darkness.

Davey was too frightened to scream. He watched in silence, with unblinking panicked eyes, as the bald man pulled out a vial filled with something purple and viscous. The man uncorked the vial and extended his arm.

The man with the hat shook his knife over the vial until a single drop of Davey's blood fell into liquid within. The liquid became dark and then changed color to a brilliant, glowing golden yellow. It illuminated the faces of the three men, who were all smiling now.

"Lovely," the one with the mustache said.

THE NEXT DAY, WHILE OUT ON his morning constitutional, the priest found an abandoned wheelbarrow containing the stiff body of a woman he had buried the day before. He shook his head. Resurrection men in this city were becoming bolder—and more dangerous. What was Edinburgh coming to?

From <u>Dr. Beecham's Treatise on Anatomy:</u>
<u>or, The Prevention and Cure of Modern Diseases</u>
(17th Edition, 1791) by Dr. William R. Beecham:

Any physician who wishes to effectively treat either disease or any variety of common household injury must first understand anatomy. An understanding of the human body and all of its component parts is elemental to our profession.

In this treatise, I will outline the fundamentals of anatomy I have discovered in my decades of study alongside illustrations of my own design. However, illustrations are no replacement for the active, first-hand discovery of anatomy through dissection, and no prospective physician will ever hope to be a service to our profession without first effectuating at least a dozen bodies and studying their component parts.

Though some of my fellow professionals in Edinburgh operate by nefarious measures, engaging the illegal services of so-called resurrection men stealing the bodies of innocents, subjects provided to my students at my anatomical school in Edinburgh are always the unfortunate men and women who suffer the hangman's noose, whom British law dictates are inclined to provide one last service to their fellow countrymen as final penance.

1

THE FROG WAS DEAD, THERE WAS no doubt about that. It had been dead already when Hazel Sinnett found it. She was taking her daily stroll after break-fast, and the frog had just been there, lying on the garden path, on its back as though it had been trying to sunbathe.

Hazel couldn't believe her luck. A frog, just lying there. An offering. A sign from the heavens. The sky was heavy with gray clouds threatening a rain that hadn't arrived yet. In other words: the weather was perfect. But the conditions wouldn't last long. As soon as the rain started to fall, her ex-periment would be ruined.

From behind the azalea bushes, Hazel looked around to see if anyone was watching her (her mother wasn't looking out her bedroom window on the second floor, was she?) be-fore she knelt down and casually wrapped the frog in her handkerchief to tuck into the waistband of her petticoat.

The clouds were approaching. Time was limited, and so Hazel cut her walk short and turned around to head swiftly back to Hawthornden Castle. She would go in the back way, so no one would bother her and she would be able slip up to her bedroom immediately.

The kitchen was hot when Hazel entered in a rush, with great clouds of steam burping from the iron pot on the fire and the thick smell of onions clinging to every surface. An abandoned onion lay half chopped on a board. The onion, the board, and a dropped knife nearby on the floor were splattered with blood. Hazel's eyes followed the trail of red to see Cook sitting on a stool in the corner of the kitchen by the fire, cradling a hand and rocking back and forth, cooing to herself.

"Oh!" Cook cried when she saw Hazel. Her red face was damp with tears and redder than usual. Cook wiped at her eyes and stood, trying to smooth her skirts. "Miss, didn't expect you down here. Just—resting my aching legs." Cook attempted to hide her hand behind her apron.

"Oh, Cook. You're bleeding!" Hazel reached out to coax Cook's injured hand forth. She gave half a thought to the frog squelching in her petticoat and the looming rainstorm, but only for a moment. She had to focus on the case at hand. "Here, let me."

Cook winced. The cut was deep, along the meaty palm of the base of her well-callused hand.

Hazel wiped her own hands on her skirts then looked up to give Cook a small, comforting smile. "This isn't going to be bad at all. You'll be right as rain before supper. You, there"—Hazel called to a scullery maid—"Susan, is it? Will you fetch me a sewing needle?" The mousy maid nodded and scampered off.

Hazel took the kitchen basin over to Cook and had her wash her injured hand and wipe it clean on a dishrag. As the blood and soot fell away, the deep cut came into clear focus. "Now, that's not so scary once the blood is washed away," Hazel said.

Susan returned with the needle. Hazel held it in the fire until it turned black, and then she lifted her own skirt and pulled a long silk thread from her chemise.

Cook gave a small cry. "Your fine things, miss!"

"Oh, pishposh. It's nothing, Cook, truly. Now, I'm afraid this might sting just a bit. Are you all right?" Cook nodded. Working as quickly as she could, Hazel slid the needle into Cook's split palm and began to sew up the cut tight with sutures. The color drained from Cook's face, and she clenched her eyes.

"Almost there—nearly done now—aaaaand there," Hazel said, tying the silk into a neat knot. She tore the thread with her teeth. She couldn't help but smile while examining her work: tiny, neat, even stitches that finally put her childhood of mind-numbingly boring embroidery practice to good use. Hazel lifted her skirts again—carefully, so as not to disturb the frog—and tore a thick ribbon of fabric from her chemise before Cook could object or cry out in shock at further damage to it. Hazel wrapped the fabric tightly around the newly stitched hand. "Now, then: remove the bandage tonight and wash the wound, if you would. I'll be by tomorrow with a poultice for you. And be careful with the knife, Cook."

Cook's eyes were still wet, but she smiled up at Hazel. "Thank you, miss."

Hazel made it up to her bedroom without any other disturbances, and she raced out onto her balcony. The sky was still gray. Rain hadn't fallen yet. Hazel exhaled and pulled the frog in its handkerchief from her skirts. She unfurled it and let it flop with a wet squelch onto the stone banister.

The parts of Hawthornden that Hazel liked best were the library—with its mottled green wallpaper and leather books and fireplace lit every afternoon—and the balcony off her bedroom, from which she could look into the tree-lined creek below and see only nature for miles. Her bedroom was on the castle's south facade; she couldn't see the smoke rising from the heart of Edinburgh, just an hour's ride to the north, and so here, on the balcony, she could pretend she was alone in the world, an explorer standing at the precipice of the sum of human knowledge, and building up the courage to take a single step forward.

Hawthornden Castle was built on a cliffside, with ivy-covered stone walls that loomed over untamed Scottish woods and a thin stream that ran farther than Hazel had ever been able to follow. Her family had lived there for at least a hundred years on her father's side. It had Sinnett history in its walls, in the char and grass and moss that clung to the ancient stones.

A handful of kitchen fires throughout the 1700s meant that most of the castle had been rebuilt on top of itself, brick atop stone. The only remnants of the castle's original structure were the gates, at the front of the drive, and a cold stone dungeon built into the side of the hill, which had never been used in living memory—except as a threat when Mrs. Herberts caught Percy stealing pudding before tea, or when the footman, Charles, had promised to stay locked inside for a whole day on a dare but lasted no more than an hour.

Most of the time, it felt to Hazel as if she lived at Hawthornden by herself. Percy was usually outside playing, or at lessons. Her mother, still dressed in mourning, rarely left her bedroom, gliding along between the walls like a ghost of death in black. Sometimes it was lonely, but usually Hazel felt grateful for the solitude. Especially when she wanted to experiment.

The dead frog was small, and muddy brown. Its thin limbs, which had flopped in her palms like a loose doll when she plucked it from the footpath, were now stiff and unpleasantly tacky. But the frog was dead, and there was a storm in the air—it was perfect. Every piece was in place.

From behind a small rock on the balcony, Hazel pulled out the fireplace poker and the kitchen fork she had squirreled away weeks ago, waiting for this exact situation to present itself. Bernard had been infuriatingly vague about the type of metal the magician-scientist in Switzerland had used ("Was it brass? Just tell me, Bernard, what *color* was it?" "I told you, I don't remember!"), and so Hazel just decided to make do with the metal objects that seemed easy enough to pluck from the household without anyone noticing. The fireplace poker was from her father's study, and even the servants didn't bother going in that room anymore in the months since her father and his regiment had been posted on Saint Helena.

A distant groan of thunder echoed through the valley below. It was time. She would breach the world between life and death, using electricity to reanimate flesh. What were miracles, but science that man didn't yet understand? And didn't that make it all the more miraculous that the secrets of the universe were out there, codes one might decipher if smart enough, tenacious enough?

Hazel delicately set the poker down on one side of the frog and then, with an air of solemn reverence, she slowly lowered the kitchen fork down to the other side.

Nothing happened.

She moved the fork and the poker closer to the frog, and then, impatiently, set them touching the frog's skin. Was she supposed to—? No, no, Bernard would have mentioned if the convict's head had been *impaled* on a spike. When he came back from his grand tour, she had been breathless with questions about the demonstration he mentioned only in passing in his letter from Switzerland, a demonstration held by the son of the great scientist Galvini. Using electricity, the second Galvini had made frog legs dance and the severed head of a convict blink as if it were alive once again.

"It was frightening, really," Bernard had said, bringing a cup of tea to his lips and beckoning for the servant to bring another ginger biscuit. "But marvelous, though, in its own strange way, don't you think?"

Hazel did. Though Bernard had refused to talk about it any further ("Why must you be so *morbid,* Cousin!"), Hazel found she could conjure up the details of the scene in her mind as easily as if she had been there herself—the man in a French-style jacket, standing onstage in a tiny, wood-lined theater, the red velvet curtains behind him heavy with dust. Hazel could see the string of frogs' legs jerking up and down, dancing like cancan girls, before Galvini whipped the cloth off the main attraction: the head of a man who had been hanged. In Hazel's imagination, his neck was cut low enough to show the purplish bruises where the rope had cut in.

We men fear death, Hazel could imagine Galvini saying in a thick Italian accent. *Death! Gruesome and terrible! Inevitable and senseless! We dance towards her as we might a beautiful woman* (Italians loved to talk about beautiful women) *and Death waltzes back towards us, beckoning, always beckoning.*

Once the veil is pierced, we never return. But it is a new century, my friends.

Here, Hazel imagined him holding a metal rod aloft like Hamlet with a skull, then raising his second rod and letting the lightning dance back and forth between them as the audience cooed. *And mankind will conquer the laws of nature!*

The audience gasped as the stage lights crackled with light, and gray gunpowder smoke popped for dramatic effect, and the convict's head came alive.

Bernard described it in a letter that Hazel had read so many times she had memorized every line: the way the convict's head had jerked when the rods were lowered to its temples, how its eyelids had scrolled open. For a moment, it might have been conscious again, blinking at the scene in front of it—the crowd of men and their wives in their best gloves and hats—and actually *seeing* them. Bernard hadn't mentioned the head's mouth opening, but Hazel found herself imagining a black tongue lolling, as if the head were bored of being trotted out for yet another performance, yet another matinee for yet another crowd.

When the performance was finished, Galvini would have bowed to incredulous applause, and then all the gentlemen would return to their châteaus and villas to amuse their hosts with their description of the evening over port wine.

It was like sorcery, Bernard had written. *Although I'd never imagine a sorcerer to be wearing such ill-fitting trousers.* Bernard had also mentioned in the letter that he purchased a hunting cape for four hundred francs and that he had seen Prince Friedrich von Hohenzollern wearing the same one.

But here she was, electricity heavy in the sky, metal on

either side of the frog, and unlike Galvini's subjects, Hazel's remained insipidly, maddeningly, unmistakably inert. Hazel glanced behind her. Her bedroom was empty—her maid, Iona, always finished tidying before breakfast was over. Hazel could hear the tinkling notes of the pianoforte trilling from the open window in the music room, where Percy was having a lesson. Mrs. Herberts was preparing lunch to take up to Hazel's mother, in her bedroom, as usual; she'd eat at her desk opposite a looking glass draped in gauzy black cloth.

Hazel held her breath and lifted the fire poker once more. There was one thing she hadn't tried yet, but—Hazel was suddenly dizzy, her mind feeling light, as if it were being pulled to the top of her skull by a string. Her fingers shook. Before she let her body stop itself, she plunged the poker through the frog's back and out through its stomach. The flesh was disconcertingly easy to pierce, the poker slipping through the brown skin easily to emerge wet, glistening in an indeterminate viscus.

"I'm sorry," Hazel said aloud, and then immediately felt foolish. It was just a frog. It was just a *dead* frog. If she was going to become a surgeon, she would need to get acclimated to this sort of thing sooner or later. As if to prove her own fortitude to herself, she wriggled the poker through the frog a little farther. "There," she murmured. "Serves you right."

"Serves who right?" It was Percy, standing behind her, his eyes sleepy and hair matted, wearing only one stocking. In her excitement, she hadn't noticed the pianoforte stop.

Though Percy was seven years old, their mother still had him dressed like a boy half that age, in a cotton shirt lined with blue piping and open at the collar. Lady Sinnett doted on him incessantly, as if he were a priceless and incredibly fragile piece of crystal. He was spoiled and selfish, but Hazel couldn't find it in herself to be annoyed with him, because the truth was, she felt sorry for him. Hazel enjoyed a rare freedom from their mother smothering him with all her attention, while Percy was hardly allowed to leave the house lest he, heaven forbid, scrape his knee on the garden path.

"It's nothing," Hazel said, turning and hiding the frog behind her skirts. "Run along now. Shouldn't you be at your lesson?"

"Master Poglia let me go early for being such a good boy," he said, grinning and showing off a row of small, sharp teeth. Hazel spotted one missing on the top. Percy rocked back and forth on his feet. "Play with me. Mummy says you have to do whatever I say."

"Does she now." The sky was beginning to clear, a sliver of blue visible on the far horizon. If this was going to work, it needed to be soon. It needed to be while electricity was still in the air. "Why don't you ask Mummy to play with you then?"

"Mummy is *bo-ring*," Percy sang, hopping on one foot and then the other. He shook his blond curls from his eyes. "If I go into Mummy's room, she'll pinch my cheeks and make me recite my Latin."

Hazel wondered if their brother George had been like this as a child, if he had been whiny and so demanding of attention, requiring a witness to applaud and kiss him on the cheek for every horse ride and lesson completed. It seemed impossible. Besides, their mother hadn't been so fearful or suffocating back then.

George had been quiet and introspective. His smiles felt like secrets shared from across the room every time. At the age of seven, Percy already knew how to wield his smiles as weapons. Did Percy even remember George? He had been so young when their brother died.

Percy sighed. "Fine. We can play pirates," Percy said as if he were making a concession, as if Hazel herself had barged into *his* room and begged him to play pirates, and only now, in his benevolence, did Percy agree.

Hazel rolled her eyes.

Percy thrust his lower lip out into an exaggerated frown. "If you don't say yes, I'll scream and get Mummy and she'll be cross with you."

Another cloud shifted. A patch of light crept up the bottom of Hazel's dress, the warmth of it amplified through her layers of skirts. "Why don't you go down to the kitchens and ask Cook what she's making for tea? I bet if you ask now, she'll make your favorite lemon cakes."

Percy considered. He frowned at Hazel and whatever she was hiding behind her skirt, but after a moment's thought, he turned and scampered away, no doubt down the narrow stairs to torment Cook and Mrs. Herberts. Hazel had bet right: there was no competition between playing with her and eating lemon cakes.

There wasn't much time left, but before she continued, Hazel needed to lock her door. There could be no more intruders. She walked inside and twisted the heavy key in its lock until she heard the satisfying thud. And then she dashed back to the balcony, where a few drops of water had fallen in the few seconds she was gone, dotting the mossy stone almost black. If this was going to happen, it would be now.

She lifted the kitchen fork again and waved it over each of the frog's limbs like a shaman. Nothing. Perhaps the demonstration Bernard had seen was a trick. Maybe there was never a corpse at all, but a man hiding under the table, his neck poking out through a hole in the wood with theater makeup deadening his skin until it was flat and colorless. What a laugh the actor—the *liar*—and the Galvini boy had probably had after the show, counting the paper money they took in, getting drunk with their fellow two-bit performers in grease makeup.

—And then the frog moved.

Had it moved? Had it just been a trick of the light? Or a breeze blowing through the valley? Hazel hadn't felt anything. Her skirts hadn't rustled. She waved the fork over the dead, impaled frog, again and again, faster and faster, but nothing else happened. And then she realized.

She pulled the giant key from her pocket and gently lowered it toward the frog, and the frog began to dance. The frog, which moments before had dangled lifeless on its pike, now jittered with energy. It still had the will to live, as if it were trying to escape. It was something out of a fairy tale, Hazel thought. *Let me off this poker,* the frog seemed to say, *and I'll grant you three wishes!* Or maybe it was out of a nightmare, like the stories in those penny-fiction pamphlets Percy's tutor sometimes slipped her with a wink. The dead come alive, and they want revenge on the living.

It was working! What was it? Magnetism? The key was a conductor for electricity, that much was clear, but what type of metal was the key made of, anyway? She would need to do a full examination, a run of trials using every combination of metals she could identify.

Gleeful, Hazel continued to trace the key along the frog's twitching limbs. But within a minute, the jerking slowed, and then stopped altogether. Whatever magic had been present in the weather, in the dead frog's humors, in the fire poker, in the bedroom key—it had been spent.

The frog was dead again, and now, from the other room, Hazel could hear her mother weeping. She had wept most days since the fever took George.

From <u>Dr. Beecham's Treatise on Anatomy:</u>
<u>or, The Prevention and Cure of Modern Diseases</u>
(24th Edition, 1816) by Dr. William R. Beecham,
Amended by Dr. William Beecham III:

The Roman fever (*Plaga Romanus*) first reveals itself through symptoms of boils on the patient's back. Within two days, the boils begin to burst, staining the back of the patient's shirt with blood (hence the name "the Roman fever," for the resemblance of several stab wounds to the back like Julius Caesar's). Other symptoms include blackened gums, lethargy, decreased urination, and aches. Colloquial names for the disease: Roman Sickness, the Boils, Bricklayer's Fever, the Red Death. Almost always fatal. An outbreak centered in Edinburgh occurred in the summer of 1815, claiming over five thousand souls.

Though the survival rate is dismal, those who do prevail retain immunity. There is no known cure.

2

IN THE CARRIAGE ON THE WAY TO ALMONT House, Hazel tried in vain to scrub black ink from her knuckles and from beneath her nails. She had been up all night the previous evening, copying notes from her father's old edition of Dr. Beecham's book on anatomy. All the while, she had kept the broadsheet advertisement flat on the desk beside her, the one she had seen nailed to the door of a public house from the window of her carriage.

"Stop, stop!" she had shouted, pounding on the door of the carriage. She scampered out, tore the advert from the door, and returned to the carriage out of breath, too exhilarated to care whether anyone had seen her.

The advertisement was folded into the pocket of her skirt. Hazel reached in with her ink-stained fingers, touching it for comfort and luck.

Bernard wouldn't care about the ink—Hazel doubted he would even notice—but Lord Almont would, and knowing his penchant for propriety, no doubt the incident would make its way back to her mother. *I do wish you wouldn't embarrass me in front of your uncle, Hazel,* Hazel's mother would say while lifting a teacup to her thin lips or pulling a thread through her embroidery as a servant added logs to the morning room fire. *It's not that I care that you make yourself look like a beggar woman when you visit town, but I do know it'll only reflect badly on you when it comes to invitations for the upcoming Season.*

Hazel couldn't even imagine what Lord Almont or her mother would have done if they knew about the broadsheet in her pocket, an advertisement for an anatomy demonstration by the famous Dr. Beecham III, grandson of the legend, and certainly the most famous living surgeon in Edinburgh, if not the whole kingdom.

Hazel practically vibrated with excitement, thinking about it.

LIVE SUBJECT! FREE ANATOMY DEMONSTRATION!
SEE DOCTOR BEECHAM, HEAD OF SURGERY,
EDINBURGH UNIVERSITY, PERFORM DISSECTION
AND AMPUTATION USING HIS
BRAND NEW TECHNIQUE. THOSE INTERESTED
MAY ENQUIRE WITH REGARD TO
THE DOCTOR'S ANATOMY SEMINAR.
8 O'CLOCK IN THE MORNING
ROYAL EDINBURGH ANATOMISTS' SOCIETY

This was the sort of event Hazel wanted to attend! Not the dreary luncheons with dowdy widowers and insufferable debutantes or the dull, endless balls. As soon as Hazel turned fifteen, her mother had begun forcing her down to London for the social season, where Hazel would be squeezed into crinoline the size of a small sofa so that she could whiz around an assortment of ballrooms in the arms of various foul-breathed boys.

In theory, going down to London for the Season meant that one of those foul-breathed boys would fall madly in love with Hazel (or her respectable dowry) and marry her, although it seemed rather pointless, because it was all but a forgone conclusion that she would be marrying Bernard, keeping the Almont title and money in the family.

There was nothing wrong with Bernard, Hazel told herself. He was nice enough, his skin relatively clear. He was, well, dull, but so were the rest of them. He was a little vain, and cared more about his clothes than most other things in the world. But he was a good listener. He had played with Hazel when they were toddlers in the mud, and so he didn't expect her to be the fragile porcelain lady other girls in their social circle pretended to be.

He had known Hazel for so long that he saw her wanting to be a surgeon as a mere quirk, not a scandal. Having a man at her side would be essential when it came to enrolling in classes and sitting for the Royal Physician's Examination, all the better if it was a powerful man with a title. Hazel ran her fingers along the crease of the broadsheet hopefully.

It was a crisp day in autumn, and the September air was as clear as it ever was this close to Edinburgh's Old Town, where those wooden buildings on top of the hill were stacked upon one another like crooked teeth in a mouth exhaling the wheezing black soot of daily life. Lord and Lady Almont lived across Princes Street Gardens—just down the hill, but a universe away from the Old Town: in the New Town, in an elegant white town house on Charlotte Square with pillars out front and enough room for their two carriages out back.

Hazel hadn't been able to get the ink off her hands after all, and so as soon as the footman closed the carriage door behind her, she stuffed her hands into her pockets with her secret hidden broadsheet.

The footman opened the door before Hazel even rang, sweat dappling his collar and his bald spot glistening.

Something was happening in the main hall: it was a swirl of activity. Hazel met eyes with Samuel, the valet, who swept past carrying an empty basin and a rag. Samuel just bowed his head slightly.

A strange man sat nearby, a beggar in dust-colored rags, occupying a simple wooden chair that Hazel had never seen before, probably pulled up from the servants' quarters. A doctor in a long coat was examining the inside of his mouth.

The beggar looked ill at ease in the well-curated manor house. Everything about him stuck out, felt out of place. His shirt was the only one in the entire hall not ironed and starched, his head the only one with hair uncombed, his face the only one uncleaned, with a ring of sweat and grime mottling the area beneath his chin where he hadn't managed to wash. The doctor grimaced and patted the man's cheek, and the man closed his mouth obediently.

Lord Almont—who had been sitting across the hall, in a wider, cushioned chair brought in from the dining hall—rose when Hazel came in. "Ah, Hazel," he said in greeting. "My apologies for the state you find the house in today. I imagine Bernard will be down in a moment. Samuel, tell Bernard that Miss Sinnett has arrived."

Hazel responded with a small, requisite curtsy before her attention returned fully to the strange beggar man. Hazel wondered what could be going on. Was the beggar a ward whom Lord Almont was taking on? A recipient of one of His Lordship's charities? A man applying for a service position and about to be roundly dismissed? Hazel couldn't imagine that Lord Almont was the one who actually did any of the hiring. And why did her uncle require a doctor's examination?

"Are we ready to proceed?" the doctor asked quietly.

For the first time, Hazel noticed the doctor's face: it was heavily pocked and scarred, with deep red lines and ridges. He wore a satin patch over his left eye, but Hazel could make out red swelling from outside its edges. The doctor's hair was long and lank and dark, held back by a black ribbon at the nape of his neck. In his hand, he held something that looked like metal clamps, glinting in the light that came through the house's entryway windows. His coat was stained at its edges, rust colored.

The beggar's eyes were wide, revealing irises surrounded by white. In his lap, he wrung a brown hat, as if he were trying to dry it from the wash. After a few seconds of terrified silence, he nodded to the doctor, leaned back, and opened his mouth.

"Perhaps the lady—" Lord Almont began, but before he could get out the rest of the sentence, the doctor had already completed his task: he had inserted the clamps into the beggar's mouth, given a quick twist, and pulled out a molar with a sickening crack.

The basin that Samuel had brought out immediately served its purpose. The beggar brought it up below his chin and used it to catch the blood and drool that came running from between his lips. He hadn't even had time to scream.

The doctor sniffed and examined the tooth, which was still glistening with blood. "Quickly now," he said to Lord

Almont. "We must act while the tooth is still fresh from the mouth if we hope to affix it to your gum."

Lord Almont dutifully reclined and opened his mouth.

The doctor applied a silvery paste to the bottom of the tooth and plugged it somewhere deep in Lord Almont's mouth with a small scalpel. The beggar whimpered softly behind them.

"Now," the doctor said as he finished, "no chewing meat for a month, unless your cook does it soft. Keep to clear liquors, and no tomatoes."

Lord Almont rose and straightened his tie. "Certainly, Doctor." From within his breast pocket, Lord Almont pulled out a few coins, examined their value, and then handed them to the beggar from as far as the extension of his arm would allow. "I believe this is the market rate for a molar these days?"

Hazel thought the lord seemed mighty keen on keeping his distance from a man whose tooth was now in his mouth. The beggar, tears dribbling silently down his cheeks, thrust the coins into his purse and left.

"My apologies, Hazel," Lord Almont said again, once the echo of the closing door faded, "for exposing you to that dreadful scene. Although Bernard did mention you tend to go in for that sort of thing." He rubbed the outside of his jaw. "Ghastly business, but a small price to pay for one's health and well-being. I don't believe you know the esteemed Dr. Edmund Straine of the Edinburgh Medical Society? Dr. Straine, may I present Miss Sinnett, the daughter of my sister Lavinia."

Dr. Straine turned toward Hazel. He hadn't finished putting away his equipment, and he still had a small scalpel in his hand, dripping red, as he barely lowered his neck in acknowledgment.

"How do you do?" Hazel said. Dr. Straine did not reply. His good eye went directly to the ink stains on Hazel's hands. She hurried to hide them in her skirts. The doctor's already-thin lips somehow became even thinner.

When the doctor did speak, it was again to Lord Almont. "Do be mindful of the toll chewing will take on the tooth, Your Lordship." Without another word, he picked up his bag, turned on the heel of his boot, and exited through the room's back door with a sweep of his black greatcoat.

"Not much bedside manner, I'm afraid," Lord Almont whispered after Straine had left. "But I'm told he's the best in the city. A protégé of the great Dr. Beecham himself, if you can believe it, before he died. You'll stay for tea, of course?"

It had been two years since Hazel's father began his post on Saint Helena—as captain of the Royal Navy assigned to oversee Napoleon's imprisonment—and since then, Lord Almont had taken it upon himself to watch over his niece. Hazel found herself taking the carriage into Edinburgh once or even twice a week to join the Almonts for tea or supper, to sit in the morning room and read Lord Almont's books, to accompany Bernard to whatever social events seemed to be unavoidable. At least George's memory didn't hover thick as smoke in Almont House the way it did in every room of Hawthornden Castle.

When she married Bernard and eventually became the new Lady Almont, the bad memories could close like the covers of a heavy book. She would get a new name and a new home. She would have a new life. She would be a new person, a person whom sadness would be unable to find.

"Ah, Bernard!" Lord Almont said as his son appeared at

the top of the stairs. "Will the two of you be lunching here? I'm sure Samuel can alert the cook?"

"Actually, Uncle," Hazel said, "I was hoping Bernard might escort me on a walk."

Bernard hopped down the last stair and extended his elbow. By the time the pair of them exited the hall, the servants had swept away all trace of the surgery performed just minutes ago.

*From **The Cities of Scotland:**
a Traveler's Companion (1802)
by J. B. Pickrock:*

They call Edinburgh "the Athens of the North" for her accomplishments in philosophy, but now it is also a testament to her architecture: white stone, broad straight avenues, columns. They began to build New Town on the flat expanse of land in the shadow of Edinburgh Castle in the 1760s, I believe (when the stench and overcrowding of the buildings along High Street on the hill became too much for anyone with any decent breeding to bear), but only since 1810 have the buildings in the Romantic Classical style truly begun to impress. Indeed, I daresay now Edinburgh boasts a more beautiful example of the Romantic Classical style than any of the capitals of Europe.

3

"PLEASE."

"No."

"*Please.*"

"Absolutely not."

"But they won't let me in without you. There's not a chance. But they can't turn me away if I'm with the Viscount Almont."

"*Future* Viscount Almont. My father is very much alive, thank you very much."

"Well, you're at least something now, right? Surely, you're a baronet at the very least. That counts for something, *future* Viscount Almont."

"Hazel," Bernard warned.

"You don't even have to look. You can cover your eyes the entire time."

"I'll still *hear* it."

Hazel clutched the broadsheet advert in her hand and gave it a shake. "Come *on*, Bernard. When have I ever asked you to do something for me? If I don't go to this, I'll never be able to think of anything else for as long as I live. I'll be bringing it up at dinner parties when we're both old and gray, and you'll wish you had gone just to shut me up."

Bernard kept walking. "No." Bernard was wearing a new top hat in dove gray, and even as he turned away from Hazel, she could tell that he was still mindful of showing it off to the best angle, so its edges caught the light just so and set off his sharp chin. His jacket was also gray, and he wore a vest of canary yellow silk.

Though the afternoon had begun with a pleasant autumn chill in the air, over the course of their walk, it had become stiflingly hot. Hazel felt a bead of sweat roll down her back, beneath layers of fabric. "Are you worried that my mother will be cross with you because—?"

Bernard turned and interrupted her. "Yes. To be quite frank, yes. I am worried your mother will be cross with me, but more than that, Hazel, I'm worried your mother will be cross with *you*. Do you have *any* idea the sort of trouble *you* would get in if your mother—or father, for that matter— found out you went to an anatomy lecture? A *public anatomy lecture*! The type of characters who attend that sort of thing! Drunkards . . . and rapists! And . . . and . . . theater actors!"

Hazel rolled her eyes and straightened the edges of her ivory gloves. Her father had bought them for her before he left for Saint Helena. "Students, Bernard. That's who attends these things. Anyway, I've worked it all out: I will tell my mother that I am going for a picnic with you at the Princes Street Gardens, and not to expect me back before nightfall. We can walk down the hill and be back at yours by teatime."

A stately carriage passed, and Bernard delayed his response until he had politely greeted the gentleman inside with a dignified nod. When he turned back to Hazel, his face resumed its exasperation. "Studying medicine is one thing. It's useful, even. My friend from Eton, John Lawrence, is off in Paris now and he's going to make a fine physician and he'll marry well and be welcome at all our dinner parties. If you wanted to pretend that you were going to become a physician—or a nurse—I suppose that would be one thing. But surgery—Hazel, surgery is the field for men with no money. No status. They're butchers, really!"

He walked forward a few paces before he realized that Hazel wasn't walking alongside him. "Hazel?"

"What did you mean, 'pretend'?"

"What did I—?"

"You said, 'pretend that' I was 'going to become a physician.'"

"All I meant was that—Hazel. I mean. You never really expected—" He stopped and then started again. "You'll be quite useful when we're married, knowing how to mend scratches and treat fevers!"

"You've always known I want to be a surgeon," Hazel said. "We've talked about it for ages. You've always supported me in that."

"Well, yes," Bernard said to his shoes. "When we were children."

Hazel's mouth suddenly tasted like copper. Her tongue went heavy. They were just a block away from Almont House, its gleaming white columns visible in the afternoon sunlight.

"Look," Bernard said, already shifting his weight to begin walking again. "Let's just get back to the parlor. Have tea." Hazel had been holding the broadsheet slack in her hands, and Bernard reached out to grab it. He ripped it in half, and then in fourths, and then crumpled the pieces. He threw them behind him into the wetness of the gutter, where Hazel watched the slips of paper disappear into pulp. "There. Let's forget that nonsense. There's a new show going up at Le Grand Leon, we'll go together soon, one evening. And take your mother. Doesn't that sound lovely?"

Hazel gave a small nod. "I think, if you don't mind, I'm going to walk a bit more. Just down the promenade. Before I take the carriage home for supper."

Bernard looked around nervously. "Without a chaperone? I don't think—"

"Just a few moments more. We're a block from your home. Look, it's just there. I'll be in sight of it the entire time."

"If you're sure," Bernard said uncertainly.

"I insist."

"Well, all right then." It was that easy. Bernard nodded, satisfied, his face affable again. He was the son of a viscount, and nothing in the world was wrong. He was steps away from his home, where there would be a roast waiting for supper. "I'll come to Hawthornden next week. Tell Percy I insist on playing him again in whist."

Hazel responded with the closest thing to a smile she could manage. She kept it on her face as she watched Bernard's long legs amble down the street, until they disappeared in the shadows of Almont House.

Only then did she allow herself to look down at the crumpled remains of the broadsheet she had kept hidden in her wardrobe, safe from the prying eyes of her mother and Mrs. Herberts, so that she could share it with Bernard. Only a few words on the page hadn't yet dissolved in the muck that ran in the gutter along the edge of the road, fragments like puzzle pieces.

LIVE SUBJECT

BEECHAM

EDIN—ANAT—

EDUCAT—

—EW TECHNIQUE

She sighed and walked toward the carriage waiting for her. Someone was outside Almont House, at the side gate, where the road curved away from Charlotte Square and toward Queensferry Street Lane, the spire of Saint Mary's Cathedral stabbing the needle of its iron cross into the blue sky beyond.

It was a woman with reddish hair—which might have looked redder if it weren't so dirty—tucked beneath a maid's cap. One of the Almonts' maids? Hazel didn't recognize her, but that in itself wasn't surprising. A household like theirs would certainly have a dozen or so maids, and they would try to stay invisible when guests were present. Maybe she was new. She looked young—very young. Younger than Hazel. She looked as though she was waiting for someone, from the way she glanced over her shoulder and down the street, but she didn't seem nervous.

Hazel stopped and watched her, curious. And then, in the blink of an eye, she was joined by a man. No, not a man. A boy. A tall boy, all vertical lines and sharp edges. The two of them were talking, and the maid furtively handed off a piece of paper.

Could they be robbing Almont House? It was broad daylight. The square was far from abandoned—several carriages had already rumbled past Hazel as she stood watching the pair. No one seemed to be paying them any mind. True, they were hidden in the manor's shadow, but surely even thieves preferred the cover of night.

Hazel crept closer, pretending to be fascinated by a small rosebush. Though she was only thirty yards away now, the two strangers didn't look up. The maid with copper hair extended her hand, and the tall boy deposited a few coins into her palm. Now that she was closer, Hazel could make out a long, slim nose extending behind the boy's dark hair. "Careful with that one, Jack," the red-haired maid said.

With the coins secured in her waistband, the maid disappeared back against the stone exterior of Almont House, slipping around the corner, back through the servants' entrance.

Strange, Hazel thought.

"Home, miss?" It was her carriage driver, Mr. Peters, calling from the end of the block. He gave the reins a quick flick and brought the horses into action.

The boy in the shadows looked up, and for a moment Hazel locked eyes with him, the hairs on the back of her neck standing at attention. His eyes were bright and clear and gray. With his long nose, he looked like a bird of prey, Hazel thought. He gave something that might have been a smile or a smirk or maybe just a trick of the light, because an instant later he was gone, trotting up toward the main road, where the smoke of the Old Town hovered black and thick, and Hazel was stepping into her carriage, back to Hawthornden, trying to conjure his face in her mind again, but the memory of it was already fading.

4

IT WAS AMAZINGLY EASY TO DIE IN EDINBURGH.
People did it every day. There were grease fires, and
stabbings in the alleys behind dingy bars. Scrapes
that you thought you could ignore turned green and oozing,
swollen and hot, until you were gone before you even had
time to see the public doctor. Thieves were hanged in Grassmarket Square, Jack had seen them himself, the way the bodies
twitched on the way down and then became still.

It was easy to die in Edinburgh, but Jack had made it seventeen years because he knew how to survive.

Jeanette was already waiting at the side gate of the house
by Queensferry by the time Jack made it down the hill. "It's
a new job," she said almost pleadingly, before he could even
apologize for being late. "I'm fixing to keep this 'un, too. The
food is good. Proper porridge for breakfast every morning,
with cream."

"It was you who told me to meet you in the middle of the
bloody day."

"I have a *job* now, Jacks, case you need reminding. Means

I can't be trotting off to your stink-holes day and night to deliver whats I know."

The hairs on Jack's neck lifted, his senses taut as a string pulled between fingers. There was a girl watching them, fifteen yards away, on the street. Jeanette didn't notice. The girl was too far away to hear them, he guessed, but she had definitely noticed them, even though now she was pretending to smell a rose. She was wealthy—her clothes gave that away, the fine fabric and real feathers in her headpiece. She was the wife of someone, must be if she was out walking in the New Town without a chaperone, but she looked no older than he was. She was maybe sixteen or seventeen. With these wealthy girls, made up like paper dolls, it was hard to tell.

Jack watched her from the corner of his eye, the way a thin line of the bare back of her neck, so white it was almost translucent, became visible as she leaned down, the gap in the armor of her frock and her hair.

Jeanette cleared her throat. "You do want it, don't you? 'Cause if you don't, I got plenty of resurrection men who'd be happy to get a double order like this. I do, Jack Currer, don't think I don't!" She pronounced every syllable of his name with a roll of her tongue: Curr-er.

"No, no, I want it, course I do." He snatched the paper Jeanette was offering him, and then fished in his pocket for the coins.

Jeanette talked out loud as she counted her payment. "One little 'un. Dead of something. Wasn't sick, so I think it must have been a wet nurse overlaying him. Fancy that. Happens all the time. These little heirs all done up proper in their nightgowns and skirts getting a feeding from a woman who nods off to sleep. Other 'un is a man. Careful with that 'un, Jack—heard a groom say he thought it was the sickness."

Jack looked down at the names and hastily drawn cemetery map in his hand. "It's not the Roman fever, Jeanette, and you'd mind yourself not to be spreading those rumors. Gets people scared."

"You're *not* scared?" Jeanette shot back.

Jack drummed his fingers against the side of his leg. He had worked as a resurrection man for years, lifted bodies decomposing with rot and disease, but somehow always maintained his health. He didn't know whether it was a god giving him mercy he certainly didn't deserve or blind luck, but he was inclined to believe the latter. "No," he said, "I'm not scared."

Jeanette just shrugged, and then scampered off to the house's back gardens, where she could sneak back in the servants' entrance and pretend she had never left.

Jack folded the paper and put it in the pocket of his trousers, and then looked up again, back at the woman who had been looking at the roses. She was staring at him, with narrow brown eyes so dark they almost looked black. She was pretty, in the way that all wealthy girls are, with their faces clean and hair combed. Her hair was light, reddish and thick and wavy beneath her hat. Her nose was long and straight, her lips curled up on one side. Jack suddenly felt naked, and a prickling heat crept up the back of his neck. He couldn't look away from her. It was like she was accusing him of something. Or conspiring with him. Was she smiling, or was that just the natural tilt of her bruise-colored lips?

Finally, to Jack's relief, the woman's eyes pulled away, and she lifted a dainty slipper to enter a handsome carriage.

Her gloves were white, and as she disappeared, Jack could just make out a spot of red blossoming at the tip of a finger on her left hand, where she had been holding the stem of a rose to pull it closer. Blood. A thorn had pierced the thin fabric, and the girl hadn't noticed. A thimble-sized crimson bloom on her ivory hands.

From the <u>Encyclopaedia Caledonia</u>
(29th Edition, 1817):

William Beecham, in full William Beecham, Baron Beecham of Meershire, also called Sir William Beecham, Baronet (born 5 April 1736, Glasgow, Scotland; died 7 January 1801, Portree, Isle of Skye, Scotland). Scottish surgeon and medical scientist, president and founder of the Royal Edinburgh Anatomists' Society, best known for his study of anatomy and the publication of *Dr. Beecham's Treatise on Anatomy: or, The Prevention and Cure of Modern Diseases.* The *Treatise,* with its detailed anatomical diagrams and updated log of maladies, provided the foundation for the next generation of medical students. It has since been re-published over a dozen times in updated editions. A rumored Scottish nationalist, Beecham is said to have refused a post as King George III's personal physician, after which he was never permitted to return to London.

In his later years, Beecham became famously reclusive, refusing patients or public lectures, and devoting his energy to the study of alchemy and the occult. Beecham's stated purpose was the quest for eternal life. Beecham succumbed to poisoning from the effects of experimental consumption of gold, mercury, and lead in high doses. *Dr. Beecham's Treatise* continues to be revised and re-published after his death by his grandson, William Beecham III.

Married to: Eloise Carver Beecham of Essex (born 1742, died 1764). Issue: John (b. 1760), Philip (b. 1762), Dorothea (b. 1764).

See: *grandson* William Beecham III

5

SHE COULD DO IT WITHOUT BERNARD, she was sure of it. It was just a matter of making certain she timed it right—she would leave after breakfast, and tell her mother she was going on a long walk in the fields beyond the house. From there, she would need to borrow one of her father's long overcoats and head out to the stables without being seen. Percy wouldn't be a problem—he had lessons all morning. And her mother's bedroom faced the eastern side of the building, so even if she glanced out the window while she was finishing her letters, she wouldn't see Hazel escaping up the drive.

A carriage was out of the question. Too noisy, too conspicuous. Someone would see her and recognize the carriage between their house and Edinburgh. No, much safer just to ride, and pull the collar of her father's winter jacket as high over her neck as it would go, and keep her head down.

Hazel had never been to the Old Town unescorted before, but she was confident she wouldn't get lost. It was all organized like a fish's skeleton—the spine of High Street from up at Edinburgh Castle down to the Palace of Holyrood below, and alleys and closes branching off from either side. She knew what the outside of the Royal Edinburgh Anatomists' Society looked like—her uncle had pointed it out once: dark wooden beams and stone, a gilded plaque next to the door. It couldn't be hard to find. She had the sixpence for the entrance fee growing warm in her pocket, thanks to her nervous habit of rubbing her fingers against the coins, but if everything went to plan, she wouldn't need them.

That morning she had continued to plan it out in her mind, step by step, while spooning porridge into her mouth across the wide oak table from her mother. Their informal dining room was perhaps the only room at Hawthornden that could be called "cozy." It was next to the kitchen and always warm, and usually smelled pleasantly of whatever meat Cook was roasting for dinner that evening. Though the walls of the house in nearly every other room were covered—with dim oil portraits and metal weapons and specimens from her father's travels kept safe behind glass—here the wood was bare, an inviting chestnut color lit by the crackling fire warming the kettle in the hearth.

If only Bernard hadn't ripped up the advert. Not that Hazel didn't have it memorized, but it would have been a comfort to be able to read it, and to reread it. The poster hadn't indicated that women wouldn't be allowed at the anatomical lecture, but it didn't have to. Besides, Hazel didn't want anyone there recognizing her and reporting back to her mother—or, heaven forbid, her uncle. No, instead she would wait until the bells at Saint Giles' Cathedral rang eight o'clock, when the lecture was starting, and hang around outside until the doors were closed. Then, when everyone was distracted by whatever miraculous new technique

Dr. Beecham was demonstrating, she could slip in, silent and undetected.

Of course, *the* Dr. Beecham, the one whose textbook redefined the field of anatomy and who had turned Edinburgh into the world capital for medical sciences, had been dead for some time. It was his grandson, Dr. Beecham III, who now served as head of the Royal Edinburgh Anatomists' Society.

Hazel silently repeated the plan over and over, like a chant: *Horse, town, lecture. Horse, town, lecture.* If she rode back hard, she would make supper, and she could pretend she'd lost track of time in the woods. Her mother wouldn't notice; she scarcely noticed Hazel at all. George was dead and Percy was the heir. What did it matter what Hazel did with her time?

"Thank goodness we're going to London for the Season."

Hazel was so distracted by her own thoughts that the sound of her mother's voice shocked her like a bolt of electricity. "I'm sorry, what?"

Lady Sinnett straightened her spine, and the veil she always wore over her face quivered. "To London," she repeated sharply. "For the Season. Don't be tiresome, Hazel."

"Yes, of course. London." A miserable few months of being trussed up like a Christmas turkey and made to smile at glossy-eyed strangers and shoved onto Bernard's arm.

"Thank goodness we're going," Lady Sinnett repeated, "given everything I've been hearing."

Hazel tried to keep her voice steady. "What have you been hearing?" Her breath tightened in her chest. So her mother knew. Knew about the lecture and the anatomical school. Of course. How could she have possibly thought to keep it hidden when—?

"The fever, Hazel," Lady Sinnett sputtered. "Obviously not where any civilized people are, but up in Edinburgh, where the buildings are on top of one another and the poor are half dead anyway—all the bad air in Edinburgh, honestly, the sooner we get to London, the better. Especially with Percy's delicate constitution."

"Oh. Yes. Right." The bells from the abbey across the field rang out the hour, and Cook swept into the dining hall to take away their plates. "I'm going to take a walk this morning," Hazel said, breaking the silence again. "A good, long walk. To get all of the good air."

From somewhere above them came the sound of Percy pounding arrhythmically on the pianoforte. "Yes, fine," Lady Sinnett said distractedly. Hazel took another sip of tea so her mother wouldn't see her grin.

THE RIDE TO EDINBURGH TOOK LESS THAN AN hour, and no one was on the road except half a dozen farmers whom Hazel didn't recognize and who didn't bother to look up at her as she sped past. She just followed the main road toward the shimmering black smoke, visible for miles—Auld Reekie, the beating heart of science and literature in Scotland. Before Hazel's father left, he had taken her and George to Almont House to listen to Sir Walter Scott do a reading from his narrative poem *Lady of the Lake*. The Roman fever had taken George less than a season later. Hazel had been sick, too, clutching her blankets and soaking her bedding with her sweat and the blood from the sores on her back. And then, one morning, with the dim yellow light of dawn across her window, she found she could sit up. Cook had wept when Hazel asked for porridge, the first food she'd requested in a week. She had survived, and her older brother, who had been stronger and smarter and braver than she, had died.

Hazel knew the Old Town was a maze of twisting streets. Even remembering what the front door of the Anatomists' Society looked like, Hazel still silently rehearsed the way she might politely stop a stranger and ask him for directions. But almost as soon as she deposited her horse at an inn and started walking along the cobblestones on foot, she picked out a pair of anatomy students in the crowd. They couldn't be anything else: threadbare black coats, stained shoes, and, most tellingly of all, copies of *Dr. Beecham's Treatise* clutched under their arms. Perfect.

Hazel followed them on foot over the rain-dappled stones until they dipped into an alley near South Bridge that reeked of day-old fish. The alley released into a close—a tight square surrounded on all sides by buildings at least three or four stories high. The buildings all seemed to tilt forward. The sky had been blue and expansive as Hazel rode to town, but here it was just a distant pocket square–sized patch of dishwater gray. Laundry and the smell of urine hung in the air.

But here she was: ROYAL EDINBURGH ANATOMISTS' SOCIETY was engraved on a brass placard next to a black door. Several of the men milling about carried the broadsheet advert in their hands. Hazel was surprised to see that most of them did, actually, look like gentlemen. She had been secretly convinced that Bernard was right, and that she was voluntarily entering a den of ruffians and theatrical actors. But, no—there were top hats and shoes of real leather. Though she couldn't recall their names, she recognized one or two men by face from the salons at Almont House, and she held her breath and pulled herself against one damp stone wall to make herself invisible. She needn't have bothered. The men were distracted by their own importance, and not one would have thought to look at anyone who happened to be standing a centimeter below his own eyeline.

Then the bells of Saint Giles tolled, louder than Hazel had ever heard, vibrating to her very core. The men murmured and scuffed their feet for a moment longer before the small door swung open and they all started jostling to get inside.

Hazel hung back, watching them, noticing their impatience and the way they greeted one another with cold reserve. And then through their capes and sweeping long coats, there stood a man who made Hazel gasp with familiarity. It was the eye-patched doctor who had given the pauper's tooth to her uncle Almont, Dr. Straine. He didn't see her, or didn't seem to, but Hazel pressed herself closer to the brick wall of the close, anyway—just in case.

It took until the bells tolled the quarter hour before the men had all made their way inside and the various groans and exclamations of recognition finally quieted. Hazel was left alone in the close when the black door swung shut.

She would give it five minutes—five good, long minutes—before she sneaked inside. She would count them off herself, count five minutes while watching the stained linens that hung out the windows above her sway softly. The Old Town wasn't so bad as all that, Hazel thought. Her mother had told her stories about the murderers lurking in every corner, the once-gentlemen turned creatures by the corruptness of the city itself. The way Lady Sinnett told it, one could scarcely go a block in the Old Town without encountering half a dozen monsters out of a penny-fiction. But here Hazel was, only seventeen, and she had made it here herself.

There, now. That would be five. She would slip in the door, covered by the darkness, and watch firsthand as Dr. Beecham—the grandson of *that very* Dr. Beecham himself!—demonstrated what the advert had promised to be "a revolution in the field of surgery." There was a smattering of applause through the door. Something had started. Now was the time.

There was only one problem. The door was locked. Hazel gave it another tug, hoping that maybe the wood had just gone slightly warped or swollen in its frame—but, no. It was firmly and tightly locked. Hazel sank to the ground, not caring that her skirts were becoming damp on the stones. She had come all this way for nothing.

"Hey!"

A voice called out to her from across the close, but its source was concealed by shadow. Hazel lifted her face, half expecting to meet with one of her mother's monsters. But, no: it was a boy. A boy she had seen before, with gray eyes and long dark hair. The boy she had seen outside Almont House. He slinked toward her and extended a hand. It was dirty, fingers pulling through holes in his glove, but his nails were clean. Hazel took it and let the boy pull her up.

He cleared his throat. "They lock up when the demonstration starts. Dr. Beecham hates interruptions."

Hazel gave him a small smile. "I figured as much."

The boy brushed the hair from his face. "You didn't go in when you could've. I was watching. I mean, I wasn't watching *you*, but I saw you."

"I was hoping," Hazel said, smoothing her skirts, "to slip

in once the demonstration started. To avoid notice. I don't imagine many women come to this sort of thing."

"Suppose not."

Hazel waited. The boy shuffled his feet and tried to wipe the dust from his hands on his trousers. Finally, Hazel spoke. "I'm Miss Sinnett," she said.

The moment she said her name, she regretted it. The boy's lips curled into a small smile, and he swept into a deep bow. "A pleasure, Miss Sinnett." He was still smiling when he came up.

The back of Hazel's neck reddened. "It's customary now for you to introduce yourself."

The boy's smile widened into a smirk, the glint of his long canine teeth visible. "Is it, now?" he said, but he didn't offer his name. Instead, he said, "If you still want to see the happenings in there, I know a way inside."

"Inside the surgical theater?"

The boy nodded.

"Yes! Please!" Hazel caught the excitement in her voice. "I mean, if it's not too much trouble."

"It's not. I don't mind." Without waiting, the boy took Hazel's hand and pulled her through an alleyway so narrow she hadn't even noticed it before, with wet stones on either side of them that smelled like mold and sweat. The cage on Hazel's skirt grazed both sides of the walls. The boy was sure-footed, hopping up and weaving through the uneven stones as if he were made of smoke. At a wooden door, he gave two hard knocks. The door opened from the inside, and in an instant, the boy had pulled Hazel through it, into a dark passage lit only by a single torch at the far end.

"Do you work here?" Hazel whispered as he guided her forward. "For the anatomists?"

"In a sense," he answered, looking back at Hazel. His gray eyes seemed to glow in the dark, and though the air was stuffy, Hazel suddenly became cold. "Here, come on."

They had made their way to the end of the dark passage. The torch on the wall made the boy's face look strange, all angles and shadows. Hazel could hear voices nearby— murmuring chatter, the melody of a booming baritone—but she couldn't make out words.

"If you want to see it, the door is here," he said.

"Aren't you coming with me?" Hazel asked.

"Nah," the boy said. "I see enough misery in real life to need to see some doctor do it for applause." Hazel wasn't sure if he was joking or not. From the other side of the wall came the sound of a man screaming. Even in the torchlight, Hazel could make out her guide raising his eyebrow as if to say, *See?*

He opened the door a crack, but Hazel couldn't see what was on the other side. She hesitated. "It's a'right," the boy said. "You'll be fine. Trust me."

Hazel nodded and lifted her skirts to slip as quietly as she could past the boy. When their bodies were pressed to each other by the narrow walls, he averted his eyes. Hazel put her hand on the doorknob and gave it a gentle push. The wooden door widened soundlessly, and Hazel realized why the boy had been so certain she would be fine: the door opened beneath the risers that the men were seated on. She was looking through their legs and past their boots, but she had a perfect view of Beecham's stage, fewer than twenty yards away.

Hazel turned to say thank you, but the boy had already disappeared into the darkness.

From <u>A Primer to the Gentleman's Field of Physician</u> (1779) by Sir Thomas Murburry:

The difference between the eighteenth-century surgeon and the physician is stark and distinct. A physician may be a gentleman of social standing and considerable means, with access to medical college and a proper education in Latin and the fine arts. It is his role to consult and advise on the matter of all ailments, internal and external, and to provide whatever poultices or medicines may offer relief.

A surgeon, by contrast, is more often a man of lower social status who understands that a genius in the study of anatomy may provide him a pathway to elevated rank. He must be prepared to work with the poor and deformed, the monsters unloved and made gruesome by either war or circumstance.

The physician works with his mind. The surgeon works with his hands, and his brute strength.

6

S E HAD HELPED THE PRETTY GIRL. HE didn't know why. She was wealthy, the type that should have helped herself. But Jack was there anyway. He had stolen through the back passages of the theater of the Anatomists' Society more times than he could count. Maybe he felt sorry for her, standing there in the close, looking more alone than was possible, her cheeks flushed pink with either embarrassment or a chill. There had been blood on her glove the last time he saw her, down in the New Town, where the buildings were straight and polished as ha'pennies and grass grew confined to neat little squares. She was out of place here, in the Old Town.

Jack shouldn't even have been lingering around the Anatomists' Society that late, that time of morning. He had already made his sale to Straine. Resurrection men were supposed to disappear in sunlight, the vampires who fed the medical students of the city. The delivery took longer than he'd thought it would—Straine had refused to pay the last guinea because the body was a week old. It was, but that wasn't Jack's fault. Bodies were harder and harder to come by: the night watchmen were tightening their fists around the kirkyards of Edinburgh. But there was no use haggling with Straine, with his rolling black eye and waxy skin and greasy hair. No wonder the Society designated him as the one to buy corpses; he practically looked like a corpse himself.

Anyway, helping the girl—it was done. It hadn't taken long, for what that was worth, and Jack wasn't going to linger. He had already made his sale for the day—in the end, the assistant begrudgingly paid the full price—and the silver jingled happily in his pocket. And now he had to get back to his job at Le Grand Leon—the theater at the heart of the city, where he swept the stage and washed the costumes and built the sets and did whatever else Mr. Anthony asked of him. Tonight, after the evening performance, after Isabella got offstage and wiped off her powdery white makeup, he was going to ask her to go for a pint—and maybe, just maybe, she would say yes.

7

THE SURGICAL THEATER WAS DARK, LIT ONLY by candles surrounding the stage and a few torches sputtering along the walls. The stage was set lower than the seating for the audience to ensure everyone would have a full view of the proceedings. Underneath the lifted benches, cast in shadows, Hazel was all but invisible. Through the smoke and the pairs of impatient legs, Hazel saw Dr. Beecham onstage, selecting a knife from a tray held by a nervous-looking assistant.

Beecham was a handsome man who looked to be in his midforties, with just a streak of gray peppering his blondish hair. The air in the theater was oppressive and stuffy, but he wore a long shirt and jacket with a collar that went up to his chin, and he wore gloves of black leather.

"Apparently he never takes them off," whispered a man sitting on the bench above Hazel to his fellow beside him. "Never without his gloves."

"Think he's scared of blood on his hands?" whispered the other man back.

Whatever the reason, Beecham's gloves remained on even

as he selected a knife from the tray, a long blade with a serrated edge, with a handle of polished silver. Beecham smiled at it, taking his time to examine the way the firelight almost caused it to glow before placing it gently back onto the tray. It seemed as though he forgot there was a theater full of men watching his every move. Hazel was so taken by watching him that it was a few minutes before she realized there was a patient behind him, a middle-aged man lying on a table with his leg covered by a sheet.

Finally, Beecham spoke. "I promised you something extraordinary, gentlemen, and something extraordinary is what I will provide. My grandfather founded this society to be a place where distinguished men of science come together to share their works and discoveries. Today, I shall bring Edinburgh into the nineteenth century." As he spoke, he turned his attention to the patient on the table and, with a flourish, whipped off the sheet covering his leg.

The audience collectively recoiled. Hazel, too, drew a sharp breath, which fortunately no one seemed to hear. The man's leg was a nightmarish thing, swollen and greenish in some parts, reddish in others, twice the thickness of a normal leg and lined with bulging purple veins.

Dr. Beecham selected another weapon from his assistant's tray: a saw. He held it aloft, almost playfully, and now the patient winced. "Now, now, Mr. Butcher. Now is not the time to be frightened."

Mr. Butcher was not capable of taking that advice. He wriggled like a worm on a hook, kicking with his good leg and thumping with his bad leg and shaking his head from side to side. Beecham dropped the hand holding his knife and sighed. "Gentlemen, if you would."

From the shadows came two men, one with a tall top hat and the other with a thick red mustache. They stood on either side of the patient's table and each put a hand on one of Mr. Butcher's shoulders.

"I assured Mr. Butcher before he came in today that our procedure would be quite painless, but he doesn't appear to believe me!" Beecham said. The gentlemen in the audience chuckled. "But I would never lie. Gentlemen!"

From within his jacket, Beecham pulled a small bottle of milky bluish liquid. The bottle was no taller than a playing card. Beecham held it high above his head so everyone in the crowd could see.

"In this bottle," he said, "is the future of surgery. A chemical compound of my own devising. It's true, what my grandfather wrote in his book, that sometimes a physician must act as apothecary, and in so doing, I have discovered something extraordinary. It is—gentlemen, if you'll forgive me—nothing short of a miracle." There were murmurs of disapproval and interest, a few canes banging on the steps, but Dr. Beecham continued: "I have single-handedly devised the secret that will render all surgery painless.

This time, even Hazel could not help laughing. Dr. Beecham smiled slightly and eyed the crowd. "Soon enough, my friends, soon enough. But before we begin, I think I should demonstrate one more of my inventions." He tilted his head, and then came a pop and a hiss and the sound of tinkling glass, and the stage erupted in blinding white light.

Hazel lifted her sleeve to shield her eyes. Beecham was the only one who didn't wince at the sudden brightness. The stage was circled with gas lamps Hazel hadn't seen in the darkness, all connected by tubes, now lit brighter than Hazel had ever seen indoors. "The future," Beecham said, "is gas lamps. With a few modifications, I've found that they make what we undertake in the surgical hall far easier."

The men applauded. Beecham nodded slightly, bowing to their praise. And then, once the crowd had calmed, he looked at the bottle in his hand. The blue-violet fluid inside seemed to be swirling. Now that the room was lit, Hazel saw its color properly, deep sapphire laced with silver. The gas lamps were so bright that neither Beecham nor the bottle seemed to have a shadow.

Beecham lifted his vial higher, and then uncorked it. For a moment, Hazel smelled a strange sweetness, like wildflowers and rot. Then, from another coat pocket, the doctor pulled a white handkerchief, embroidered with the initials *W. B.* He held the handkerchief aloft like a magician before plunging it into the blue bottle. When he withdrew the handkerchief, Hazel got another momentary whiff of the wildflower-rot smell. There was another scent uncorked in the vial, too, something specific, but Hazel couldn't identify it.

Dr. Beecham approached the terrified patient, holding the handkerchief. Though the two stocky men held him down firmly, the patient continued to wriggle as much as he was able. Beecham smiled, but he didn't show his teeth.

He turned to the audience. "Gentlemen, I give you *ethereum*. Or, what I have taken to calling in the laboratory 'the Scotsman's dodge.'" There were murmurs of confusion and interest in the stands. A few of the men stomped their feet, which caused a spider to fall into Hazel's hair.

While the patient struggled, Dr. Beecham pressed the handkerchief firmly against his face, muffling his cries. The struggling stopped. The men in the stands were silent. Beecham gracefully plucked the bone saw from his assistant's tray and began his work sawing at the disfigured leg.

It took fewer than five strokes back and forth and less than a minute before the leg fell with a sickeningly wet thud into the sawdust below. Beecham's face never changed, even as a spattering of blood painted a bright red line from his forehead to his upper lip. He exchanged his saw for a long metal instrument with a hook on its end, and then pulled at a few of the still-bleeding veins inside what remained of the patient's leg. He tied each of them into a neat square knot, and then nodded at another assistant, who began to wrap the bleeding stump in linen.

Throughout the entire thing, the patient never woke or cried out. He slept like a child with pleasant dreams. "The Scotsman's dodge, gentlemen," Dr. Beecham said quietly.

The room erupted into wild applause. Several more spiders fell onto Hazel. Whether it was the angle, or the candlelight, or the look of supreme confidence on his face, Hazel saw exactly how much Dr. Beecham resembled the ink etching of his grandfather from the first page of *Dr. Beecham's Treatise*. The small nose, the lowered brow, even the deep dimples that revealed themselves with only the hint of a smile. It was uncanny. It was unmistakable. The only difference was the blood still slowly dripping down the living Beecham's chin.

Beecham's assistants got to work tidying the stage, wiping the blood from the table, and carrying the mangled leg away. The sawdust where the leg had fallen was so dark with blood it almost looked black, even in the grotesque brightness of Beecham's lamp. By the time they were finished, the patient was blinking himself awake. "Is it—?" he said.

"Over," Dr. Beecham said. The audience erupted once more.

Hazel was dizzy with the heat and the smell of hot, coppery blood and visions of what she had just seen. A surgery! With her own two eyes! Flesh, mottled and damaged, cut away to reveal the clean bright red beneath, those veins and arteries tied with the deft skill of a master with an embroidery needle. And, most thrilling of all, that concoction, that ethereum, whatever it was that had put the patient to sleep.

Finally, Beecham raised one arm to silence the ecstatic crowd. "My anatomy lectures will begin again this term. Payment is due in full on the first day of class. I warn you, the course is extremely demanding, but I can tell you this: not a single pupil of mine has ever failed his Physician's Exams."

He smiled to more rapturous applause.

A class! There it was. The answer Hazel had been looking for without even knowing she was looking. The invisible string that had pulled her here from Hawthornden, to this very spot at this very moment. No more slipping into her father's study to memorize an already obsolete edition of *Dr. Beecham's Treatise* with the spine falling apart, or the tiny experiments she could cobble together with materials from the garden. She could spend an entire term learning from an actual surgeon, examining bodies, solving cases. She could be the one to cure the Roman fever! She would be the savior of Scotland—how could her mother possibly take issue with her then, when she was famous and celebrated?

Even on Saint Helena, her father would get word, letters and newspaper clippings. The prisoner Napoleon would drop dead with shock at the news of a brilliant female physician, and then her father's posting would be over and he could come home again. If her mother thought Hazel would be going to London for the Season, she was sorely mistaken. There was no way. They would need to tie her to the horses to get her to leave Edinburgh at a time like this, when the nineteenth century was finally starting, and Hazel had a chance to be in the middle of it!

Hazel decided it would be safer to wait until the room was mostly empty before she made her way back through the passage to the outside world and exited to the street. Slowly, the crowd started to file out, with about a dozen men elbowing one another to get to the stage to try to shake hands with Dr. Beecham, in the hope that some of his genius and importance could be transferred palm to palm.

Finally, the air in the room shifted, and it seemed as though most of the gentlemen had left the theater. The assistants were finished wiping the table, and they, along with Dr. Beecham, had retreated to a back room. Hazel found the hidden door again, and she pressed through the narrow passage until she was once again on the street.

It was dusk already. Hazel had no idea how long the demonstration had lasted, but the city had become strange around her. The air smelled heavy with grease and fish. Hazel needed to get home. She would already have missed tea-time, and her mother would probably be furious, but Hazel could feign having got lost in the woods or something. She would ride as fast as she could and—

"Miss Sinnett, was it?" A voice like knotted wood dipped in honey interrupted her thoughts.

Hazel turned, and found herself face-to-face with the

one-eyed doctor she had met at her uncle's house. "Dr. Straine." Hazel's heart pounded as she gave the closest approximation of a curtsy she could manage.

The doctor was shorter than she had first supposed. His bearing, the way he carried himself, and the long curtain of his black cape gave him the look of a vulture, but Hazel was astonished to discover that now, just a yard away, they were almost exactly the same height.

"I shudder to think what a young lady of your social stature is doing in the Old Town." His lips pursed and his one visible eye narrowed. "Without a chaperone."

Hazel's hands became slick with sweat in their gloves. She forced her face into an imitation of a smile and willed herself not to look at the door to the Anatomists' Society. "Just a walk to enjoy the weather," she said.

The obviousness of the lie reflected back plainly on his face. Dr. Straine flexed his fingers. The leather of his gloves creaked. "A shame," he said, "that women aren't permitted in the Anatomists' Society. I always found the fairer sex to be a—calming influence on the sanguineous urges of men."

"Indeed," Hazel replied dryly.

Straine's eye seemed able to penetrate through Hazel's clothes and skin, down to her bones. Finally he spoke again. "Give your uncle my best." He turned on his heel, and before Hazel could respond, he was gone.

The streets were indeed changed. It was even darker now, with strangers leering from windows and doorways. Hazel gathered her skirts around her and walked quickly back to the main street, where at least the last glimmer of sunlight was still reflecting on the cobblestones.

By the time Hazel made it back to Hawthornden, the

only fires still burning were in the kitchen. Hazel took a candle to slip up to her bedroom without anyone noticing her. Cook was playing cards with the scullery maid; Hazel could see their shadows stretched along the galley wall and hear Cook's booming laughter. She made it up the staircase and saw that the door to Lady Sinnett's bedroom was closed. Hazel's maid, Iona, was dozing in the chair by the low smoldering embers. She roused herself to unlace Hazel's gown and help her to bed. "Were you—?" she began. Hazel shook her head. She was suddenly so exhausted she could barely speak. The entire weight of the day seemed to hit her at once, leaving her limbs heavy, as if her blood were molten lead.

As Hazel lay flat and deadened on her mattress, she replayed the demonstration over and over, trying to capture every detail in her memory, carving it like a lithograph in her brain. It wasn't until she was a moment from sleep, and the tiniest thread tethered her to consciousness, that she realized with a jolt what the third smell in that violet bottle of ethereum was. It was a memory locked deep inside her mind, through its curving hallways and maze of rooms, from when Hazel was lying in the very same bed, dizzy with nausea and dehydration. She had been certain the sickness was going to take her. Dr. Beecham's magical bottle had smelled like wildflowers, and mold, and death.

8

AZEL HAD EXPECTED A STERN LECTURE AT least, a birch switch across the knuckles or a fiery "just wait until we tell your father about this won't he be furious." It was true, when Hazel's mother wasn't trapped in mourning for George, she was so obsessive in her doting over Percy she could barely see beyond her own crinoline, but still—surely *some* consequence would come for what she had done.

But, no. When Hazel awoke late the next morning, with the sun coming thick and yellow through her curtains, she found that her mother hadn't even left her rooms yet. Iona told her that Lady Sinnett hadn't come out for dinner the night before.

Her mother hadn't been like that before George died. When George was still around—when George and Hazel's father was still around, come to think of it—they had been, well, a normal family. Teatime in the library. Readings around the fire. Christmases at Almont House. Hidden afternoons when Hazel's father would walk her to the tiny spring beyond the woods at Hawthornden and point out the types of grouse that waddled through the branches around them. But then came her father's posting—a *very* prestigious posting, Lady Sinnett was quick to remind them all—and the fever that took George. And now it was just the three of them at home: Hazel, her mother, and Percy. Percy, the little princeling spoiled rotten, her mother's pride and joy, kept safe and hidden away like a pearl in an oyster so he would never get sick—like George. Lady Sinnett devoted all her time and attention to Percy now, his schooling, his clothing, the very air he breathed, and when she spoke to Hazel, it was more often than not just to ask if she had seen Percy anywhere.

Hazel wouldn't see her mother until a few days later, when she was fussing over Percy's bacon at breakfast. Hazel slipped into her seat unnoticed while Lady Sinnett dabbed at the grease on Percy's cheeks with a handkerchief.

But then to Hazel's astonishment, her mother turned to her. "Bacon, dear?" Lady Sinnett said, extending a plate in her black-gloved hand. It had been more than a year since George's death, but her mother still wore a costume of full mourning. Her dress was black taffeta, and she wore the brooch with George's hair in it at the middle of her chest.

Hazel accepted cautiously. It seemed like a trick. If it was, the noose would be tightening soon. Perhaps her mother *had* noticed that she was gone, and her seeming indifference had just been a con, to lull Hazel into a false sense of security.

"Percy, darling, why don't you run along and tell Master Poglia to start your lesson?" Lady Sinnett said, smiling.

Percy eyed his sister suspiciously, but then obeyed his mother and pranced happily enough from the dining room.

Lady Sinnett took a studiously casual sip of tea. "So, Hazel. The theater—Le Grand Leon, of course—has a premiere tonight. Some charming dance piece, I imagine. I thought you and I should attend."

Hazel nearly choked on a piece of toast. "You and I? Together?"

"Of course," Lady Sinnett said. "Shouldn't a mother make a social engagement with her daughter?"

"I suppose she could. What will Percy do?"

"Percy's too young for the theater, darling. Besides, who knows what he could come down with at a theater. He'll be fine with Mrs. Herberts. How silly of you to ask." Lady Sinnett waited for Hazel to say something else. When she didn't, Lady Sinnett carried on. "Well, wonderful. I'll tell Iona to put you in that new silk. The arsenic green. It makes your eyes look, well, not quite so brown."

So Hazel wasn't in trouble after all. She was so relieved she just nodded.

Lady Sinnett took her agreement and smiled back at her, pleased. "I know I'm still in mourning, but I suppose I can wear the pearls that my mother gave me, and the emerald ring from your father. Bought it when we were engaged, don't know how he ever afforded it, he was just a lieutenant at the time. And there I was, daughter of a viscount, and so easily captured by thoughts of romance and"—she gave a short, rueful laugh—"love. You know, I grew up at Almont House with a summer cottage in Devon and an apartment in London for the Season." She noticed the strange look on Hazel's face. "Why are you staring at me like that, like you're a cat caught on a ledge? It does nothing for the wrinkle on your forehead."

Hazel struggled to take a sip of tea. "I think this might be the most you've spoken to me since"—she knew enough not to say George's name—"since Father left."

Lady Sinnett scoffed. "Oh, honestly, Hazel. Ridiculousness doesn't suit you."

They sat for another few moments without speaking, with only the clink of forks on china and occasional pops from the fire puncturing the silence. When Lady Sinnett spoke again, her voice was different. Thick and serious. She didn't look at Hazel's face. Instead she gazed out the window, at the foggy expanse of field and the stables beyond.

"Hazel, when your father dies," she said, "the house goes to Percy. You know that. All of it—the house, the property, what money he has, what money *I* had coming into this marriage—it goes to Percy."

As if on cue came the sound of Percy running and laughing along the upper gallery. His steps and laughter echoed. "All of that is to say," Hazel's mother continued carefully, "that it would behoove you to get your cousin to formalize your engagement sooner rather than later."

Hazel laughed. "Formalize? Mother, we've been practically engaged since we were children."

Lady Sinnett didn't laugh. She tightened her thin lips. "Has he asked for your hand yet?"

"Well, no, but—"

"Do not play games with your future. It permits the possibility of losing." Lady Sinnett rang the bell for the scullery maid to come clear the table. "I'll take my infusion in my bedroom," she said, and rose to exit. Looking back at Hazel, she added, "Tell Iona to lace the corset tight tonight. Nip the jacket in if she has to. Let Bernard see you tonight as a woman, not as a childhood companion."

The fire popped again as a log fell. The bacon suddenly felt very thick in Hazel's throat.

B Y THE TIME HAZEL AND HER mother arrived at Le Grand Leon, most of the other carriages had already dropped off their passengers. Lady Sinnett wore gray, a dress with unfashionably long sleeves. Hazel's dress was red. She hardly ever wore it—a silk dress with chenille thread embroidery at the hem and sleeves that her mother had brought back from Paris—but Hazel's stomach had turned when she looked at the arsenic green dress Iona had laid out on the bed for her. Something drew her to the red, hidden away in the back of her clothing press. She had forgotten about this dress. It was softer than her crinoline, and sheer around her shoulders.

"Lady Sinnett, you *do* look well!"

The large bosom of Hyacinth Caldwater met Hazel at eye level as they were walking up the steps into Le Grand Leon. Mrs. Caldwater had gone through two husbands already, and she looked as though she was already on the prowl for a third. Her dress, in a shocking pink, was cut low at the bosom. Her cheeks were brightly rouged in a way that would have been considered girlish for a woman half her age.

Lady Sinnett's face became tight as a drum. "Mrs. Caldwater. How nice to see you," she said, looking as though it was anything but.

"It's been *ages*! Still in half mourning? Oh, you poor dear. So lovely to see you out and about. You haven't invited me over for tea like you promised, I haven't forgotten! Ha ha ha! And *ooooh*!" Mrs. Caldwater looked over at Hazel and squealed in delight. "This isn't Hazel. No. No! It couldn't possibly! How big she's got. I swear, she's quite grown up in the meantime. You're not hiding her away, are you?"

Lady Sinnett looked past Mrs. Caldwater, hoping for someone who could pull her into a different conversation. "No," she said absently, "I'm afraid Hazel is a reader, she hardly ever leaves Hawthornden if she can help it."

"A *reader*. How fascinating. What are you reading, my dear? Novels?"

Hazel looked to her mother before she answered. "I only just began *The Antiquary*, by the author of *Waverley*. My father ordered it and sent it along to me."

Mrs. Caldwater clasped her hands together. "Such a little mind she has, Lavinia."

Hazel's mother tugged at her hand. "We really must be getting to our seats now."

Hyacinth Caldwater called up the stairs after them, "And *don't* forget that tea, Lavinia, I shall be *scandalized* if you continue to avoid me!"

"Dreadful woman," Lady Sinnett murmured as she and Hazel continued through the throng of people. "Oh, look, there's Bernard and your uncle."

Bernard bowed to Hazel and Lady Sinnett as he approached. "I trust you're well, Hazel? I must say, that red absolutely suits you."

Hazel couldn't force her face into a smile. She looked at Bernard, and all she saw was that smug, blank look on his face from that day on the street. *When we were children,* he had said. If he only knew what she was capable of doing! If he only knew what she had seen!

Lady Sinnett elbowed Hazel hard in the ribs. "Very well, thank you, Cousin," Hazel said coolly.

"We trust we'll see you down in London for the Season, Bernard?" Hazel's mother said quickly, smiling like a serpent. "Hazel has so been looking forward to the masquerade ball that the duke always throws at Delmont, haven't you, darling?"

Hazel looked away. "Mmmm," she said.

"I wouldn't miss it," Bernard said. "Ah! It appears as though my father is calling me to our box. If you'll excuse me, ladies." He bowed again and swept away into the crowd.

Hazel and her mother made their way up the rest of the stairs to their own seats, in a box on the upper right side of the theater. The curtain, thick and dusty velvet in acid green, hung in front of the stage. The orchestra was still warming up, and Hazel took the time to scan the crowd to see who else had come out tonight.

Bernard and Lord Almont were sitting in a box across the theater next to, of all people, the Hartwick-Ellis twins, Cecilia and Gibbs. Hazel hadn't seen Cecilia for some time— when was the last time? Since the Morris ball? That was a summer ago. Cecilia had grown taller; her neck was long and narrow as a stork's. She had always been fair; tonight her blond hair was curled into ringlets on either side of her head. Hazel couldn't miss them, nobody could; she was shaking them about from side to side, trying to get the light to catch them while she giggled obscenely. Her brother, Gibbs, looked glum as always, a blond boy whose eyes, nose, and mouth all seemed too small and too close together on a face large as a dinner plate.

"Cecilia looks well," Hazel said to her mother.

Lady Sinnett didn't reply. Her eyes were fixed like daggers on Cecilia and, Hazel saw, on Bernard. Bernard, who seemed to be laughing along with Cecilia, who happily dodged each assault by her ringlets and genially patted her gloved hand when she clasped his hands in hers. Were they . . . flirting? It wasn't possible. Cecilia Hartwick-Ellis had about as much personality as a bowl of rice pudding. The pair of them—Cecilia and Gibbs—probably couldn't count to five if they started at four. They certainly hadn't read that many books between them.

At that moment, Cecilia gave a laugh so ridiculous and false that Hazel heard it from across the theater. And Bernard—Bernard seemed to enjoy it. There was a flush creeping up his neck onto his cheeks. He had done something different with his hair tonight—it was swept forward and his sideburns were long, as if he were pretending to be that scandalous poet Lord Byron. Bernard whispered something into Cecilia's ear and she laughed again, throwing her head back and making her curls shake. Hazel couldn't stand to look at it. She wasn't sure whom she was more embarrassed for.

Finally, the gaslights of the theater dimmed and the orchestra began to play, a dreary dirge in a minor key. When the curtain parted, it revealed a stage nearly empty. The backdrop was a misty moor, all gray and brown, with a false dead and gnarled tree and a low-hanging orange moon. A redheaded dancer in a white flowy gown like a nightdress pranced onto the stage, soon joined by a man who was supposed to be her husband. Hazel tried to focus on the plot and ignore what was happening in the box across the theater. In the dance, the woman's husband was called away to some vague and distant war, and the woman grew depressed in his absence, swirling herself across the stage and reaching her arms toward the heavens—or rather, the rafters above. Every day, the woman went to her window to wait for her love, and every day she was disappointed.

And then a man *does* come, a man dressed in all black with the mustache of a villain and dark, willful eyes, wearing the jacket of her former lover. Perhaps it *is* her lover, back from the war, the woman thinks! They dance together, she's seduced. But as they dance, the mysterious man's costume falls away. He wasn't her husband after all; he was the Devil himself. Bereft at her mistake and betrayal, the woman pulls a dagger from her writing desk and stabs it through her breast. Red ribbons meant to stand in for her blood flutter down to the stage. The dancer falls. Her true husband finally comes home to find her body lying cold, and the curtain comes down. A tragedy.

A little heavy-handed, thought Hazel. But Le Grand Leon was never the place for subtlety. Last month, they had premiered another story with more or less the same plot—a beautiful young virtuous woman led astray—only that time it had been by a foreign vampire who tempted her with gold and jewels before he consumed her heart.

IT'S THE LESSON YOUNG GIRLS EVERYWHERE were taught their entire lives—don't be seduced by the men you meet, protect your virtue—until, of course, their entire lives depended on seduction by the right man. It was an impossible situation, a trick of society as a whole: force women to live at the mercy of whichever man wants them but shame them for anything they might do to *get* a man to want them. Passivity was the ultimate virtue. Heaven forbid you turn into someone like Hyacinth Coldwater. Be patient, be silent, be beautiful and untouched as an orchid, and *then* and *only then* will your reward come: a bell jar to keep you safe.

Lady Sinnett had kept her hand clenched in a claw on the armrest of her seat for the entire performance. Before the applause had even ended, she yanked Hazel out of her seat and down the staircase, out of the theater and into their carriage.

She waited until they were a sensible distance from the theater and onto the quiet lane that led back to Hawthornden, and then she turned to Hazel. "Do you," she said through clenched teeth, "have any idea what is going to happen to you?"

"What do you mean?" Hazel said.

Lady Sinnett swallowed and pressed her tight lips together. "The world is not kind to women, Hazel. Even women like you. Your grandfather was a viscount, yes, but I was a daughter and so that means very little. Your father owns Hawthornden, and when he—when your father dies, Hawthornden will go to Percy. Do you know what happens to unmarried women?"

Hazel knit her eyebrows together. "I suppose . . . I mean—"

Lady Sinnett cut her off with a sad, rueful chuckle. "Nowhere to live. At the mercy of your relatives. At the mercy of your little brother and whomever he deigns to marry. Begging your sister-in-law for scraps of human decency, praying that she's kind."

Hazel didn't know what to say. She just stared down at her lap.

Her mother continued, fingering the edge of her veil. "I

realize—I realize that since George left us, I maybe have not been as *attentive* to you as I might have been. I may not have stressed the importance of your marriage to Bernard Almont, because I assumed you knew it."

"I do know it."

"Yes, I thought you did. Smart girl, always reading. Not everyone will be so forgiving of your little—quirks—as your cousin is. The books on natural philosophy you steal away from your father's study. There will be none of that when we go to London. I guarantee Cecilia Hartwick-Ellis doesn't dirty her dresses with mud—or ink from books."

"Only because she doesn't know how to read," Hazel mumbled to the glass of the carriage window.

Lady Sinnett sniffed. "Let your fate be on your own head, then. I have given you all the motherly advice I can."

They spent the rest of the carriage ride in silence. Hazel stared at the dreary darkness through the window and watched the dead branches whip past them as the horses pulled them away from the city and toward home.

9

TWO STAGEHANDS WERE MISSING FOR THE opening performance that night. Jack grumbled as he filled in for them before the show, putting costumes where they belonged, checking the gaslights along the edge of the stage. He liked to be in place by now, high in the rafters, ready to raise the curtain on Mr. Antony's cue.

Isabella stretched in the wings, her face already powdered, her flowing muslin costume on. She looked beautiful like this, Jack thought, with her yellow hair pulled high on her head and her cheeks rouged. But Jack always thought she looked beautiful. He spent every show in the rafters, up above the stage, watching her—watching the way she seemed to glide through the air like a fish underwater. Effortless. She turned to see him staring at her and smiled at him. Jack smiled back.

"Oi! Lover boy!" Mr. Anthony called out. He was securing a rope and balancing a cigar on his lower lip. "Make sure you get that tree set for Act Two. Carafree ain't here, so his job is yours now." He gave a heavy sigh. "You can handle it, right, Jack?" Mr. Anthony had lost an arm fighting the French in the West Indies, and in its place had a limb of leather stuffed with what might have been horsehair coming out at the seams between the false fingers, although Jack had always known better than to ask.

Jack swept his hair out of his eyes. "Course I can. But where is Carafree? And where's John Nickels? Not like them to not show up."

"You didn't hear, you mean?"

"No, course not. Hear what?"

Mr. Anthony glanced around and moved in closer to Jack, turning his back on a group of giggling chorus girls. "Dead."

"What? Both of them?"

"As doornails. They're saying it's the bricklayer's back again. That it took Carafree before he even felt a fever and John Nickels quicker than that."

"No," Jack said quickly. "No, the boys at King's Arms like to talk and scare each other, is all. I bet Carafree and John Nickels are both on a carriage to Glasgow, laughing their heads off about the gambling debts they're leaving behind, and I bet they didn't think a lick about leaving me with all of their extra work."

Mr. Anthony shrugged. "That's not what I heard, mate. I heard it's the fever back again. Took a whole family living at Canongate last month."

"It's not the Roman fever," Jack said confidently. "It couldn't be. They'd close the theaters. We'd be out of a job."

Mr. Anthony gave a hearty, miserable laugh that turned into a hacking cough. "Sonny boy, if the fever is back, you and I will have to worry about a lot more than a job." The dance mistress rang the bell for the start of the show. Jack gave one hopeful glance back at Isabella, in case she was still looking at him, but she was distracted, pulling up her stockings. And so Jack just nodded at Thomas Potter, the lead actor, and climbed the ladder along the back wall to get to the galley above the stage.

The rafters above Le Grand Leon felt to Jack like a great ship—there were the ropes and wooden beams, the thick sails of canvas for painted backdrops, and among them all, dipping and swinging and pulling and releasing, there was Jack. He didn't know where he had been born—somewhere off Canongate, he imagined—but this place was the closest to home he had known.

A few miserable years were hazy in his memory, years after he ran away from his overworked, overdrinking mother; years of begging on High Street and performing card tricks for the ladies in the Princes Street Gardens and wrestling the other sharp-elbowed boys for the bones thrown away behind the butcher's shop. He had lived for some time near there with a group of thieves in Fleshmarket Close, where the smell of the curdling blood that ran from the butcher's down onto the street clung in Jack's nose during all waking and sleeping hours. Munro had been there, too—a boy a few years older than Jack, who wore fisherman's pants even to sleep and had a nose broken so many times that what was left on his face was crooked in half a dozen directions. It was Munro who'd first taught Jack to become a resurrection man.

"You see there?" Munro said to Jack one afternoon when they were watching a hanging at Grassmarket. The sorry murderer's hands were tied behind his back, and he had to ask the hangman to take off his cap for him, revealing his hair slicked wet with sweat. The man was being hanged for beating his wife with such viciousness that she died, as had the baby she was carrying in her belly. For weeks, boys in the streets had been selling broadsheets with drawings of the man and details about the crime.

Jack and Munro stood and waited for the body to drop through the wooden floor, for the gruesome bounce, and for the twitching to stop and the cheers of the crowd to go quiet. When the body at last lay still, a horde of men fought their way forward to grab the corpse. "There, all them men coming to get the body?" Munro said. "You see them?"

Jack bit into a mealy apple. "Who wants the bones of a dead murderer?"

"Don't be daft," Munro said, snatching the apple out of Jack's hand and biting into it himself. He made a face but took another bite. "They're trying to get the body to sell it to the doctors. The students up at the uni. They needs bodies to study on and stuff. A body goes for two guineas and a crown. If it's pregnant, it goes for three guineas, but that's harder, seeing as they rarely hang a woman with child." Munro tilted his head toward the gallows, where four or five men were working furiously with penknives to cut pieces of the noose. "They'll be selling those pieces of rope as keepsakes. Meant to ward off evil spirits, I guess. Or ward off murderers. Or maybe meant to ward off your own bad luck in being hanged yourself.

"But the real money's in the body," Munro said, sucking on the apple core. "Problem is, everyone knows when a hanging is, everyone's fighting over the body. But a body is a body whether it was hanged or not, and doctors don't care so much about the law as you might think."

And so Jack Currer became a resurrection man. He kept

a spade and slipped into kirkyards after dark to dig up fresh bodies—sometimes alone, usually with Munro, sometimes with Munro and whatever poor boy showed up at Fleshmarket in need of a good meal.

Were they going to get in trouble? No more than the trouble they got in just being poor and living on the streets of Edinburgh. Body snatchers were a vital organ of the living city itself. It was filthy, and the fancy folks liked to look away, but they were essential nonetheless. Everyone knew they were doing it; police hardly cared, so long as they didn't take clothes or jewels from the graves. Wealthier families had iron cage mortsafes, or solid stone slabs above the graves to protect them from people like Jack. Poorer families sometimes had someone sitting and watching, a sentinel who would stay beside the grave for three or four days, until the body decomposed enough to no longer be valuable to doctors for study. (Both of those were easy enough to get around for a professional like Jack—start from twenty yards away and dig a tunnel straight through and underneath. Pull the body out, and no one ever knows.)

Mostly, though, it was the unloved who made Jack's living, the bodies buried shallow and forgotten. They would be invaluable to Jack, and to the doctors he sold them to. Whatever little those poor souls did in life, they did plenty in death.

He had thought that starting work at Le Grand Leon would mean giving up that life, the long nights of digging until his shoulders ached, of pulling bodies bloated with gas and shit, of worms that wriggled into his shoes. He had a place to sleep, nestled into the canvas laid across the planks above the stage, and Mr. Arthur made stews for the crew out of cabbage and potato skins and whatever bits the crew could scrounge up.

The way Jack liked to think of it, he had a better view up here than even those posh folks in their fancy box seats, and all he had to do was make sure the curtain and right backdrops unfurled at the right time. Those people in the audience were stuck in their seats, wearing their silk—which would wrinkle if you stood wrong, let alone jumped a garden fence—and shoes that pinched their feet. But the want of money creeps up on you like a fox in the darkness.

And there was Isabella. Always Isabella, dancing on the stage below him night after night. How could anyone *not* fall in love with her after seeing the way she moved, the way the lanterns onstage made her blond hair glow—made all of her glow? She was the closest thing to an angel Jack had ever seen in Edinburgh.

Jack had worked as a stagehand at Le Grand Leon two months before he started stealing bodies again in the night.

"Ye all right?" Thomas, the lead actor, called up to Jack from the wings during an applause break. Thomas was already dressed in his costume for the next scene, when he appeared as the devil, disguised as the lady's former lover. Jack nodded. Thomas was from Birmingham—God knew how he had made it to Le Grand Leon, but he liked to tell anyone who would listen that he was going to save up enough money to make it down to London to perform Shakespeare for the king. He was handsome in that broad-shouldered actor sort of way, the type of handsome that had the ladies who do the costuming giggling behind their hands. Jack tended to disappear into the shadows, but that was by design. Like a nocturnal animal, the best way for Jack to remain safe was to remain unseen.

Life at Le Grand Leon was like living inside a music box.

The gilt-edged ceiling was painted in four sections meant to represent the four seasons, each with its own collection of potato-shaped cherubs with cheeks the color of roses and skin the color of ivory. And like a music box, there was the dancer, center stage, Isabella Turner. Jack could imagine her like one of those porcelain ballerinas he saw in the window of the antique shop on Holyrood Street, a ballerina balancing on one foot, the other extended out behind her, her arm lifted, her entire body taut like a pulled bowstring. Spinning onstage slowly, to the sound of windup music.

Back when he was living in Fleshmarket Close, he had passed that antique store every day. But he finally built up the courage to walk in only last week. The woman behind the counter had glowered at him, and glowered even harder as she watched him pick up the music box in the window.

"How much for this?"

"More than ye can afford, I reckon," she said, but not so unkindly as she might have.

"I have work. I do, I swear it. Work down at Le Grand Leon. How much for this one, here?" The ballerina in the music box was blond, like Isabella.

The shop owner sighed and drummed her finger on the counter. "I've seen you out there before, haven't I? Looking in the window." Jack nodded. "Least I can do for her is ten shillings."

Jack's eyes nearly fell out of his head. That was as much as he made in a month of work. But he had come with his mind made up. He reached into his pocket and pulled out the coins. "Take it, then," he said. And he left the shop before he could talk himself into changing his mind. It was for Isabella, and it was perfect. It would just mean another night at the kirkyard, and he would steal and sell a thousand bodies if it meant buying Isabella the things that would show her how much he adored her. Let him spend every night in the dirt if it meant getting his mornings with her.

THE SHOW ENDED WITH THE USUAL APPLAUSE, and Jack lowering the heavy green velvet curtain, wincing as the rope squeaked on the way down. Isabella beamed at the audience, extended her arms as if she were about to take a dive, and lowered into a curtsy that anyone might have mistaken for a lady's. And then she ducked back behind the safe wall of the curtain, and her smile fell. The magic spell was over, they were all human again, and the audience was filing into their carriages and complaining about the weather.

Jack would have to be quick if he wanted to catch Isabella before she snuck out the back door and went home. He pulled the music box out from beneath his overcoat, where he had wrapped it to keep it safe, and climbed one-handed down the ladder, keeping it level.

He could hear Isabella in her dressing room—the sounds of movement, the scratch of a candle being lit, the rustling of a skirt—but he couldn't force himself to knock. Not yet. For the hundredth time, he ran his fingers along the smooth edges of the music box. And then Jack took a deep breath and rapped hard, twice, on the door.

The door swung open before he even finished knocking. It wasn't Isabella—it was the dance mistress's daughter, Mary-Anne, a flinty-eyed girl of eight or nine who tidied up and did the hemming on the costumes. "She ain't here," she said flatly, looking Jack up and down. Her eyes landed on the music box.

"Do you know where she went?" he asked her, trying his best to twist his mouth into what he hoped was a roguish smile.

Mary-Anne just shrugged. "Didn't come back after curtain that I saw."

Jack sighed. And then he heard Isabella's laugh. He would have known it anywhere, from a thousand miles away, the way her voice pealed like a bell. It was coming through the window from the alley. Jack pushed a crate against the wall and stepped onto it to look out the window below. Why did he do it? Why didn't he just go inside? Why didn't he just go to bed, realize that Isabella not being in her dressing room was a kindness of fate and he should forget about her? But half a lifetime in the rafters had given Jack the instinct of silently looking onto other people below. And when Jack stood up against the window, he could see Isabella outside, her arms wrapped around the lead actor, and the lead actor pulling her into a kiss.

The music box slipped from his hand and clattered to the floor. Jack fell from the crate, toppling two false trees. "I'm all right!" he shouted to the people staring, although nobody had asked.

When it hit the floor, the music box had opened and begun to quietly play its tinny melody. When Jack picked it up, he realized that the ballerina had chipped and broken. Gone were her arms and her head and neck and torso. All that was left was her leg, anchoring her to her tiny stage, and the pink hoop skirt of her dress. But she kept spinning, until Jack slammed the box closed.

He climbed back up into the rafters, where he had made his bed and hid his few paltry belongings. He shoved the music box back under his spare coat. He didn't want to see it anymore; just looking at it made him burn with humiliation. Isabella had been a fantasy, she always had been. What did he think, he would buy her one stupid music box and she would swoon? He didn't even know if she liked music boxes! He was a fool. No, worse than a fool. He was a romantic fool.

Jack wrapped himself in a discarded curtain and pulled out the wine he kept nestled under some rope, and he drank deeply until the theater was dark and he was left alone in the silence—just the rats in the walls, and mice in the seats, and his own solitary heartbeat.

𝕰𝕕𝕚𝕟𝕭𝕦𝕣𝕘𝕙 𝕰𝕧𝕖𝕟𝕚𝕟𝕘 𝕲𝕒𝕫𝕖𝕥𝕥𝕖

November 11, 1817

SIX MORE DEAD FROM MYSTERIOUS ILLNESS

Six deaths in the last fortnight in Edinburgh's Old Town have several officials fearing another outbreak of the devastating Roman fever. Four of the bodies remain unidentified—three male, one female—but the other victims have been identified as Davey Jaspar, 12, a shoeshine, and Penelope Marianne Harkness, 31.

Mrs. Penelope Harkness worked as an innkeeper at the Deer and Stag, where she was described by patrons as kind and easy with a laugh. She reported feeling feverish on Friday evening. Her landlord discovered her deceased Sunday morning when she failed to come down to church.

"It's a terrible situation," stated William Beecham III, head of the Royal Edinburgh Anatomists' Society and Chief Surgeon at the King's University Hospital. "I examined the body myself, and I was horrified to find the lesions on Mrs. Harkness's back consistent with Roman fever. Obviously, we hope that the disease has not returned to our city, but I must advise caution and vigilance."

The Roman fever ravaged Edinburgh two years ago, the summer of 1815, with over two thousand dead.

10

AZEL KNEW WHAT WAS COMING. THOUGH Lady Sinnett abhorred newspapers and tried to keep Hawthornden tightly sealed as a cocoon, still, she knew about the rumors and the fears that had begun to bubble over from Edinburgh proper. If the fever was making a return, Lady Sinnett would do whatever it took to keep Percy safe. Even still, it came sooner than Hazel expected: the trunks packed in the hallway, the frantic arrangements made for an apartment in Bath.

"But we always spend Christmas at Hawthornden," Hazel had said as she watched her mother carefully wrapping her jewels in linen.

"Not this year," she replied. "This year we're going to Bath, for a holiday before London."

A dozen times a day, Lady Sinnett gently pressed the back of her cold hand to Percy's forehead and cooed. "The warm waters at Bath will do you well, my darling," she repeated. She flitted through the house like a trapped moth, opening and shutting windows at random, murmuring about "good air" for Percy.

The day before the trip, Hazel began to cough conspicuously. That evening, she complained of a chill. The next morning, Hazel didn't go down to breakfast. She told Iona to tell her mother that she felt feverish. From her bed, Hazel could hear her mother's shriek a floor below. There was frantic movement and inaudible whispering, and then came a soft knocking on Hazel's door.

"It's me, miss," Iona said softly from the other side of the wood. "Your mother asked me to stay on the other side of the door, in case you're catching. She asks what the symptoms are?"

Hazel thought for a moment. "Fever, definitely. I think maybe just fever. And blurring vision." And, why not? "And my tongue has gone green."

Footsteps. And then footsteps back. Hazel could sense Iona's hesitation in the hallway. "Your mother—Lady Sinnett wonders if perhaps it might make more sense for you to rest here, at Hawthornden, and join them in Bath only once you're well." Lady Sinnett shouted something from down the stairs. "Or even," Iona amended, "wait until they're in London for the Season and meet them there. Just to make sure you're well, miss."

Hazel grinned from beneath her sheets. She had heated the bedpan to use to warm the sheets, and brought a glass of water that she could have used to pat against her hairline if her mother needed proof that she was feverish, but she might have known that Lady Sinnett would be too frightened to get closer than the landing. "I think that'll be just fine," Hazel said. And then, realizing that her voice had sounded perhaps a bit *too* perky, she added, "If that's what Mother thinks is best. For Percy's safety."

There were more footsteps, heavier this time, and Hazel

knew that her mother was now in the hallway outside her door. "Hazel," Lady Sinnett said, "do take care of yourself. Iona and Cook will be here. And I've told Lord Almont to send an extra ladies' maid if you need one." A pause. "You understand, don't you?" Lady Sinnett asked. "We could delay the trip, but . . ."

"It's perfectly all right, Mother," Hazel called back. "In fact, I insist upon it. I imagine I just need rest. And there's no sense in risking Percy's health. I will rest up at Hawthornden and join you in the South when I'm well." She added a theatrical cough. "I'm too sick even to leave bed at the moment."

"Well, all right," Lady Sinnett said after a moment. "I'll see you again soon. I've left the address of the apartment in Bath. Please write to let us know how you're feeling."

"I will."

There was the swish of skirts on the wooden floor. For the next hour, Hazel was silent, listening to the sounds of the house as they made their final arrangements for the trip down to England, the dog barking as trunks were brought outside, Cook wrapping pies for the road, the horses getting strapped into place. Finally, there were the final footsteps of Percy and Lady Sinnett leaving their rooms, and the echoes as the household went outside to wave them off.

Hazel waited until the sound of the carriage on the gravel drive faded away. And then she waited another half an hour—about as long as it would take them to get to the end of the drive and to the gate where the Hawthornden estate met the main road. And then Hazel flipped her blanket down, got out of bed, and called to Iona, asking for a cup of tea. She had done it. She had *months* alone, without Lady Sinnett, without Percy—with everyone who mattered thinking that she was too sick to leave the house.

Iona returned with the teapot and two cups. She set the tray down gingerly, and then looked up at Hazel and smiled.

"Do you think I'm mad, Iona?" Hazel said quietly, more a statement than a question.

Iona shook her head. "And besides, there won't be much time for madness when you're the Viscountess Almont. Might as well get it out of your system now."

Hazel tried to resist the smile pulling at the corners of her lips. "And my mother—she didn't suspect a thing?"

Iona laughed. "Course not. So worried for Percy, I think she would have left you here for looking pale at breakfast. Poor boy."

"Poor boy? Poor *Percy*? He gets all the attention in the world."

"It's not good to be smothered like that. Boy needs fresh air and a little mud on his knees every now and again."

"George rode every day, and look where he ended up. Oh—oh, Iona, I'm so sorry."

Iona had been madly in love with George since he came back from Eton for summer holiday having grown a thin mustache and about six inches. She'd followed him around like a lovesick puppy, repeated his words back to the rest of the servants, and spilled tea from nerves if he was ever in the room.

"He was just so beautiful, wasn't he?" she said now.

Hazel nodded, and she pushed away the thought that had seemed to bubble to the surface of her brain like scum on a lake every day for the past two years: *Maybe it should have been him, and not me.* It was a nibbling rat of a thought, illogical, terrible, and cruel. Hazel knew all of that. And yet.

Iona gazed out the window, her eyes flat and misty, some distant memory of George playing across her face.

"You know," Hazel said, "the footman Charles has become quite handsome in the past few years, I've noticed. And he can't take his eyes off you. I've caught him more than once lingering in the library, hoping to catch you setting up the fire. The boy is positively lovesick."

"Charles? Truly?"

"And he won't be a footman forever. Before my father left, I remember him mentioning to the steward that Charles would make a fine valet."

Iona was lost in thought, or fantasy, for a moment, and Hazel watched a smile twitch at the edges of her lips. "And you say he stares at me?"

"Honest to goodness."

The light from the window reached Iona's cheeks beneath her cap, and Hazel would have sworn she was blushing.

"Well, enough of that nonsense. We have a task at hand," Iona said. She stepped back and squinted one eye to get a better look at Hazel. "You do look a good deal like your brother, I think. From the side. The same nose, same eyebrows." The two of them glanced involuntarily toward the hallway, where George's portrait hung on the wall. Iona was being kind, Hazel knew. Hazel was pretty enough, but people had remarked on George's striking good looks since they were children.

"The important thing," Hazel said, "is that he wasn't too much taller than I am."

ITH IONA'S HELP, HAZEL WAS SOON wearing one of George's muslin shirts, a waistcoat, a jacket, and a pair of trousers. "These britches are nice. Although perhaps they don't look quite modern enough," Iona had said, holding up a pair of knee-length pants while they were going through George's clothes press. "Although I suppose they were the style a few years back."

"No," Hazel said. "Trousers. With braces. I'm to be a medical man, not a dandy."

By the time they finished and dusted off a hat from a top shelf, Hazel Sinnett could easily have passed as a gentleman.

"These boots are going to be too big, I'm afraid," Iona said, pulling out a fine black leather pair of Hessians that were meant to reach midcalf, but on Hazel would go up to her knees.

"No matter," Hazel replied. "We'll stuff the toes with stockings. There must be an overcoat somewhere—even one of Father's . . ."

"A cravat?" Iona asked.

"No, I'm trying to be George, not Beau Brummell."

Iona's eyes went wide. "You can't be telling them that you're George. But surely they'll know that George is d—"

"They won't know George Sinnett from Adam, I assure you. But I think you're right to use a false name. How about George . . . Hazleton?"

Iona wiped the wetness from her eyes and smiled slightly. "I think that suits you well, *Mr.* George Hazleton."

"Besides," Hazel added, "if I'm paying the tuition for the whole semester in good sterling up front, I doubt they'd care if I introduced myself as Mary Wollstonecraft."

From the <u>Memoir of</u>
<u>the Rev. Sydney Smith</u> (1798) by Sydney Smith:

No smells were ever equal to Scotch smells ... Walk the streets, and you would imagine that every medical man had been administering cathartics to every man, woman, and child in town. Yet the place is uncommonly beautiful, and I am in constant balance between admiration and trepidation.

11

HE WALLS OF THE CLASSROOM WERE BLACK, peeling wood. The entire place smelled like sawdust and embalming fluid. Bookshelves lined the back of the room from floor to ceiling. Hazel tried to get a glimpse of their contents before she took her seat—she recognized a row of various editions of *Dr. Beecham's Treatise*, each one becoming thicker than the last, but there were also books in French, German, and Italian. Some had titles in languages Hazel couldn't even identify. One book was bound in tan leather that Hazel realized, brushing the spine with her finger, might be human skin.

Around the classroom's perimeter were specimen jars that had already captured the attention of the other boys who would be taking Beecham's course: animals preserved in dingy yellow fluid, human organs, full sets of grinning teeth. Hazel noticed a jar containing a pair of tiny human fetuses, no larger than the palm of her hand, conjoined at the head. There were disembodied hands and feet, and an entire row of milky gray brains in sizes ranging from walnut to swollen grapefruit. And then forming a morbid gallery on a high shelf running across the top of the wall were the skulls, at least a dozen of them, mostly with strange deformities, all in various states of decay.

Above them, the skeleton of a massive sea creature, perfectly preserved and wired in place, dangled from the ceiling as if it were still swimming through an invisible current. Hazel was so absorbed in the strangeness of her surroundings that she didn't notice Dr. Beecham himself standing behind the lectern until he gently cleared his throat and stretched his fingers in his gloves to make the black leather creak.

The other students were just as taken aback as Hazel: immediately, they all scrambled to their seats.

Dr. Beecham stood there while the room quieted down, letting his eyes linger on each student, one at a time. When Beecham's eyes reached Hazel, she couldn't help but feel her scalp become itchy underneath her hat. The pins she and Iona had used to fasten her hair were suddenly sharp. Before putting on George's clothes, she had fantasized that they would offer more freedom than her own corset and bustle and skirt. But now, sitting in ill-fitting men's pants, and with a shirt's collar up to her chin, she found herself distinctly uncomfortable, sweat dampening the thick fabric at her underarms.

Beecham's gaze dropped to Hazel's desk, to her well-worn edition of *Dr. Beecham's Guide,* peeling at the spine and spotted with brown. He gave a small, disapproving tut at the book's deterioration, but then he mercifully passed his gaze onto the next student, a boy who couldn't have been more than fifteen, still unable to grow whiskers.

"Welcome," Dr. Beecham said finally. "Before we begin in earnest, I must offer one brief comment on a personal note. There are some—perhaps not among this group sitting before me, but surely among the various drawing rooms of London and Edinburgh and Paris—who may think that my elite position at the university and within the Anatomists' Society is thanks to my grandfather. I assure you: I owe nothing to nepotism."

Beecham waited to see if anyone would challenge him. Nobody did. Who would dare? Surely, Hazel thought, no one who had seen Beecham's demonstration at the anatomy theater, the speed of his blade, the use of that . . . ethereum. The most senior Beecham would die all over again if he could ever have seen how much further surgery had come since his death.

Dr. Beecham stood with his posture impossibly straight as he continued his introduction. He adjusted the seam on the black leather gloves he was wearing as he spoke. "I warn you now that the course on which you are now embarking is not an easy one. It will challenge you physically. It will challenge you mentally. You will come face-to-face with the strange, the macabre. The medical field is at the cusp of great change, and I intend, with my students, to lead a charge into the future. We shall learn basic anatomy, basic physiology, surgical techniques. The fundamentals of the apothecary. By the end of my course, you shall be well prepared to sit for your Royal Physician's Examination before Christmas, after which you will be certified to work as a physician anywhere you choose in His Majesty's empire. The field of medicine is deadly. I would be remiss if I neglected to mention that I have lost more than one student in the time that I've been teaching. I like to think I have the experience to know, looking at the students now, exactly who among you will not have the fortitude to make it." He paused. The students shifted uneasily in their seats. "Blood will stain your hands. You might find that blood may even stain your very souls."

From behind the lectern, Dr. Beecham withdrew a rabbit. A live rabbit, apparently indifferent to being held aloft in front of a classroom, placidly gazing out toward the students. There was a wave of giggles, Hazel's among them. Beecham raised one eyebrow and pulled the rabbit into his chest, stroking it with his long fingers.

"All that is to say," Dr. Beecham said, "if you wish to leave this class now, I won't hold it against you. In fact, I think self-knowledge is a form of wisdom. The field of medicine is arduous. I would be lying if I said I haven't lost more than one patient over the course of a semester." He pulled out a small scalpel from his pocket and examined the blade as he spoke. "To infection. To disease. To a mishandled blade. Even once"—he placed the rabbit on the lectern. It gave a small hop, but then settled in silence beneath Beecham's hand—"to shock."

And then Dr. Beecham brought the scalpel down onto the rabbit. Hazel gasped, but fortunately she wasn't the only one. Beecham withdrew a handkerchief to dab at the blood splatter that landed across his forehead. "I repeat. If you wish to leave this class, do it now." The boy next to Hazel looked close to fainting. He shoved his chair out and ran from the room. "Any others? No? Good."

Beecham rang a small brass bell he'd pulled from behind the lectern, and an assistant in an apron came in, carrying a box of rabbits, all of which mercifully were already dead. The rabbits were distributed amongst the students, along with scalpels that looked as though they had been in use for years. Hazel peeled a brownish drop of dried blood off her scalpel's handle.

"You have all been given a rabbit," Beecham said. "I have

taken the liberty of doing the killing for you. The term starts with anatomy, but until more men start breaking His Majesty's laws, human subjects are in limited supply, to say nothing of their considerable price. And so, for your first day: rabbit. Your task will be identifying and articulating the major organs: brain, heart, stomach, lungs, bladder, liver, spleen, large intestine, small intestine." He wrote the name of each body part in chalk on the board behind him and underlined it.

Hazel looked down at her rabbit, a thin wiry thing with mottled brown fur. The smell of it reminded her of the kitchens after her father and George went hunting. She looked up again to see Dr. Beecham impatient and expectant. "What are you waiting for?" he said to the class. "Begin!"

The scramble started immediately, as the boys around Hazel slashed their knives into their animals and began to hack away at the innards. Hazel paused a moment and examined the animal in front of her. She waited to lift her knife until she could perfectly picture all the slices she would make—as few as possible. And then Hazel cut.

"FINISHED. I MEAN: FINISHED, SIR." A few of the boys near Hazel lifted their heads in disbelief. They were covered in sweat.

Dr. Beecham looked up from the newspaper he was reading at his desk at the front of the room.

"All the organs," he said. "Not just the first one on the board."

"I know, sir. I've got them all."

Beecham rose and walked slowly over to Hazel's table,

where she had neatly removed all the requisite organs and placed them in organized rows next to the now disembow-eled rabbit. "Brain, heart, stomach, lungs, bladder, liver, spleen, large intestine, small intestine," Hazel recited, point-ing them out one by one.

Beecham blinked a few times in disbelief. "What's your name, young man?"

Hazel's mouth went dry. "George. George Hazelton, sir."

"Hazleton. Hazleton, don't believe I know the name. Is your father a physician?"

"No, sir. He serves in the Royal Navy. But he had an inter-est in natural philosophy, and I studied his books."

"His books."

"Yes. Actually, I've learned the most from your grandfa-ther's book. *Dr. Beecham's Treatise.*"

Dr. Beecham smiled. "I'm well familiar. You couldn't have found a better primer. Class, drop your scalpels. Mr. Ha-zelton has outdone you all." He leaned in to examine what remained of Hazel's rabbit. "I say, in the years I have taught this course, not a single student has ever managed to cut so cleanly and swiftly. Bravo."

A boy behind Hazel coughed loudly. "*Bootlicker,*" he coughed again. The boys around him laughed. Hazel had spent enough time with her brothers to know what he meant: she was sucking up to the teacher. The cougher had several large moles prominently placed on his face, and long side-burns perhaps meant to draw the eye away.

"That's quite enough, Mr. Thrupp."

Thrupp rolled his eyes as Dr. Beecham made his way back to the front of the classroom.

"Now, what's say we all get caught up to where Mr. Hazelton already is," Beecham said, beginning to draw a diagram of a flayed rabbit on the chalkboard.

Hazel felt something wet and cold hit the back of her neck.

A rabbit heart, which landed on the floor behind her, still leaking blood. Thrupp's cronies laughed and Thrupp smirked at her, and Hazel felt a slimy wetness drip from her neck down into her shirt.

Her cheeks burned, but Hazel forced herself not to break eye contact with that boy as she reached down and picked his rabbit heart off the floor. Looking straight at him, she brought the rabbit heart up and squeezed it, hard, in her first.

The laughing stopped, and Hazel turned back to listen to the rest of Dr. Beecham's lecture, too pleased with herself even to care about the unpleasant squelching of the blood and viscus between her fingers for the rest of the afternoon.

7 October 1817
No. 2 Henry Street
Bath

My dear Hazel,

After a nightmarishly long journey—awful, the weather, just awful—we arrived in Bath. The air already suits Percy, but I'll get him into the natural hot springs straightaway as a preventative measure. Who knows what terrible diseases he might have picked up from the bad airs on our travels? We shall be here for several months and then head to the London apartment, where I hope you will meet us. I've told Lord Almont that I expect Bernard to propose within the year, so do try to arrive in London engaged if you can.

—Your mother, Lady Lavinia Sinnett

P.S. I hope your condition has improved. Do write if anything takes a turn for the worse.

12

THE WEEKS PASSED FOR HAZEL IN A HEADY daze. Though her childhood afternoons spent on the floor of her father's study memorizing his old copy of *Dr. Beecham's Treatise* had given her a leg up on the other students initially, it soon became obvious that she would need to absorb everything she could in class if she hoped to pass the Physician's Exams at the end of term.

She took notes as quickly as she could to keep up with the pace of Dr. Beecham's lectures, which jumped from the lymphatic system to skeletal structure to the use of leeches in modern bloodletting; he reminded them not infrequently that the class would only be getting more difficult, especially once they started to watch human dissections. *That* was the real heart of the course, what students paid the fees for: the chance to see a professional efficiently autopsy a body. Whether the bodies were procured from public hangings or resurrectionists, Hazel wasn't sure. George had been buried in the family kirkyard outside Hawthornden, so Hazel's family never had to concern themselves with the rabble in the heart of Edinburgh's Old Town, the men who slinked into kirkyards with spades at night to bring the freshly buried back to the surface.

Initially, Hazel worried that her disguise wouldn't hold, that experts of the human body would see her—in an oversized hat and trousers that even Iona's hemming couldn't get to sit quite right—and easily identify her for what she was: a young woman in her brother's clothes. But the classroom was dim, lit by torches and candles, and her fellow students were so focused on their own notebooks, frantically scribbling to keep up with Beecham's words, that no one paid her much mind.

Well, no one but Thrupp, the boy with moles and a smirk like that of a boar ready to charge. When it became clear that Hazel (or rather, George Hazelton) was the best in the class by far, Thrupp delighted in taking every opportunity to torment her. One morning, Hazel found her ink replaced with a small pool of blood. The next, there was a piece of brain pinned to her desk with a penknife. But even he couldn't muster enough energy to *really* make Hazel's life difficult, when he needed to be focused enough to keep up with the material.

The Physician's Exams loomed, but there was another, more immediate threat: for all his welcoming bravado, Beecham was fanatical about culling the class if anyone fell behind. On day two, one poor boy forgot his quill and was kicked out. On day four, two boys were dropped from the course without ceremony because they were unable to identify the major systems of the body.

"You there! With the blue vest. Name me the symptoms of the Roman fever, *Plaga Romanus*. Nom de guerre, 'the bricklayer's fever,' or 'the sickness.' Well?" Beecham had shouted the question at one of the students the previous week. The boy's face went blank with terror. Hazel imagined it was exactly the same face one would make if they just happened to notice a lion running toward them full speed.

"Uh—er—well. Fever?" the boy had squeaked out. Thrupp snickered. Dr. Beecham waited for the boy to continue, his eyebrow raised expectantly. The boy looked desperately around the room for help. When none came, the unfortunate boy rose from his seat, bowed deeply to Dr. Beecham, and then sprinted from the room.

As they moved into their second month of classes, the room—once overflowing with boys jostling and elbowing each other for room at the desks—contained only a dozen students.

Beecham seemed pleased by the development. "Good morning," he said, smiling, as he arrived. "The crème de la crème remains. We shall have some fine physicians among you, there's no doubt about that." Under her hat, Hazel couldn't help but smile herself.

Beecham taught the day's lecture (on setting broken bones and the ligaments of the legs), but as the students were packing up their notes, he raised a hand to keep them in their seats. "Tomorrow will be a little different. A hanging in Grassmarket occurred last night—some poor murderess—and we have been lucky enough to secure the specimen." There was chattering of excitement. Thrupp punched his companion jovially in the arm. "Though usually I would wait until a little later in our seminar for human dissection, fresh meat follows no man's schedule!"

TOO IMPATIENT AND EAGER TO SLEEP, Hazel arrived the next day to the classroom nearly an hour early and found it empty. Dr. Beecham's lectern was replaced with a long table. Hazel prepared her quill pen and blotter and waited. The other students gradually filed in, some politely smiling at Hazel, most ignoring her. Ten minutes before class was scheduled to begin, two assistants came in through a door on the side of the classroom, carrying a mass under a sheet. They placed it gingerly on the table and pulled the sheet back.

There it was. A dead body. A woman who could have been around fifty, but might have been as young as thirty—it was hard to say. Gray curled at her temples, and her face was heavily lined, puffy but still, somehow, serene. Beecham had said she was a murderess, but nothing about her face looked like someone who had killed. There she was: a strange, naked, alien thing, waiting for a knife to split her as final punishment for her sins.

From outside the room came the echoing clang of the church bells on the hour: class was supposed to start. But Beecham, who every morning had been there before Hazel arrived, wasn't there. The students became restless in their seats.

"Maybe it's a test," said Gilbert Burgess, a nervous boy with a flop of blond hair who could never remember the bones of the hand. "Maybe we're supposed to dissect the body. And the Doc is watching somewhere! Waiting to see what we do!"

Thrupp sucked air in through his teeth. "And maybe you're supposed to stuff your fat face with cotton, Burgess."

Burgess slinked back into his seat.

Hazel cleared her throat. "At least we can see Burgess's face. Is there a nose beneath those pockmarks, Thrupp?"

Even Thrupp's cronies laughed at that one, until he elbowed one of them hard in the ribs. Burgess gave Hazel a small, grateful smile.

"Oi," Thrupp barked at Burgess. "You're lucky you have this pretty boy to protect you. You fancy yourself some sort of gentleman with those lined coats, Hazleton?"

"Yeah," Hazel responded with the most masculine swagger she could manage. "I do. And the ladies seem to like it just fine." Burgess laughed at that, a full throaty laugh, and Thrupp retreated with an eye roll.

It did seem as though they were supposed to do *something*. The clock struck ten minutes after, and then fifteen. Hazel was just about to go to the Anatomists' Society headquarters at the end of the block to ask if Dr. Beecham had been held up when the back door swung open. But it wasn't Dr. Beecham standing there. Hazel knew who it was by his bearing and cape and the bump of his cane on the wooden floor, before she even saw his eye patch.

"Good morning," said a voice like wet gravel. Dr. Straine made his way to the front of the room and stood before the naked body. His one good eye landed right on Hazel. He had met her as Hazel. He knew who she was. She tried to disappear beneath the collar of George's large shirt. She quickly prayed to whatever god was listening that her disguise would hold.

Dr. Straine lifted a scalpel and an eyebrow. "Let's begin."

13

"THE FEMALE ANATOMY," DR. STRAINE SAID, looking directly at Hazel, "is a strange beast. This woman here—hanged yesterday, eleven o'clock, Grassmarket, for the murder of one of the guests of her inn. Seems a rather small, weak person to have been capable of that."

Some of the boys in the class laughed. Hazel didn't.

Dr. Straine wiped his scalpel on his jacket. "My name," he said, "is Dr. Edmund Straine. I will be conducting the anatomical portion of your studies from here on out. Dr. Beecham, well connected and *famous* as he is, prefers to leave this part of the course to me. As you may have already learned, Beecham is not one to get his hands dirty." Straine waggled one hand in the air and pantomimed putting on a glove. "And one imagines it's difficult to fit in students when one's social calendar is filled with teas and autograph signings. But no matter. As I said, it is finally time for you to learn anatomy."

Thrupp scoffed. "We've learned plenty of anatomy already," he said.

Dr. Straine almost smiled. "No," he said. "You have learned theory. Dr. Beecham is an excellent physician and quite a learned scholar. But I'm afraid Beecham has never quite mastered the art of surgery the way I have. Yes, *art*, Mr. Thrupp—the delicate balance of understanding a body as both flesh and vehicle for a living soul, of feeling the hum of it under your knife . . ." Straine's good eye took on a distant, faraway quality, but he shook his head and then returned to staring straight at the students. "It also seems Dr. Beecham has grown too accustomed to the fine living rooms of lords and gentlemen to want the stink of a corpse on his body," he said, smirking. "All of which is to say, twice a week on Tuesdays and Thursdays, I shall conduct your lectures on anatomy. Dr. Beecham's lectures will concern treatment and remedies. Be warned, I am not as easy to impress as my esteemed colleague. And I ensure that the details from my lectures form an integral part of the Physician's Exam at the end of the term. So those among you with the faintest shred of hope of success: pay very close attention."

Without any further ado, Dr. Straine brought the scalpel down on the body of the dead woman on the table and pulled the knife through from her breastbone to her navel.

The classroom always had a strong odor: of days-old blood, and iron, and the strange pickling liquids that were used in the specimen jars that lined the walls. But Straine's first cut of his dissection unleashed a wave of something awful into the air. Several students gagged audibly, although Hazel managed to swallow the bile that rose into her mouth.

"You there," Straine said, using his still-dripping scalpel to point at Gilbert Burgess. "Name."

"Gilbert Burgess, sir," he replied. He looked positively green.

"How many chambers in the heart, Gilbert Burgess?"

Burgess shook. If it had been Beecham asking him, Hazel was certain he would have known in an instant. But something about Straine, whether it was the eye patch or the cape or the stern line of his mouth, turned him into a figure of terror.

"Er—six, sir?" Burgess said, his voice nothing more than a squeaking whisper.

Straine pounded the floor of the classroom with his cane so hard it made the entire floor shake. "Who knows? Hands up, don't be shy. You, there." He pointed directly at Hazel, who realized to her own astonishment that her hand had gone up of its own volition.

"George," she said softly. "George Hazelton. And it's four, sir. The right ventricle, left ventricle, right atrium, and left atrium."

"Correct," he said through clenched teeth. "Continue then, Mr. *Hazelton*. Name the four valves of the heart."

Hazel closed her eyes and tried to remember the diagram from the pages of *Dr. Beecham's Treatise*. "The aortic valve, sir. The tricuspid valve. The pulmonary valve and—and the bicuspid valve." She smiled, and relief flooded her body.

"Very good, Mr. Hazelton," Straine said quietly, although his tone might have been mocking. "Please stand, and come to the front of the room."

Hazel's feet obeyed and she walked to the front of the classroom until she was standing close enough to Straine she could pick up the scent on him: port wine and something sour like lemons gone bad.

"Remove the heart, Mr. Hazelton."

Hazel swallowed hard, held her breath, and obeyed, avoiding looking at the face of the woman whose body her hand had just entered. She held the heart, heavier than she expected, cold with viscous slime.

"Now," Straine said. "Identify the valves you named."

Hazel looked at the heart, an alien thing painted in blacks and purples. It was oddly shaped, nonsymmetrical, fatter on one end than the other, coated on one half with a thick beige plaque. It looked so entirely different from the object drawn in neat black lines in Hazel's textbook that she couldn't even be certain which way was the top.

"I can't, sir," she said finally.

"You *can't*?" Straine said with a cruel edge in his voice. "But you so ably identified them when you were seated?"

"It looks very different in person, sir."

"Where is the gallbladder, Mr. Hazelton?"

Hazel looked at the mess of viscera beneath her. Reds and purples swollen and pressing against each other, everything strange and bulbous. That was the stomach, she knew the stomach . . . and that was the large intestine. And the lungs. But anything smaller seemed lost in the sea of deteriorating flesh bloated with the gas of decomposition. Hazel's vision blurred and her breath caught in her tightened chest. "I'm not certain, sir."

"How about an easier one, then? The liver."

Hazel forced herself to look down again at the corpse's open belly, but the place where she thought the liver ought to be was filled with something else—*maybe the small intestine?*—and nothing else was where it was supposed to be either. She had been quiet, staring down for long enough for the giggles to start up in the classroom. Hazel suddenly came back to the realization that everyone was watching her. "I don't know," she said at last, quietly.

"Sit down, Mr. Hazleton."

Hazel's cheeks stung as she returned to her seat.

"Let this be a lesson to you all," Straine said, his eye fixed on Hazel. "What you read in books might help if you intend to show off in class, but it will do very little when you're faced with a real body. Do you imagine that you'll be operating on drawings in books, Mr. Hazelton?"

"No, sir," Hazel murmured.

Straine's thin lips twitched. He didn't look at Hazel for the rest of the lecture. By the time the sun had set and Straine finally released them, Hazel's hand ached from the effort of taking notes fast enough to keep up with his lesson. Hazel gathered her notebook and rose to head home, already fantasizing about the bath Iona would run for her at Hawthornden.

"*Mr.* Hazleton." Straine's voice called out from the gloom. "Please stay a moment."

Hazel's heart pounded in her chest. Burgess gave her a sympathetic look but then quickly turned and scampered out the door before Straine could ask him to stay back as well. Hazel tried to tilt her face down beneath her collar and her cap. In the weeks she had been dressing like George, no one had seen through her disguise. (Thrupp calling her a "pretty boy" was the closest anyone had come, and even that had made the hair on the back of her neck prickle.) But Straine had seen her, in Almont House. They had been introduced. And something about the steely look in his good eye gave Hazel the impression that he never forgot a face.

"Do you take me for a fool?" he said slowly, letting each

syllable linger on his tongue, after Hazel had come as close as she dared.

"Sir?" she squeaked.

"Do you," he said again, "take me for a fool?" His voice was soft.

"No, sir—of course not," Hazel managed.

"I am not one for masked balls, *Mr. Hazelton*. That is the type of frivolity afforded to the wealthy, the landed gentry who have nothing better to do with their time than to amuse one another with nonsense until they eat themselves to death. Some of us have had to *work* for a living, Mr. Hazleton, to earn our way through discipline and effort and ingenuity and"—his hand flicked up toward his missing eye—"sacrifice. I do not teach because I enjoy culling the sniveling herd of dimwits who want to play doctor, nor because I find it so gratifying to demonstrate, year after year, the most *basic* principles of anatomy. I teach for money, Mr. Hazleton, and I teach because I think it to be my duty to educate the men who will actually go on to serve as professionals in my city."

"Sir—"

"Let us drop the ruse now, Miss Sinnett. If you do not, as you claim, imagine me to be a fool, then pray tell why do you continue to believe yourself so easily able to fool me?" Hazel's blood turned to ice. Slowly, she lifted her arms to remove her brother's top hat, revealing the hair held up by pins underneath. "An amusing game to you, I'm sure."

Hazel looked at the hat while she spoke. "Sir, I *am* sorry for the deception, but I assure you, it was never meant to be a game. I do mean to learn anatomy, and I *do* mean to be a surgeon."

"Hah!" Straine's laugh rattled the skeleton of the aquatic beast hanging from the ceiling, but no joy reached his eye.

Hazel burned. "If you think just because I'm a woman that I'm incapable of learning—"

Straine interrupted her with another chilling laugh. "You *do* take me for a fool then, Miss Sinnett. My, what a shame. I might have thought you were smarter than that after all. No, unlike some of my more regrettable colleagues, I wouldn't object to teaching the rare woman who had a mind capable of natural philosophy and the study of the body. Yes, on the whole, the female brain is smaller, more susceptible to *hysterics* and emotion, less inclined to reason. But there's no reason to believe that a specimen might not emerge from the female sex able enough to be taught."

There was a chance then! Was this an olive branch? Was there a possibility that Straine saw Hazel as that exception? Maybe if she shed her costume and begged forgiveness, she could continue in his class. She opened her mouth to begin her apology, but before the word was formed, Straine continued.

"No, I refuse to teach women for a simple reason: I do not waste my time nor energy on dilletantes. There is no place in our world for a woman to practice medicine, Miss Sinnett, sad as that might make you. Another consequence of growing up without the glow of privilege is that one becomes quick to dispel illusion and fantasy. No hospital will hire a female surgeon, nor any university. Even less willing, I imagine, would be a patient to suffer beneath the knife of a woman. So you have come here under the foolish pretense that you are *not* a niece to the *Viscount Almont*, daughter of a lord, that you will *not* marry some equally frivolous child of society and devote the remainder of your life to bearing his brood and holding dinner parties. Am I incorrect, Miss Sinnett?"

Hazel didn't know what to say. He continued to stare at

her. His face had no hint of kindness or mercy; it was a cruel face lined with something that might have been close to pity.

"Perhaps you attended this class with good intentions. Perhaps you told yourself it wasn't a lark, and perhaps you even believed it. But I do not waste my time on students who will not go on to be doctors, regardless of their sex. Unfortunately for you, Miss Sinnett, your sex precludes it. Although it seems to me that your intelligence would have precluded it as well. Do not set foot in my classroom again."

Hazel could feel her eyes sting with tears. She tried to blink them back, but it wasn't working. Her eyes became hot and red, and a tear caught on her cheek.

"Do not attempt to stifle your tears on my account," Straine said. "Women have such trouble controlling their emotions. You're dismissed, Miss Sinnett."

The tears threatened to become sobs. Hazel's brain swam with a thousand things she might say—excuses, insults, retorts—but they all dissolved when she tried to speak. She stood as if bolted to the floor, while Straine turned back to his parchment and made a few notes, working as if she weren't there. She stood for what might have been only five seconds or an eternity before she ran from the hall. She was in a stupor for the ride back to Hawthornden, made dizzy with shame and embarrassment and anger all at once. It was only when she was finally in her bedchamber, when she cast George's clothes off and threw them across the room, that her sobs finally escaped her chest. She keeled over then, naked but for her chemise, and wept.

14

AZEL DIDN'T LEAVE HER BEDROOM UNTIL the sun was already high. Her room was stuffy and hot. She had sweated in the night, which left her chemise clammy. Iona had left tea and toast on a tray by the door, but it was impossible to know how long ago that was; the tea had long since gone cold and the toast soggy. Hazel forced herself upright with a moan as the memories of the previous day flooded back. It was the look in Dr. Straine's eye that stuck with her, an expression she couldn't quite parse. At the time, she had thought it might be pity, but now when she conjured it back, it seemed closer to resentment. He resented her, and everything she represented, simple as that.

Could she blame him? Who was she? The rich daughter of a respectable lord and captain of the Royal Navy, niece of one viscount and future wife of his heir. She had had a negligent mother who let Hazel nurture her childlike fascination with physiology while Lady Sinnett was more focused on protecting the heir, and an absent father with a library he left at home. No matter how much Hazel read, however naturally the study of the body came to her, Dr. Straine was right.

Her entire future would be attending balls down in London and preparing menus for her husband's guests at Almont House. If her husband permitted it, she might be allowed to hold a salon and invite prominent thinkers into their parlor, but *they* would be the men of discovery and action. It would be her guests who came with their stories and ideas. Hazel would be seated neatly on a divan, listening. That was the closest she would come to the world of science—the edge of the bubble, permitted to listen and serve tea and smile gamely and offer her thoughts only if they were disguised as harmless witticisms. Her path was finite and certain. Educating her in anatomy would be like teaching a pig to read before the slaughter.

Hazel looked over to the corner of her room that she thought of as her own little scientific library and laboratory: the divan next to the balcony, invisible under towering stacks of books she had pulled from her father's office. Certainly there was *Dr. Beecham's Treatise,* but also *Modern Studies in Chemistry: A History of the Royal Physician in Practice,* as well as *Home Remedies, 1802.* That corner was also where Hazel kept her notebooks—stacks of them, years' worth of scribbling, mostly nonsense, most probably illegible—and her favorite specimens. There were butterflies secured to boards with sewing needles, their wings trapped in full extension. A taxidermy hawk sat on the mantel, a gift some distant cousin had once given to George, which he eagerly passed along to Hazel when he saw the way she'd stared at it. It was the beak Hazel couldn't stop staring at. The bird was dead (and, if Hazel was being honest, only mediocrely stuffed), but its beak was still monstrously sharp, like the bird could choose to swoop down from Hazel's mantel at any moment to dissect a mouse for supper.

Now all of it looked pathetic. The books, the specimens she had gathered, the medicinal herbs she had picked from the garden and labeled so neatly, the notebooks—just looking at it all made Hazel sick. Before she could talk herself out of it, she flung the blanket from her bed, walked over to her laboratory corner, picked up a butterfly imprisoned within a glass case, and smashed it on the floor.

Her heart pounded. It felt good to destroy something. She did it again, with another case, this time containing an Egyptian beetle her father had brought back for her. It shattered against the floor in shards, with bits of glass glistening like gemstones in the carpet. Hazel brought her arm across a pile of books and threw them all to the ground. She tore pages from her notebooks in fistfuls. The broken glass was everywhere now, pricking her feet, and while she could see blood spots emerging on her legs, she barely felt any pain at all. Her ears rang with an echoing sound of laughter that she realized with a shock was her own.

It was useless, pointless, foolish. *Humiliating.* She had been so proud of reenacting the Galvini experiment that Bernard had described to her, so proud of performing a *parlor trick.* It wasn't anything *novel* or *helpful* to anyone. She hadn't contributed to the world. She had made a frog dance for her own amusement. She had been the dancing frog all along. *How diverting! Look, quick, come see: a woman who fancies reading about blood and gore! Pay your tuppence, go inside, she'll even pretend she's going to be a surgeon someday! Don't worry if she stains her skirts with bile—one of her servants will clean it off for her. Her father will buy her another gown. Pay another ha'penny, and you can see her in a man's jacket!*

Hazel continued tearing through her books until she had an armful of crumpled pages. She kicked open the door to the balcony, and before she thought better of it, she threw all of it over the railing, into the ravine far below.

The pages separated in the air, some caught by the wind. For a moment they were suspended, flying like a flock of broken birds. And then they fell. Hazel watched until the pages disappeared beneath the canopy of foliage.

Hazel returned to her room and saw with fresh eyes the damage she had done. The floor was strewn with bits of broken glass, with pieces of insects and feathers. A bottle of ink had spilled on her dressing gown; a stain black as oil was seeping up from the hem. Her copy of *Dr. Beecham's Treatise* was splayed open on a bust of David Hume.

Iona stood in the doorway, her face a mask of shock and horror. "Miss!" she said.

"I'm so sorry, Iona." Hazel gingerly pulled a stray pen from where it had embedded itself like an arrow in a portrait of her great-grandfather. "That must have made such an awful racket below."

"Your feet, miss!"

Hazel looked down and understood why Iona had looked so horrified. Her feet were red, as if she were wearing a pair of colored stockings, covered in blood. "It doesn't hurt so bad as all that. I'll wash them in the tub and be right as rain. And I'll clean all this up. I am sorry. I must have—temporarily lost my mind."

Iona chewed at a nail nervously. "Miss, your— I mean, Lord Bernard Almont, is at the door for you."

"Bernard? Now? Whatever for?"

"I can't say, miss."

Hazel examined herself herself in the looking glass. She was still wearing her chemise, which was stuck to her in places with sweat. Her hair was half down and wild without a bonnet, knotted and matted and flat from sleep. Her hands were covered in ink and blood, scraped all over as though with a schoolboy's pen nib. "Please tell Bernard—er, his Lordship—that I'm indisposed at the moment, and that I will call on him later this week."

"Yes, miss," Iona said, and scurried from the room with one last mournful glance back at the mess in the corner of the room.

Hazel sighed. She put a chair upright that had fallen on its side. The low murmurs of Iona's sweet voice echoed from downstairs. Hazel heard Bernard's rough reply, although she couldn't make out the words, and then came footsteps.

Iona reappeared. "He insists on seeing you, miss," she said. The two women made eye contact.

"All right," Hazel said dully. "I suppose we don't have time for a bath, but I can at least brush my hair while we find some clean stockings." The two women worked with single-minded focus on making Hazel look as close to presentable as they could manage. After Hazel plucked half a dozen glass splinters from her palms, Iona helped her slide on her sturdiest pair of gloves, in a deep maroon that wouldn't show if one of her scratches began to bleed. After fifteen minutes of their best efforts, Hazel looked . . . well, not *good*. She still had dark bags under her eyes from crying, and her skin was sallow; her hair, which as it turned out would have required at least an hour of careful brushing to look presentable, was concealed beneath one of Hazel's least favorite hats. But she looked *human* and at the very least well enough to meet her cousin, a boy who had seen her splashing naked in the mud when they were toddlers.

"Bernard," Hazel said when she reached the top of the landing and saw him standing below, "to what in the world do we owe the pleasure of your company?"

"You might apologize for keeping me waiting," Bernard said to his cuff link.

Hazel furrowed her brow. "All right, then. I'm sorry, Bernard."

Bernard puffed up. He was in a coat she had never seen before, bright robin's-egg blue, paired with a yellow waistcoat and matching trousers. Hazel would have guessed he was in costume as Young Werther if there was any chance at all that Bernard had read it. He carried a bouquet in his hand of white lilies wrapped in ribbon. "For you," he said, thrusting them at her. "They told me at the market they represent purity. And devotion. My father mentioned that you might have taken ill."

Hazel forced herself to smile and dutifully lifted the lilies to her nose to smell them. *The women at the market lied to you,* she wanted to say. *They said what it took to make a sale. They saw you in your bright blue coat and knew you wouldn't know that white lilies are funeral flowers.* "They're beautiful," she said. "Thank you."

Bernard's chest puffed out even further. "So, how are you feeling? Still sick?"

"You know how my mother overreacts when it comes to Percy's health. I had a chill for a single evening, and she had to whisk him out of the country for his well-being."

"I'm relieved to hear that," he said, straightening his shoulders. "Not about your mother. I mean that you're feeling well." He cleared his throat and then continued. "I came to ask if you might promenade with me today in the Princes Street Gardens."

This time Hazel couldn't even feign enthusiasm. She thought of the mess she'd left in her room, the shattered glass and torn pages that represented all the wasted effort of her young adulthood, and when she opened her mouth, the first thing to come out was a guttural, sarcastic laugh. "You must be joking," she said.

Bernard looked as though she had poured a kettle of hot tea down his shirt. "I—I can't imagine—" he sputtered.

"No. I'm sorry, I didn't mean that. I just meant"—*my entire life has gone up in flames, all my work has been for nothing, and also I'm covered in blood*—"that I still have a *bit* of the chill. I'm not quite well enough to . . . promenade."

Bernard looked her up and down critically. "Well," he managed, "I suppose you are wanting for a bit of color."

A sliver of glass stabbed at Hazel's heel from within her shoe. She bit her tongue to keep from yelping. "Well, if that's all," she said through gritted teeth, "I'm afraid I must cut our visit short."

Bernard looked taken aback. "What?"

A lightning bolt of pain shot up Hazel's calf. "My apologies, Cousin. I have to ask you to leave now."

A shadow crossed Bernard's face, something darker than Hazel had ever seen in his expression. Her cousin, usually jovial and good-natured, had grown up, and she hadn't noticed. His jawline had sharpened, his brow lowered, his mouth tightened. "So," he said, "to be clear. You're *refusing* my offer of a promenade."

"Bernard, I'm sorry, but I have more important things to worry about right now than traipsing around Princes Street Gardens, pretending to be interested in whatever you have to say." It was far crueler than she'd meant, but the words bypassed her brain and came right out of her mouth.

Bernard looked as if he had been slapped. He stood with his mouth open like a trout for a few moments before he smacked his lips together. "I assume I'll see you at the ball, of course?" he said finally. The Almonts' Ball was an annual affair in Edinburgh, a chance for Lord Almont to show off his latest art acquisitions and for everyone else to show off their most expensive gowns.

"Certainly, Bernard," Hazel said glumly.

"Well then, it appears we have nothing more to discuss. I bid you good day, then, Cousin." He left with a flick of his blue coat and left a blinking Charles to close the door after he was gone.

"Ughh. Finally!" Hazel said, throwing the lilies onto a side table and ripping off her shoes and stockings. She massaged her massacred foot. "I'll need a hot bath to get this glass out. I'm sorry again for the mess, I'll tidy it as soon as I'm, well, whole again. Honestly, the nerve of him, barging in without warning, acting like I committed some sin for not wanting to *promenade* with him. What is a 'promenade,' anyway? Just walking slower than any natural human gait so you can show off a new outfit to people distracted by how badly they want to show off *their* new outfits. It's a pointless exercise in self-absorption that doesn't even *work* because everyone involved is too self-absorbed to provide the admiration their fellows are in such desperate need of. And as if Bernard would need to be circling around the Gardens like a show pony to get people to notice his clothes; I swear, one could see that blue jacket from Glasgow. Ooof, just got it there." Hazel withdrew a particularly barbarous shard of glass from her foot with her fingernails. "Charles, bring me a basin, will you? I should dispose of these bits of glass before they find their way into my other foot."

Charles, who had been dutifully standing by the door, obliged. Iona approached, chewing the cuticle of her thumb. "If I may, miss? It's possible that you were a *bit,* well, harsh with him."

Hazel wet her thumb and ran it along a red stain on her leg. It came off. Good. Just dried blood then, and just a little scratch. "Harsh? He's a man, isn't he? He has the entire world at his feet. I think he can handle my turning down a *promenade.*"

"He is your betrothed, though," her maid said to the floor.

"Not *yet.* Much as my mother wishes it were the case so she could get rid of me once and for all."

Iona swallowed and twisted a strand of hair around her finger. "Perhaps, then, you should be sweeter to him, to ensure—"

"Oh, Iona, please. I will have my entire life to be sweet to him if he wants it. Can't I have a single afternoon of mourning my future?"

Charles returned with the basin, and the three of them moved back to Hazel's bedroom to begin the slow work of undoing the damage she had wreaked in her frustration. "Seems a pity," Charles said, picking up a beetle that had fallen from its casing. "To throw these fine things away."

Hazel plucked the beetle from his fingers and held it up to the light. The beetle was black, but where the afternoon sun hit it, it almost glowed an iridescent blue. "We won't throw them away, Charles. Let's just sweep up the glass and put the specimens back. I'll replate them tomorrow."

"Very good."

Hazel watched Charles as he worked with the broom. And then she watched Iona watching Charles, and something close to benevolence rose like a tide in her chest. "You know," she said, "Bernard wasn't actually wrong about it being a lovely day to *promenade*. I can tidy the rest of this up myself. Why don't the two of you go down to the Gardens? Take one of the carriages."

The two servants stared at Hazel with astonishment.

"To the Princes Street Gardens, miss?" Charles asked.

"Together?" Iona asked.

"Absolutely," Hazel said firmly. "Now, it's chilly, be sure to take a jacket and scarf—but the sun is out, and heaven knows how rare that is in this part of the world."

Iona's face flipped between terror and delight. The effect was close to the look of an adorable but deranged woodland creature. "Are you sure you can manage on your own? Without me?"

"Iona, not to diminish your impeccable service, but I can absolutely manage an afternoon without you. I might take a walk down the ravine."

"A *promenade*?" Iona said with a wicked glint in her eye.

"Very witty."

"Will you be all right without a chaperone? Even with your mother gone, I worry—you know, appearances and all that."

"Iona, I have been going to Edinburgh unchaperoned for weeks now."

"Oh," she said. "I forget when you're dressed like George."

"Now, the two of you be off before it gets any later. I'll tell Cook to leave you dinner in case you stay late."

Charles's grin could have lit all the lamps in Hawthornden at once. The two of them rose and awkwardly maneuvered themselves out the door, each trying to politely defer to the other, until Charles bowed and Iona went ahead and then tripped on her laces. "Steady, now!" he said, gingerly touching her elbow.

Hazel finished tidying the mess she had made of her amateur laboratory in half an hour, collecting and smoothing the papers she hadn't thrown from the balcony and pressing them between the covers of books to get the creases out. The emotions of her confrontation with Straine seemed so much smaller now, more distant, as if they had shrunk to a size where she could deposit them neatly into a hatbox and then forget about them at the back of a closet.

She heard humming coming from the kitchen, and smelled something from down in the kitchen. Cook was making fish pie, one of Hazel's favorites, and no one ever seemed able to do it justice like Cook. Hazel rounded the corner into the kitchen to find Cook patting a heaping mound of mashed potatoes into a giant dish. A pot of cream sauce simmered gently on the fire.

Cook beamed when she saw Hazel. "Hand looks worlds and universes better," she said proudly, holding up her palm where Hazel had sewn her cut closed. "Not a bit of bile—tell you the truth, I was a bit worried about that but didn't want to bother you, with you so busy these days. Your *illness* and all that." Cook's smile revealed the gap between her teeth, and Hazel couldn't help but smile back.

"No pus is just fine," Hazel said. "Here, let me see." The cut, which had been furious, was now just a thin line of pink, embroidered with Hazel's needlework. "I think I can remove these sutures now."

"I was very careful with them, not letting them strain or stretch."

"That's wonderful. It's healed beautifully." Hazel removed a pin from her hair and, holding Cook's hand up against the light of the fire, slowly pulled at each stitch. Cook winced and averted her eyes, but Hazel's fingers were nimble, and the work was done before Cook had a chance even to cry out. "There," Hazel said. "I don't even imagine it'll leave a scar. A small one, if it does."

"I'd hardly be a cook without scars on my hand, miss."

"Well, I hope you'll be content with one less. I did come down to tell you to save Charles and Iona plates. They might be out late this afternoon. I told them they could go down to the Princes Street Gardens together."

Cook clapped her hands. "Oh, good for them, now!"

Susan, the kitchen maid, let a stack of dishes clatter into the sink. "'S about time!" she huffed. "I've been telling that boy to do something. He looks moony at her all day, it's a wonder he's able to get anything done."

The warmth of the kitchen—of Cook, of the fire, the smell of fish pie—filled Hazel and pushed out all the bad feelings of the morning and previous day. Her hands had felt sure and adept with the needle and with the pin, removing the careful stitches. She had liked the feeling of competence, of seeing Cook's injury, knowing how to address it, and then being able to do so. Maybe she had been foolish for thinking there was a path forward to work as a surgeon in the public sphere, but perhaps she had been equally foolish for pretending it was pointless not to learn all she could in the meantime. When she married Bernard, she would leave Hawthornden, and her makeshift laboratory and her father's books. She would be going to Almont House with only her trousseau and her mind. With her mother and Percy in Bath and her father abroad, this might be the final time in her life she had the opportunity to attend lectures without being discovered. Maybe there was an answer.

"Would you mind keeping a plate warm for me as well?" Hazel asked. "I have an errand to run in Edinburgh, and I might be back late."

15

THE SIGN WENT UP ON THE giant oaken front door of Le Grand Leon on a frosty November morning, nailed in by Mr. Arthur, who made sure the notice was straight before sighing and going back inside.

"So it's true, then, is it?" said Thomas Potter, the lead actor. His mouth was tight, a straight line. He glanced back at Isabella, standing behind him, looking out nervously from under a curtain of blond hair.

"Ay," Mr. Arthur said. "And with the state of this city, God knows if we'll be open next season, so you all best start looking for other ways to earn a living."

Isabella tugged at Thomas's jacket. "Thom, what are we going to do about—?"

He turned to her. "We'll figure it out. I'll figure it out." Tenderly, he kissed the top of her head.

Jack had been sitting in the rafters listening. He had been listening for days, to conversations between Mr. Arthur and the theater owner, between the theater owner and the choreographer. For the last week, their show had been playing to mostly empty rows of seats, the worn red velvet gathering a thin layer of dust. It was too risky for the well-to-do to venture into the theater when they were faced with the threat of a plague. And so they stayed home. And so, at least for the time being, Le Grand Leon was closing.

"Yer welcome to stay, Jack," Mr. Arthur said the next day, when all the actors had gone, handing Jack a heavy ring of brass keys. "In fact, I'd appreciate it if you did. Ward off thieves. Can't pay ye much—or anything, really—but it'll keep a roof over yer head if ye need it. It'll be good to have ye here to keep the place upright. In case, ye know."

"In case what?" Jack asked, taking the keys.

Mr. Arthur smiled sadly. "In case we come back for next season," he said. He patted Jack genially on the shoulder and walked up the aisle and out toward the lobby, leaving the boy in a theater filled only with echoes and ghosts.

Jack would need to steal another body soon if he wanted to eat.

16

AZEL HAD HALF EXPECTED THE DOOR to the Royal Edinburgh Anatomists' Society to open directly from the street into the operating theater, the one she had seen only from beneath the risers. But instead, after Hazel raised and dropped the brass knocker on the door, a footman in a powdered wig politely ushered her inside to a handsomely appointed lounge that looked like an upscale salon, or a gentlemen's club. A bright orange fire burned merrily, its crackling the only sound in the otherwise silent room, where ten or so whiskered men scattered among the velvet settees sipped brandy and read newspapers.

One entire wall of the room was occupied by mounted animal heads, taxidermy zebras and rhinoceroses, a lion and one heavily scarred elephant, though its ivory tusks had been removed. The opposite wall was made up of massive bookcases so tall they required a sliding ladder to reach the volumes on the topmost shelves. Hazel tried to sneak a glance at the titles, but most of them were too faded to read. The volumes on the bottom were all in Latin.

The fire made the room unusually warm, and Hazel

resisted the urge to tug at her petticoat and loosen her stays. The weeks wearing George's old clothing had made her forget how stifling the layers of fabric of women's dress could be, especially when one was dressing to look as refined as possible. And Hazel was. She had dressed herself like a soldier sheathing himself in layers of armor, with all the protection that could be afforded to her by wealth and decent taste. The dress was a sensible blue, trimmed with black lace velvet and cording. A lavender ribbon tied the collar at her throat. She looked, in other words, like a well-respected woman of Edinburgh society, and while the footman at the Anatomists' Society might privately have wondered why she didn't have a chaperone, he would be too low ranked to imagine challenging a woman like Hazel or refusing her entry. Being a woman had closed many doors to Hazel Sinnett, but it had also revealed to her a valuable tool in her arsenal: women were almost entirely overlooked as people, which gave her the power of invisibility. People *saw* women, they saw the dresses women wore on public walks through the park, and the gloved hands they rested on their suitors' elbows at the theater, but women were never *threats*. They were never challenges worthy of meaningful consideration. The footman might have refused entry to a beggarwoman or even a strange or foreign man, but Hazel—dressed like wealth— would be free to walk past him if she did so swiftly and feigning confidence. And so she did.

Dr. Beecham was sitting at a small table alone, a cup of strong tea steaming beside him. Books and papers were scattered around the table. A large tortoiseshell served as a paperweight. Even with the heat of the fire radiating from the grate, he was still wearing his usual jacket with the collar raised up to his chin.

"Hello, Dr. Beecham?" Hazel said quietly. A few of the nearby gentlemen grunted at the disruption and then returned to their reading.

Dr. Beecham finished making a note and then neatly returned his quill pen to the inkwell. "I don't believe I've had the pleasure of meeting you, have I? Please forgive me if we've been introduced; I'm afraid my memory isn't quite what it used to be."

"That's a—an interesting question, Dr. Beecham," Hazel said. "I'm— My name is Hazel Sinnett." Hazel removed her bonnet and smoothed her curls away from her face. "But I met you as—"

"George Hazleton." Beecham stood up and extended his hand.

Hazel shook it, bewildered.

"Yes, of course. Straine did mention— But I get ahead of myself. Miss Sinnett, please do sit. Can I offer you a cup of tea?"

Dazed, Hazel sat opposite Beecham at the table. (The nearby gentlemen scoffed at Hazel for sitting, but returned to their reading even quicker than they had the last time.)

"Fascinating," Beecham said, staring at her face as if he could see the bones and muscles at work beneath her skin. "I can't imagine how I didn't recognize it immediately. Absolutely fascinating. The clothes came from—a shop somewhere? A tailor?"

"They were my brother's." And then before she could stop herself, she added, "He died."

A shadow crossed Beecham's face. "My apologies. My

sincerest apologies. I had a son who—" He looked beyond Hazel for a moment, and then shook his head. "It's no matter. It's a pleasure to finally meet you in person, Miss Sinnett."

"So, hold on a second. You—?" Hazel began, but then thought better of it. She blinked a few times. "So you're not upset with me?"

Dr. Beecham smiled sympathetically. "No, I confess I am not upset with you. A little, well, disappointed in my own skills of observation, but . . . no, no. Not upset. Interested, really."

"Interested?"

"In you. As a specimen. It's very rare to see a woman with your interest in the natural sciences. And even rarer, I must say, to see one with your aptitude. Tell me—were you always interested in anatomy?"

And so, as a cup of tea was placed in front of her and Hazel settled into the surprisingly comfortable velvet chair, she found herself telling Dr. Beecham everything. She told him of her lonely childhood behind the gray walls of Hawthornden, hidden in her father's office and reading books on medicine and alchemy by candlelight long after she was supposed to be in bed. She told him about her father abroad, and her distant mother, trapped in perpetual mourning, obsessed with the health of her younger brother, the new heir. From the time she was able to write her own name, she had wanted to study the body, to learn the rules that governed it, to understand how to master it: this strange vessel that contained the soul. How fragile it was, Hazel had realized when she was a child scraping her knee and seeing blood pearl up from beneath her stockings. She would spend hours tracing the thin blue-green veins beneath her skin.

Beecham listened attentively, stirring more sugar into his tea and nodding along as Hazel spoke. "And that's how I came to your anatomy lectures," she said in conclusion.

She had left out how she sneaked into the operating theater to watch Beecham perform surgery with that miraculous ethereum. There seemed no need to get that boy, the body snatcher, in trouble.

"I swear it was with no malice or intent to mock you. I just couldn't think of another way. Please, if you let me continue in your classes, I will work harder than any student you have ever taught, and learn more diligently. If you could just speak to Dr. Straine, or convince him to allow me to continue my studies . . . I will be discreet, if you require, and I *will* find a way to work as a physician somehow. I don't know how yet, but I will. Your teachings will not go to waste. I swear, I will pass the Physician's Examination somehow, and I will be a credit to your course, I know I will be." She was a little out of breath when she stopped. Her mouth had moved faster than her brain.

Beecham added another spoonful of sugar to his tea and took a thoughtful sip. He winced and added yet another spoonful of sugar.

To Hazel's surprise, a small, leathery head extended from the tortoiseshell on the table.

"Oh, hello, Galen," Beecham said. He fed the tortoise a bit of a biscuit and stroked his shell absentmindedly before returning his attention to Hazel. "You know," he said, "I don't share the same *ideas* about female physicians as our friend Dr. Straine. When you've lived as long as I have, my dear, you take novelty wherever you can find it, and you are nothing if not novel."

Dr. Beecham couldn't have been older than fifty, but Hazel understood his point. "Does that mean," she began slowly, "that I might be able to continue in your class?"

Beecham cleared his throat and gestured for a server to bring a fresh pot of tea. "I'm afraid that if Dr. Straine is unwilling to let you attend his demonstrations, there's nothing I can do to undermine him. I did, when he spoke to me the other day, attempt to convey to Dr. Straine the notion that an exceptional medical mind could in fact come in the female form, but alas. A stubborn old bat."

"But surely," Hazel said, "as the *head* of the course. As a fellow lecturer. Your grandfather founding the society, surely there's *something*—"

"Miss Sinnett. Much as it pains me to say, it's possible that Dr. Straine has a point. The anatomical demonstrations can be quite . . . gruesome. Skin flayed out and organs puffed up. Perhaps it's best after all that your delicate female sensibility be protected." He took a large sip of tea and sighed with satisfaction. "And the classes only get more challenging from this point on. Incredibly rigorous. And then there's the Physician's Examination. A grueling affair. Yes, perhaps it *is* best after all—"

A spark flared in Hazel's brain, and she spoke before logic or reason could extinguish it. "What if I sit the Physician's Examination? Even without the lectures. What if I'm allowed to sit the Physician's Examination anyway?"

Dr. Beecham tilted his head and lifted his quill to his lips. "An experiment," he said.

"Yes," Hazel said quickly, "exactly. An experiment. To test my abilities. And if I pass, I receive my qualifications, *and* you permit women to enroll in your lecture from here on out. Yours and Straine's."

A fresh pot of tea was deposited on the table, and Beecham thanked the servant with a warm smile before turning back to Hazel. As he leaned forward to refill his teacup, Hazel thought she saw a glimpse of something glinting and gold, almost glowing, inside his breast pocket. But before she could get a better look, Beecham reclined. "I do warn you, if you intend to sit the Physician's Examination, you'll find it nearly impossible without the benefit of studying from subjects. I doubt *anyone* could pass without dissections. John Hunter himself would flounder."

"I'll manage. I can assure you: I will manage. And I will not be the last woman to attempt to enroll in your course, Dr. Beecham, I assure you of that as well. When I pass, the others will see it's possible. And I *will* pass."

Now Beecham looked positively merry. His eyes glistened with excitement. "I do love a game, Miss Sinnett."

"So we have a deal, then," Hazel said, extending her hand.

Beecham brought his hand toward her, but then lifted it away with a sharp flick. "The conditions: You will sit the Physician's Examination at the end of this term. If you pass, I shall open the course to any women who wish to attend, although I warn you there may not be quite so many with your peculiar predilection as you seem to believe. *And,* in the unlikely event that you do pass, I will also offer you an apprenticeship—with me—at the university hospital, where as you must know, I serve as Chief of Surgery. A rare and *highly* sought-after apprenticeship." He brought his hand down, ready to shake, but this time Hazel hesitated.

"And what if I do fail? What then? All wagers have stakes, do they not?"

Beecham chuckled, but not cruelly. "Very good, Miss Sinnett. I consider this more an *experiment* than a wager. I imagine the stakes of your failure would be self-evident. For one, I'd be unable to convince my colleague Dr. Straine to permit other females to attend lectures in the future. Let's say that if you do not pass the Physician's Examination, you'll be unable to sit it in the future. This larger experiment, of a female surgeon, will be considered concluded."

Hazel nodded, and they shook.

Beecham's hand was cold, she could feel the ice of it even through his glove. "Well, then," Beecham said. "I look forward to seeing you at the examination. Ah, one final thing!" He raised a finger while he shuffled through the pile of books at his elbow. "Aha. There we are. A newer edition of *Dr. Beecham's Treatise*. For you to study from. I happened to notice that the one you brought to class was a little out of date. And a tad worse for the wear, if you don't mind my saying so."

Hazel took the book. The light from the fire reflected off the shiny gilded letters on its cover:

DR. BEECHAM'S TREATISE ON ANATOMY
OR, THE PREVENTION AND CURE OF MODERN
DISEASES
by Dr. William Beecham
24th Edition, 1816

"Thank you," Hazel said, flipping through the pages. She noticed a few notes in the margins. "You're sure you don't mind? Are there notes in it?"

Dr. Beecham waved her off. "Just scribblings, I'm sure. And now, if you'll excuse me, I must return to my notes. *Terrible* deaths are happening in the heart of the city. Just terrible."

Hazel sat up at attention. "I've heard about them! They say it's the Roman fever back again. You! You were in a paper, speaking of it."

"Yes, I found myself examining the bodies. Terrible, truly terrible."

"Do you think it's true then?" Hazel asked quietly. "The Roman fever is back again?"

Dr. Beecham looked stricken. He nodded. "It does look as though that's the case. And there seems to be so little interest in the public when it's the poor who die. So few who care."

"My brother, who died—it was of the fever," Hazel said, avoiding the doctor's eyes. "My brother George. The last time it struck Edinburgh."

"George," Dr. Beecham repeated softly. "George. Of course. My deepest, most sincere condolences on his loss, truly." He stared beyond Hazel into the distance for so long that Hazel wondered whether she was supposed to leave. Just as she was about to stand, Beecham spoke again. "*Morte magis metuenda senectus*. Do you know Latin, Miss Sinnett?"

"Only some, I'm sorry to say. Is it—er—something like, 'We fear old age—'?"

"'Old age should rather be feared than death.'" Beecham once again assumed that far-off expression, and he and Hazel sat in the silence for a few moments, listening to the fireplace continue to crackle and the whiskered men around them sniff and flip the pages of their newspapers. Finally, Dr. Beecham spoke again. "Well, I do hope that you study hard and pass the examination, Miss Sinnett." The reflection of the fire glinted orange in his eyes. "Especially if the Roman fever has returned to our fair city. It might be you who finally discovers the cure."

From <u>A History of the
Royal Physician in Practice</u> (1811):

The philosophy of medicine during the Tudor period was dominated by the notion of the four humours, found in the writings of Hippocrates (ca. 460 B.C.) and further developed by Galen of Pergamon (ca. A.D. 129), the noted physician of Ancient Rome.

Physicians operated under the understanding that each individual had a dominant *humour,* or fluid, that governed their personality, and any ailment could be understood in the context of either an excess or deficiency of said humour. The four humours were: blood, phlegm, yellow bile, and black bile.

BLOOD	*Sanguine*	*Hot and moist*	*Friendly, frequently joking and laughing; have rose-tinted appearance and good skin*	*Air*	*Spring*	*Liver*
PHLEGM	*Phlegmatic*	*Cold and moist*	*Low-spirited, often forgetful; will grow white hair young*	*Water*	*Autumn*	*Brain*
YELLOW BILE	*Choleric*	*Hot and dry*	*Bitter, short-tempered and miserable; skin might appear greenish*	*Fire*	*Summer*	*Gall-bladder*
BLACK BILE	*Melancholic*	*Cold and dry*	*Lazy and sickly; black hair and black eyes*	*Earth*	*Winter*	*Spleen*

17

"O I!"

Hazel had been so distracted as she exited the Anatomists' Society, so buoyed by her own purpose and determination, that she had taken a single, confident stride past the threshold back out onto the rain-dappled stones of the Edinburgh close and immediately collided with a stranger.

"I'm so s— It's you!"

Hazel had meant to utter an apology, but she looked up as she was straightening her skirts and saw him: the boy from before the surgical demonstration, who had pulled her into the narrow alley and escorted her, like her own Virgil through Hell, to the secret place underneath the riser seating. He stood before her now, seemingly also too stunned by their surprise encounter to speak, and Hazel was able to get a good look at his face.

Yes, it was him, the boy from before, with a tangle of black hair that reached the nape of his neck, and the thin hooked nose bumped in the center. And then there were his odd gray eyes, which up close, Hazel saw, had irises rimmed in navy blue. Blue was laced in his clear gray eyes like poison dissolving in water. He was tall, at least six feet, but his trousers hit only at his ankles, even though someone had released the hem to make them longer. His shirt, too, was too short at the wrists, although Hazel identified no fewer than four spots where tears had been carefully sewn closed with clumsy but small stitches.

"Miss Sinnett," the boy said, revealing his pointed canine teeth as he spoke. "Or was it Lady Sinnett? Either way, it seems we meet again."

"Hazel is fine. And I'm sorry to say I can't do you the honor of remembering your name, seeing as you never gave me one."

The boy grinned and winked, although it might have just been him squinting against the setting sun that had managed to slip through the entryway of the close from High Street and illuminate them both in the pale yellow of late autumn's final efforts at sunshine. "And you're not going to. I don't find myself cavorting with high society ladies like yourself too often, so it doesn't strike me as an introduction one needs to make."

"We've already met. Twice," Hazel reasoned.

"Aye, but is it really meeting if I haven't given ye a name?" he said, and this time he winked for real.

Hazel felt an unfamiliar warmth creep up from her navel to her chest, a terrible excitement that she had felt before only while setting up an experiment, still anticipating its results. It was the feeling of anticipation, of wanting to know what would happen next, combined with the sensation of having drunk a full glass of champagne on an empty stomach.

The boy extended his hand, and Hazel reached out to take it.

The moment their skin touched, the champagne bubbles in Hazel's stomach foamed with frenetic energy. It was Galvanism, Galvini's electric shocks—there was no other way to describe it—a current of lightning that flowed from his hand through hers and directly into her pounding heart.

"It's lovely to meet ye again, Hazel Sinnett," he said, shaking her hand. His own was so big that her hand all but disappeared in it.

From the mouth of the close, where it met High Street, a boy called out between cupped hands: *"Oi! Currer! Quit flirting!"* He looked older than the gray-eyed boy, but he was shorter and stockier, as if his body were a compact square of muscle. "You got the back pay, yeah? Just give me my half so I can head to the pub. I swear to God, Jack, don't stiff me on this one, mate. Bailey already cut my credit at the Arms, and I need a drink something fierce now, I do."

Jack groaned and pulled his hand from Hazel's. "Dammit, Munro! I've got the money. Just head down to the pub now, and tell Bailey to put your first drink on my tab. Trot along, now!" Jack purposefully tried to avoid looking back at Hazel, his cheeks flushed with embarrassment.

Munro looked unconvinced, but he disappeared beyond the stone alley anyway. Jack watched him go, until he turned around to see Hazel standing in place with an eyebrow raised. "Jack . . . Currer, is it?"

Jack Currer, the gray-eyed boy, swept down into an exaggerated bow. "At your service."

Hazel noted the dirt beneath his fingernails and mud encrusted on the bottom of his shoes. She eyed the plaque of the Anatomists' Society and then looked back at Jack. "You're a grave robber, aren't you?"

Jack lifted from the bow with his own eyebrow cocked. "No," he said. "No, no, no, no. Never a grave robber. Very careful about that. You see, if you don't take anything but the body from the grave, they can't get you on grave robbing."

"So you're a *body snatcher*, then."

Jack checked over his shoulder to see if anyone nearby was listening. They were alone in the close, the door to the Anatomists' Society firmly shut and the alley beside it empty. He leaned in. "I prefer 'resurrection man.' Makes it sound a bit more *romantic*, don't you think?"

"So that's how you knew the passage down to the surgical theater. You sell *bodies* to them, the physicians."

"Sometimes."

Hazel studied him even more closely now, top to bottom. He looked to be about her age, maybe a year older. His thin fingers twitched as they spoke. "And how much do you charge for something like that?" she asked. "A body."

"That depends. Are you in the market for one?"

"That depends," Hazel replied. "Do you make deliveries?"

4 November 1817
No. 2 Henry Street
Bath

Dear Hazel,

Your brother Percy has taken ill with a cold. He sniffles all day and spends half the night up with a cough. It is enough to make my poor heart weep. I take him to the hot springs twice a day, and the apothecary has given us laudanum drops to help him sleep. I beg of you to keep him in your prayers, and ask the Lord for a swift recovery. A dreadful cold!!!

—Your mother, Lady Lavinia Sinnett

18

AWTHORNDEN CASTLE WAS BUILT ATOP A craggy hilltop, and if you followed the narrow garden path down and to the left of the building's stone facade, you might discover the small wooden door tucked into the slope itself, directly under the property. It was a mottled door, sun bleached and swollen from rain and damp, and nearly invisible in the dark, moonless night— with a small metal grate at eye level that slid open with a clank when Jack Currer knocked.

"Who's there?" said a voice on the other side of the door. A woman's voice, Hazel's, feigning confidence and taking on an artificial masculine deepness to scare off someone foolish enough to intrude.

Jack raised the lantern he was holding to illuminate his face. "Don't be daft, it's me. Who else would know how to find the hidden door in the middle of the night to the bloody dungeon you have built into the side of a castle?"

"What's the password?"

"Oh—er . . ." Jack looked down to his palm, where he had written the words in ink. Sweat made the letters bleed together. "*Morto . . . vivios . . . bo*—No, no, wait. Something *docks*?"

Hazel sighed and opened the heavy, creaking dungeon door. "*Mortui vivos docent.*"

Jack pushed his wheelbarrow past Hazel and into the underground chamber. "I'm sorry, I skipped my Latin lessons at Eton."

Hazel had to press her body against the damp wall to avoid getting run over. "But clearly not your etiquette lessons."

Jack finished pushing the wheelbarrow and let the handles fall. He exhaled from the effort and wiped his hands on his trousers, leaving a streak of ink. "*Mortui vivos docent,*" he repeated. "So what does it mean?"

Hazel stared at the dark mass hidden under the blanket of Jack's wheelbarrow. "'The dead teach the living.' I read that in a book."

The dungeon was lit with torches burning in the wall and a handful of gas lamps set on the workman's table. There was no window to the outside world, save for the sliding grate in the door, which Hazel shut firmly once the door was closed and locked. On the table was a collection of strange silver tools. Some Jack recognized, like the knives and the bone saw. But others had curved edges and handles like scissors. They were a mismatched set, some already rusted, some clearly made from fine silver. The collection of a magpie who hoarded what she had been able to find.

Nailed into the wall were two pairs of manacles, where a prisoner might be strung up from his wrists. "Is this place used?" Jack asked, a little fearful. "As an actual dungeon, I mean."

"It can be," Hazel said.

Jack laughed.

"The truth is," Hazel said, "I don't think it's ever been used for a real prisoner. It's been empty my entire life. Until now."

Jack picked up a small scalpel with a wooden handle and twirled it in his fingers. "Until now, when you've made it your own private laboratory."

"Something like that."

"Your mum and dad don't mind? Their little girl sneaking out at night, under the cliffside, fraternizing with resurrectionists?"

"My father is on a Royal Navy post on Saint Helena, supervising the exile of Napoleon. My mother is"—Hazel hesitated to come up with the right words—"on holiday, in England. She never really pays any attention to me, even when she is here." There was something about Jack's face—the way his lip curled up at its edges, his cool gray eyes that seemed endless, as if they were windows into an expanse of calm ocean that went for miles—that made her want to tell him things, to open up and say the things she had never said out loud. Maybe it was because she had never had anyone to say them out loud to.

"So," Jack said, stepping closer to Hazel while the torchlight danced across his face. "You're in a big castle, all alone. I didn't think that ladies were ever alone."

The unfamiliar electric shock charged through Hazel's body, and she suddenly became aware of how foolish her actions might have been. She had told a stranger where she lived, invited him inside, and then told him that she lived without protection. Jack could be dangerous. He could be a member of a band of thieves who would arrive as soon as Jack gave the signal, and a horde of criminals would pillage Haw-thornden and leave her bound and gagged in a corner.

Hazel involuntarily reached for her biggest knife on the table. "Maybe I'm not a lady," Hazel said.

Jack flicked his eyes up and down her body, and then began to laugh with such earnestness, a genuine childlike warmth, that Hazel somehow knew his plan had never been to rob her.

Her heart pounded, and she gave thanks for the dim gas lamps and torchlight that hid her blush. Hazel cleared her throat. "So, the specimen. It can go on the table." She used the knife in her hand to gesture.

"Right you are." Jack pulled his eyes from hers and moved toward the wheelbarrow.

She averted her eyes as Jack maneuvered the corpse, as he laid its limbs neatly into position so that it might only have been sleeping under a shroud. "Sheet on or off?"

"Off," Hazel said. "Might as well be off. I'm going to be looking anyway. How much do I owe you?" She pulled a coin purse from beneath her apron. "Six guineas, I think?"

"It's a fresh corpse, dug it up just tonight! Ten guineas."

"Just because you dug it up tonight doesn't mean it was buried tonight. Certainly doesn't smell like it. Seven guineas."

"Nine, or I take it straight back to the Old Town and give it to the barber on Haymarket Street. He's a good customer, always pays what I ask."

"Eight guineas, and three shillings," Hazel said. She held out the heavy coins in the palm of her hand.

Jack hesitated, and then swiped them into his own hand. "Deal."

Once Jack had secured the money in his pocket, he withdrew the sheet with a flourish and revealed the shriveled corpse beneath: a young woman, shrunken and waxy. The smell dominated the dungeon now, sickly sweet rotting meat and eggs gone bad, a warm larval musk.

"Here," Hazel said, offering Jack an orange filled with cloves. She was already holding one up to her own nose. "It helps with the smell."

Jack accepted gratefully. "Did you read about this in a book too?"

"Actually, I did," Hazel said.

The body had cold blue eyelids and hair like straw. If Hazel had to guess, she would have said that the two of them were exactly the same age. The woman—the girl—had lived a hard life, Hazel could see that, reading her body as one does a book. Her feet were frostbitten and mangled at the soles from poor shoes. Her fingernails were yellow and broken. She had bruises running up every limb. At the back of her head, there was a section where her straw-yellow hair had been shaved, revealing the scars and circular suction marks from a wet-cupping operation. The girl had gone into a hospital for the poor, and they had treated her by sucking blood from the back of her skull with knives and hot glasses. Hazel had never seen it done, but she had read about it. Seeing the scars in person—bright purple suction bruises in perfect circles, like the woman had wrestled with a terrifying deep-sea creature—made the procedure seem far more brutal than Hazel had imagined it to be from the pages of her books.

The girl had another scar, too, running at least thirty centimeters down the center of her chest between her breasts, sewn up tight by stitches so neat they were almost invisible.

Hazel wondered what ailment had been addressed. Perhaps someone had tried to save her life.

Jack had been paid, but he still lingered, looking over Hazel's shoulder at the corpse. "Did she—you know—was it the fever?"

"The Roman fever?" Hazel said, perplexed.

Jack nodded. He had heard the rumors. The priest who spoke over her body at the burial had prayed to God that they would be delivered a cure.

"No," Hazel said, "definitely not."

Jack came closer. "How do you know? It's what everyone's saying she died of!"

"Really? No, here, look—" Hazel used the sheet to tilt the body away from them, to show Jack the corpse's smooth back. "No buboes. No boils at all. That's what the Roman fever is named for."

"Not because it came from Rome?" Jack had heard more than one stagehand at Le Grand Leon curse "those damn *Eye-talians*" for the sickness that threatened their business.

"No, certainly not. It's because the primary symptom, after the fever, is these boils, filled with blood. And then they burst and look like wounds from a stabbing. Like Julius Caesar on the steps of the Senate. Rome. *Plaga Romanus.*"

"From a book?" Jack said.

"Actually, that one I know firsthand."

Jack inched half a step closer. "So," he said, "*can* you tell what she died from?"

In answer, Hazel lifted her largest knife and made a long incision vertically down the corpse's chest, just as she had seen Dr. Straine do in class. She paused, looking down in disbelief. She looked up at Jack, down at the body, and then up at Jack again. "As it happens," Hazel said, "I can tell you exactly what she died from. She doesn't have a heart."

"A heartbeat? Well, yeah, she's dead—I could've told you that much."

"No," Hazel said. "Look. She literally doesn't have a heart."

Jack looked into the yawning void of the body's chest. It was all so *red*, and so *wet*, he didn't know what he was looking for.

"Just there." Hazel gestured with the knife, toward the center of the woman's chest. "Beneath the rib cage. In front of the lungs."

"I don't see anything," Jack said.

"That's sort of the point."

The heart was gone. In its place, nothing. Just the vacuum of other viscera and darkness glowing red by candlelight. The veins had been crudely cauterized, the larger arteries sewn shut. No animal had eaten the heart from her chest; it was stolen.

"So," Jack said, leaning against the damp dungeon wall to steady himself, and nearly singeing his jacket on a torch, "Someone cut her open, and—and—cut her heart out? Jesus, why?"

Hazel looked down at the body. Even with her chest pulled open, the dead woman somehow looked serene. "Maybe she had enemies. Do you know who she was? Her name or anything?"

Jack shook his head. It had been too dark in the kirkyard to get a good look at the gravestone.

"Maybe it was an accident," Hazel said softly. She glanced back at the scars from the body's wet-cupping. "Maybe she was brought to the poor hospital and someone was trying to save her but didn't know how."

"Save her from what?"

Hazel could only shrug her shoulders.

Jack wanted to stay. He couldn't explain it—he wished there were a reason for him to linger, to press his body up close against Hazel's and breathe in the metallic smell of lightning that clung to her, a peculiar smell mixed with bergamot and castile soap. He wanted to watch her hands, deft and gloveless, do their work. Her face was stone, deep in concentration, impossibly beautiful in the sharpness of its planes.

"So I'll just be off now," Jack forced himself to say. He lifted the cloved orange to hand it back to her, but Hazel waved him off.

"Keep it, for next time."

"There's going to be a next time?" Jack asked.

"Are you turning down a paying customer, Jack Currer?"

"I wouldn't dream of it. I just think I should probably ask the lady what she's planning on doing with these dead bodies."

"I thought that would be perfectly obvious by now," Hazel said. "I'm studying."

Jack opened his mouth to reply, but just sighed, shaking his head in cheerful disbelief.

He maneuvered the wheelbarrow back toward the small door and the inky black grass beyond it.

"Jack, I need a body that actually did have the fever . . . if you can find one. I want to examine it. I want to see if I can cure it." She hadn't admitted out loud, not even to herself, that curing the Roman fever was indeed her ambition.

Jack didn't scoff or laugh at her. He just nodded.

Hazel pressed another few coins into his hand. "Payment," she said. "In advance."

"I'll see what I can do."

Hazel turned back to the body.

Jack stood in the doorway and watched as she took several deep breaths to steel herself and then began to make a slow incision across the corpse's scalp. Hazel didn't look up from the brain she had just unsheathed, its milky-gray curves visible beneath a sliver of bone-white skull.

"Goodbye, Hazel Sinnett," Jack said, pulling the creaking door closed behind him. The hinges clanged.

Jack had already made his way several steps along the garden path when he heard her whispered call back to him through the darkness: "Goodbye, Jack Currer."

19

HE GENTLE KNOCKING STARTLED HAZEL OUT of her hypnotic focus. She was dissecting a stomach to see if she could diagram its blood vessels. She dismissed the noise, thinking it must be the sound of a small bird, one of the small black ones that chittered around the trees along the drive, but then the rapping returned, a little more frantic. *Knock, knock, knock!*

"Miss!" It was the hushed and panicked whisper of Iona. There was another round of knocking. "Miss, please."

Hazel sighed and wiped a small scalpel on her apron. She had been using it to pull apart the layers of the stomach lining and she had been making excellent progress. But reluctantly, she trudged to the door, realizing only as she moved how sore her neck and shoulders were. She must have been at work for hours, so focused on the task in front of her that the time had slipped away. Hazel cracked open the door, astonished to find that there was daylight on the other side.

Iona looked terrified, and then she glanced down at Hazel's blood-streaked apron and looked even more terrified. "I wasn't sure whether or not to bother you, but . . ."

After so many hours in the dimness of her slowly dwindling candles, Hazel had to lift her arm to shield her bloodshot eyes from the brightness of the outdoors. "Did you *have* to bother me, then?" she said. Hazel had gone so long without speaking that her voice had a strange croak to it, and the words were sharper than she'd intended. "I'm sorry, I didn't mean for that to come out that way. What do you need, Iona?"

Iona wrung her hands. "It's just, tonight, I mean, in a few hours. It's the ball."

The day was overcast, thick gray clouds hanging low in the sky. This was Scotland. It was *supposed* to be dreary. So how was it still *so* bright? Hazel wanted to retreat like a mushroom back to the shadowy dankness. "What *ball*?"

Iona looked behind her, as if there were another servant who might relieve her of the unpleasant duty of having to relay this information to Hazel. "The, er, the Almonts' ball."

Hazel blinked while the information connected inside whatever part of her brain was responsible for that sort of thing. "Oh, *bollocks. Bollocks, bollocks, bollocks!*"

Iona gazed at her sympathetically. "It's already past noon, miss."

"Past noon? Already? How?!" She had worked all night and then all morning, and hadn't realized it. She stepped outside the dungeon onto the muddy brown path, and one glance at Iona's face revealed to Hazel how much she reeked. Her hair was matted with a gummy combination of ink and cadaver gore, to say nothing of what was probably beneath her fingernails.

"It'll be all right," Iona said, although everything about her expression made it abundantly clear that she thought it would almost probably not be all right. "I told Charles to start the bath."

"Figures," Hazel said, taking long strides up the hill and back toward the castle's main entrance. "The single party of the Season I can't miss." Iona scurried behind her. It would be a long and miserable afternoon and, Hazel knew, an even longer and more miserable evening to come.

20

I T TOOK TWO ROUNDS OF WASHING Hazel's hair with her mother's fine rose hip bar soap and another hour of brushing it out, but eventually Iona managed to make Hazel look somewhat presentable in time to arrive at Almont House late, but not late enough that it would be considered unforgivably rude. Hazel had let Iona tighten the laces on her boned corset firmly enough to allow her to fit into her blue velvet gown with the lace trim, and even she had to admit—as she glanced at her reflection in the glass of the Almont entry hall—that it suited her. The midnight-blue color made the pink flush of her cheeks look rosy and her eyes look bright, in spite of having stayed up all night.

"Cousin!" Bernard said, bounding to meet her at the entrance to the ballroom and extending his arm. "Welcome, finally. You look, well, marvelous."

Hazel stifled a yawn by turning it into a polite smile. She rested her gloved hand gracefully on Bernard's elbow and allowed him to escort her into the room. It was well-lit and warm, full of bodies and swirling crinoline. Hundreds of candles stood tall as soldiers in gilded chandeliers. Somehow, a dance card was secured around Hazel's wrist, and a flute of champagne deposited into her hand.

Gibbs Hartwick-Ellis had grown a miserable little mustache since the last time she saw him at the theater; he was pressed into a corner, politely trying to extricate himself from a conversation with the boorish Baron Walford, who was leaning forward and all but pinning poor Gibbs in place.

Hazel shot Gibbs a sympathetic look. She had been placed next to Walford at one of her parents' dinner parties, and even after studying cadavers, she still retched to recall his breath—to say nothing of the creepy way the Baron's glass eye seemed to roll in its socket of its own volition.

Hazel didn't see Cecilia, but Mrs. Caldwater was impossible to miss. The trill of her high-pitched laughter all but vibrated the crystal. Hazel would turn a quick circle about the room, make her presence known, and then return to the cadaver in her dungeon. (She had forgotten to visit the ice shed—the body would last only another few hours before the flesh began to disintegrate beyond all practical use.)

She could say she had a headache. Or she was feeling faint. No one seemed to ask too many questions about a woman feeling faint, nor about the broader cultural phenomenon of an entire society of women who seemed to swoon en masse. A fainting woman was so easily explained: either the weather this time of year was unseasonably warm or cool, and if it was neither, then certainly the lady's corset had been laced too tight. No doubt all of the swooning made the men around them feel so useful and strong, to be able to lift a woman up from a heap among her skirts and fan her face until her eyelashes blinked her back to consciousness.

The band launched into an upbeat waltz, and Bernard laced his fingers with Hazel's and pulled her in tight. Slightly too tight. The heavy velvet was causing her chemise to stick to her skin, and Bernard's hand was unpleasantly sweaty. Maybe she wouldn't need to fib about feeling faint after all.

Hazel tried to loosen her hand in Bernard's grip, but he just pulled her in tighter. "How lovely to see you up and out, Cousin," he said coolly.

Hazel dipped into a shallow curtsy. She tried to recall exactly how rude she had been to Bernard the last time he stopped by Hawthornden. "Bernard, when I saw you the other day—I was sick. I really wasn't up for company."

Bernard lifted a gloved hand in forgiveness. "Forgotten," he said. "Although I would be remiss if I didn't tell you that people are whispering. You haven't been yourself of late. Missing social functions. You've become practically a ghost. *Nobody's* seen you for weeks. One *might* think you've been avoiding me," he said. "Silly, I know."

"I've been sick. That's all, Bernard."

Bernard smiled, but the smile didn't quite reach his eyes. They seemed to be spinning faster than the other dancers around them. "I've stopped by Hawthornden quite a few times, you know. To pay a visit. Your carriage was gone."

"Was it?" Hazel said, hoping her voice was light. "How unusual. And what an unusual thing to notice."

Without warning, Bernard wrapped his arm around Hazel's waist and pulled her body against his into a waltz frame. She almost gasped at his presumption. "Visiting another suitor, were you?" he sneered.

Hazel almost laughed in his face. "No," she said, stumbling as she tried to follow his lead on the dance floor. "I can quite assure you, there is no other suitor."

Bernard's eyes were flat and cold. He looked more like his father than Hazel had ever noticed before. "There were boots in your entry hall," he said through clenched teeth. "A gentleman's boots. Someone intimate enough to take his *boots* off in your home, although I can't imagine who that might be. If it's someone at the club, I assume I would have heard of it. I swear to God, Hazel"—he clenched Hazel's hands so hard they ached—"if you're humiliating me, I . . ." He released Hazel's hands in lieu of finishing his thought. His hair, so neatly parted and pomaded, shook slightly with his emotion.

"Bernard," Hazel said softly, "those were George's old boots. I swear it. I wear them to walk in the gardens, and down to the stream, to not muddy my own." She was relieved she could at least tell only part of a lie.

"Oh." His face softened. "Well, then. Perhaps I can interest you in a stroll out to our winter garden? I assure you, it's quite lovely in the fall, with the weather mild as it's been."

Hazel glanced around. No one was giving them more than a cursory look. Even Miss Hartwick-Ellis, usually so jealously observant of whatever Hazel happened to be doing, was cheerfully flirting with the son of the Danish ambassador, her eyes scarcely leaving the handsome blond for long enough to blink.

"Perhaps we should find a chaperone?" Hazel said.

"Oh, pishposh." Bernard grabbed Hazel's arm and guided her toward the door to the servants' entrance. "You wanted to go to some dreadful *surgery* in the Old Town alone with me!"

They were standing in the servants' entrance to the kitchen, a dank little passage with only a few flickering gas lamps. A footman strode by, carrying a tray of pastries, and politely averted his eyes.

Hazel tried to pull away, back toward the party. "Well, we wouldn't have actually been alone at a surgical demonstration, but—"

Before she could finish her sentence, Bernard pressed his mouth to hers. The wet worm of his tongue slithered along her closed lips until it found purchase and pried her mouth open.

His lips were cold and strange, his tongue clammy. Some part of Hazel's brain told her to slap him, to yank herself away. A thousand harsh words formulated themselves neatly, but she seemed completely unable to get them past her throat. Her body, likewise, was suffering from a strange paralysis. All she could do was stand there, eyes open like a fish, waiting for Bernard to finally pull away with a self-satisfied smack of his lips. He wiped the lower half of his face with his sleeve and waggled his eyebrows.

Hazel's stomach flipped over itself, and she tried not to grimace looking at Bernard's face—the ruddiness of it, the dead flatness in his eyes, his thin lips still glistening with sweat. So that was a kiss. That was the thing she had read about in novels and poems, that had inspired great artists. It was wetter than she had imagined, and colder.

Finally, Hazel's voice returned to her and she pulled

away from Bernard's grip. "I don't know *what* in heaven's name you thought you were doing, but you'll have us *both* ruined. If anyone saw what just happened—"

Bernard put his hands on his hips and puffed his chest forward. "What? A servant? You're hardly ruined, Haze. *I* still want to marry you, so consider yourself quite set."

For a moment, another life flashed before her, a life in which she begged on the streets, moved to Yorkshire, posed as George Hazleton forever. Maybe she could become a midwife, the mad lady in a tiny cottage in the woods with a stocked apothecary of roots and herbs and foul-smelling teas, who helped women in need. She would be a surgeon, a teacher, a witch—a cautionary tale told in threat to trembling debutantes before their coming-outs. A myth.

But the flash of an alternative life only lasted for a moment before it disappeared like powder in an open palm on a windy day. There was no life for her except to become the Viscountess Almont, to marry Bernard. His would be the first and final kiss she would ever know.

Bernard leaned forward and kissed Hazel again. "Come on," he said, grabbing her arm once more. "Let's go back to the party."

Hazel let him escort her back through the servants' entrance and into the golden din of the ballroom. She floated numbly, paying no mind to Bernard as he strode over to the band and whispered in the ear of the lead violinist, who then stopped the music.

The dancers stumbled for a beat and tripped over their skirts. Bernard held aloft a crystal goblet and struck the side a few times with a knife to get the room's attention. Lord Almont stood nearby, beaming.

"Hello, hello, all," Bernard said in a voice effortfully deep. "Yes, hello. My father, the viscount, and my mother, the viscountess, and I wish to thank you all for joining us at our little get-together. The annual ball is a tradition that I so greatly enjoy and one that I hope will continue for years to come. My apologies for interrupting the festivities, but I have a little announcement to make. The lovely Miss Sinnett and I are engaged. Or at least, we are but a moment away. Hazel, my dear, will you marry me?"

Hazel's vision became a tunnel, dark and fuzzy at the edges. A ringing echoed through her ears, and her tongue turned to sand in her mouth.

All eyes in the room turned and found Hazel, and the smiles of the crowd grew wolflike. Hazel's dress was suddenly unbearably hot, so itchy at her neck and her sleeves that she felt hives rising beneath the fabric. The room was quiet but for the tinkle of champagne glasses. They were waiting for her to say something, to give her answer.

Unable to manage anything else, Hazel lifted the sides of her mouth into what might have been a deranged half smile.

"Aha!" Bernard shouted.

The applause sounded like gunfire. Hazel deflected the well-wishes and pats on her hand. She found that she had trouble breathing in her dress. Maybe it wasn't the dress; maybe it was the room, the house, her life. The black at the edges of her vision was growing, and the syllables on her tongue sounded thick and heavy as she tried to tell somebody that she needed to leave.

"Poor thing must need something to eat!"

"Must've had too much champagne! Har har!"

"Get the poor dear to bed."

"Heaven knows she won't get much rest once it's her *wedding* bed!"

Some gentle soul guided Hazel back to her carriage. "Please give Bernard my apologies," she heard herself mumble to whoever it was, before her driver cracked the whip over the horses. The carriage lurched forward, taking Hazel back to the safety of Hawthornden. But she knew safety was temporary. Her future was coming for her even as she was riding away from it, pulled by four horses, as quickly as she could.

21

I N HER NEW MAKESHIFT LABORATORY, HAZEL had cleared the table, prepared a blank page of her notepad, and replaced all the candles with fresh tapers in anticipation of Jack Currer coming to make another delivery that morning at ten o'clock. She was in a foul mood. The events of the Almonts' Ball kept replaying themselves in her brain, no matter how much Hazel tried to push those thoughts away and focus on the impending examination. The examination needed all her time and attention. The Bernard situation could wait.

But with Jack Currer coming, Hazel found her mind was too restless to study. By half past ten, Hazel had resharpened all her quills and laid them flat on the table, shortest to longest.

By eleven o'clock, most of the candles had burned down to waxen stumps. Finally, just before the bell rang noon, Hazel heard a knock on the door to the dungeon. "Finally," she murmured to herself. "Come in! It's unlocked."

The door creaked inward, revealing a sliver of overcast gray sky and Jack, alone. "There you are. Is the body out front? Broken wheelbarrow, I suppose. Marvelous, just marvelous.

If we need an extra pair of hands to carry the body, I can go get Charles, but I'd prefer if we just handled it ourselves."

Jack didn't look up from the earthen floor.

"What?"

"There's no body. I didn't go last night."

"Sorry?"

Jack's shoulders lifted to his ears. He looked as though he would rather be anywhere but there. Hazel noticed the deep purple shadows beneath his eyes. "There's no body," he said again, simply.

Hazel's eyebrows knitted together, but she forced herself to remain composed. "When will I be able to expect the body, then? One with the fever."

"There ain't going to be any more bodies." He looked away and showed a heavy bruise across his left cheek.

Before she could think better of it, Hazel strode forward and lifted Jack's face in her hands. Jack's hair was particularly lank and dull, and his eyes were flat.

His work as a resurrection man kept him up nights often; he was accustomed to going hours without sleep. But the previous night had been different. The exhaustion had started in his soul and crept outward. He had counted the seconds until sunrise from his paillasse in the risers at Le Grand Leon, willing his eyes to shut, not being able to force them to stay that way.

Jack jerked his chin away from Hazel's hands and shrugged his jacket higher onto his shoulders.

"I don't understand," Hazel said resolutely. "I paid you in advance. You've only given me one body. If I'm to cure the fever—let alone pass the Physician's Examination—I'm going to need at least several—"

"Well, you can find yourself another resurrection man, then, can't you now."

Hazel gave a barking laugh. "It's not as if you advertise in the evening newspapers."

Jack didn't smile. "Look, I'm sorry. I'm sorry, and I have your money back here if you want it." From deep in his pocket, he pulled out some coins, gave them a cursory glance, and then dropped them onto the wooden table, where Hazel had been expecting a corpse. "But I can't get you any more bodies, at least not until—" Jack didn't know how he was supposed to finish that sentence.

"Until what?"

Jack sighed. "My partner—er, or, he's not really a partner, more like a colleague, really. Munro. He's, well, missing. He went on a dig the other night, few nights back—alone, I thought, but maybe not—and anyways, he didn't come back."

Hazel gazed at him quizzically. "Well, maybe he made other plans. Left town. Visiting some family."

"He wouldn't do that without saying goodbye. And he's not the first one, is the thing. Resurrection men going missing more often than not these days."

"You think someone is *killing* resurrection men?"

"No, I don't—I mean, it's probably coppers cracking down. One of us probably accidentally got the body of a wealthy somebody or his wife, and now the police want all our heads to make him happy. These sorts of things happen for a bit, lawmen getting overeager. They lose interest in us soon enough."

He almost mentioned the story Munro had told him, months back, about the three strange men who had approached him after a resurrection. At the time, Jack had thought it was just one of Munro's tall tales, the type of ghost story he spread to make himself seem tougher and more interesting, like how he also claimed he could shoot a sparrow with a pistol at sixty paces. Jack had made fun of him for it, and Munro was embarrassed and bought the next round.

"But, anyways," Jack continued, "it's just too risky to go alone now, and I don't have a lookout, so unless I want to join Munro in a cell or, or wherever he is, that's it for now."

Hazel picked up the coins Jack had refunded her. She ran her fingers along the metal edges. "What if you didn't have to go alone?" she said carefully. "Would you do another dig, for a body, if you did have a partner?"

"I suppose," Jack said.

"Well, lovely. We'll go tonight, then." Hazel strolled past him, out of the dungeon. "And I'll be a very generous partner, let you keep all the money. Really, I *should* be asking for half."

Hazel was on the garden path and already halfway back to the castle before Jack broke from his astonished daze and caught up to her. "Wait! Wait, wait, wait. That's madness. I'm not doing a dig with a lady."

"You won't be," Hazel said. "You'll be doing it with me. I have plenty of old boots lying around, and I've gotten very comfortable in my brother's trousers. I'm not sure how much help I'll be with regards to digging, but as a lookout, I'm unmatched, I assure you."

Jack's head spun with everything she had just said. "Wait," he repeated. "Wait, wait. No. If the guards catch us, they'll think I've kidnapped you. They'll think I'm taking liberties with some—some daughter of a—whatever your dad is."

"Captain of the Royal Navy. It's actually my mother with the title, the daughter—now sister, I suppose—of a viscount."

Jack groaned.

"Well, pishposh to that," Hazel said. "I'll be dressed as a man."

"Oh, will you now? I'm sure that will be very convincing."

"More than you know. And anyhow, we won't be caught."

"We can't do this."

"We certainly can. I need a body. You need the money from a body, but more immediately, you need a partner to assist you in your resurrection. And here I am. Have you identified a body? One with the fever?"

Jack nodded reluctantly. He had scoped out the burial in the cemetery of Saint Dwynwen's, outside Edinburgh's city center. It was a body with no family, just two assistants from Saint Anthony's, the poorhouse hospital, dropping the body off wrapped in a sheet, and a priest to murmur a few prayers and bury it in a cheap wooden box. There wasn't even a headstone, just a simple wooden cross. Jack had overheard the priest murmur sadly to the groundskeeper as he shook his head: the fever had come fast for him.

"It's dangerous," Jack said. "Not just the risk of getting caught. People catch the fever from bodies all the time."

"I had it already," Hazel said simply. "You?"

Jack shrugged. "Been doing this long enough and haven't got it. Something lucky in my blood, I suppose."

"Well, then it's settled," Hazel said. "You and I will dig for the body together."

"See, that's the problem with wealthy people. You just assume you can do anything you want, whenever you want, and everything will just somehow *work out for you*!"

By this point, Hazel had reached Hawthornden's heavy wooden front door. She turned back to Jack before entering.

"Well, sometimes you *can* just do things. Who gave you permission to be digging up bodies from graves in the first place?"

"Nobody!" Jack spat. "It's a crime! That's the whole point of it."

"And now it's a crime that we're going to do together."

Jack could only laugh, and Hazel smiled back at him.

Their eyes met, and Hazel blushed. "Well," she said. "You should get some sleep. There are guest rooms if you . . ." She gestured to the castle behind her.

Jack shook his head. He couldn't imagine what it would feel like to stay as a guest in one of these grand houses. He doubted even his exhaustion would allow him to sleep in such strange surroundings.

"The guesthouse out front is empty, too, at the end of the drive, if you prefer."

"Nah, I best be headed home to my own bed for a spell."

"Well, then. Meet back here at midnight?" Hazel asked.

"Wear dark clothes," Jack warned in answer.

"I'm not a fool, Jack Currer, no matter what you might think of me."

"Oh, I assure you, Miss Sinnett, I've taken you for a lot of things, but a fool was never one of them."

22

JACK WAS ALREADY WAITING OUTSIDE WHEN Hazel came out. He was leaning against the low stone wall built a century ago to contain the sheep, using his long fingers to peel an orange and then tossing the pulpy rind onto the grass. When he saw her approach, he gave a low whistle. "Well, look who made it," he said, scanning her from top to bottom.

Hazel did a mocking little curtsy. She was wearing George's trousers and shirt, but on her feet she had an uncomfortable pair of dirty boots that had belonged to Charles. None of George's shoes seemed suitable for a jaunt to a graveyard, and Charles had been more than happy to trade his workman's boots for a pair of George's leather riding ones.

The familiar flutter returned to Hazel's chest when she saw Jack lounging there, as if he were reclining in a boat on the Thames. Only the flicker of his fingers as he finished peeling the orange revealed his nervousness.

It wasn't uncommon for Jack to go a few weeks without doing a job with Munro. Their partnership was a matter of convenience, and often Munro would prefer to partner with a newcomer out on a dig, with the assumption that he could swindle him out of his proper share. But none of Jack's old contacts from Fleshmarket had seen Munro, and the innkeeper at the inn by the docks where Munro had been staying for the past few months said he hadn't come by to collect his things. A sallow-skinned sliver of a woman, she had let Jack up to Munro's rooms for the low price of a charming smile and a thin lie about being Munro's brother. The room looked exactly as Munro would have left it before a dig: soiled blankets on the unmade bed, an extra pair of shoes in the corner of the closet, and—Jack knew to feel for it amid the matted straw—a purse of coins sewn into the filthy mattress's underside. There was the smallest chance that Munro might have skipped town without saying goodbye, but he never would have left without his money. Jack had neatly replaced the coin purse and made a silent promise to Munro as he closed and locked the door that he would figure out what happened to him. Even if he was dead, Munro deserved a proper Christian burial. Even sinners deserved a headstone.

Jack licked the juice from his fingers and let the acidic tingle of the citrus wake him up. "I have to admit," he said, stepping closer to Hazel and seeing her hair hidden under her hat, "you as a man is more convincing than I imagined."

Hazel rolled her eyes. Behind Jack stood a wheelbarrow containing two spades, some burlap, and candles.

"I've got some strikers and a candle, too, case we need some light, but it's best to try to adjust your eyes as quickly as possible, I've found. We'll have the walk for that."

The cemetery behind Saint Dwynwen's was not too far up the road, less than an hour's walk. Whatever the danger that was coming to resurrection men, it was smarter for him to stay out of the city for a while, avoiding the high-profile area of Greyfriars Kirkyard, right in the heart of Edinburgh's Old Town. Too many distractions, too many people, too much risk.

Maybe it was an abundance of caution, but he hadn't consulted with Jeanette about finding the body. He didn't have any reason to suspect Jeanette of having something to do with Munro's disappearance, but he didn't have any reason to trust her, either, and staying alive meant trusting only himself. And apparently—he thought to himself—trusting some noblewoman's daughter playing dress-up, for some reason. Really, why was he trusting her?

He tried to reason through it: one of the first lessons he'd learned in the narrow closes and tight hidey-holes of the underbelly of Edinburgh was never to rely on someone with less to lose than you did. He knew the way it was for these society girls, the restrictions placed on them, how precariously they balanced on the precipice between promise and ruin. Imagine what would happen to her reputation—to her family's reputation—if it got out that she was off sneaking around at night, unchaperoned, with a poor boy who worked in a theater. It was in her best interest not to get caught tonight too. That was the logic of it, anyway.

But, if Jack was being honest with himself—if he allowed himself to acknowledge the tiny, hidden truth nestled somewhere in his brain—he didn't have any good reason to trust Hazel Sinnett, but he did so anyway.

She was unlike any girl he had ever met—the sound of her syllables narrower and more refined than those of Jeanette or even Isabella. The girls at the theater wore thick oil makeup; there was something startling about standing close to Hazel, being able to see her freckles and the fine downy blond hair along her cheeks.

Jack couldn't explain it. She wasn't more beautiful than Isabella. She was small, and arrogant, and wealthy. Her nose was sharp, her features were boyish, and her lashes and eyebrows were too pale for her dark hair. And yet.

And yet.

Since Jack had met Hazel Sinnett outside the Anatomists' Society, he had found himself tracing her jawline in his mind before he went to sleep. He could see the thin arc of her pale lips, the freckles almost invisible on her cheeks. Her face was burned into his memory, and it remained there: an echo but undiminished. A haunting. From the moment he had first looked into her wide brown eyes, the warm brown of burnished wood or polished amber reflecting the sunset, Jack had trusted her, and he would keep trusting her for far longer than his survivor's instinct warned him was prudent.

"Did you say 'walk'?" Hazel said. "Why would we walk? I told the stableman to prepare a pair of horses. You do know how to ride, don't you?"

"Of course I know how to ride," Jack lied. "I just didn't want *you* to have to worry about your servants knowing about your midnight . . . comings and goings. Didn't want to cause a scandal and all that."

Hazel glanced back at him sideways, leading the way to the stables. "My house has always been a little odd. My father's absence, my mother's— Well, in simple terms, my brother died, and my mother went into mourning, and neglected to come out of it. All of which is to say no one really cares what I do or where I go, especially since I never had to bother with the whole nightmarish spectacle of a London coming-out, me being practically engaged since I was a baby and all."

"You're *engaged*?" Of course she was engaged, Jack thought, women like her were always engaged. They were practically bred for it. Sows groomed for the slaughter.

Hazel paused. Her familiar answer caught itself on her tongue, and the memories of what had happened at the Almont ball came flooding back, bringing with them waves of emotion: terror first and then, surprisingly, relief, at the inevitable finally having happened. Hazel laughed, a full-throated laugh that startled a few nearby birds into scattering from their trees. "I suppose I am engaged."

"I'm not sure that's the typical reaction. Most brides are excited for that sort of thing."

"I haven't really said it out loud before. It sort of felt like a bad dream up until now."

"Why? Ugly guy? Pockmarks? No, let me guess: He's pushing sixty, with a potbelly?"

"Actually, no. Eighteen in March, fairly handsome from what I understand these things to be. Lord Bernard Almont. You don't know him, do you?"

Jack shook his head. "Know the house, though," he said before he could stop himself. Hazel gave him a queer look. "Everyone knows Almont House, I mean. Big 'un. In the New Town." And then, to change the subject quickly: "So how come you don't want to get married? Live in that big house, get money and all that?"

"I don't believe they let viscountesses dissect dead bodies," Hazel said.

"Well, how could they possibly fit it into their demanding social schedules?"

"It would certainly stain their gloves."

Jack pushed a lock of hair dangling in his face behind his ear. "So they let women engaged to be viscountesses dissect dead bodies?"

"Only if they don't find out." Hazel smiled as she opened the stable gate, and led Jack toward a maple-colored horse tied to a post, with a saddle already affixed. She ran her hand along the horse's muzzle.

The horse had a glossy coat, Jack could see that, and a velvety pink lining around its nose, but the thing that drew most of Jack's attention was the horse's alarming, colossal height.

Hazel read the fear on his face. "I know, they're larger than the usual ponies one typically sees around here. My father had them brought up for us from London. Arabians. But they're lovely, really. This one is mine. Miss Rosalind," Hazel said, stroking her brown mare's haunches tenderly, to which the horse responded with an affectionate whinny. Hazel saw the look on Jack's face and rolled her eyes. "I was *young* when I named her. I didn't know what you were supposed to name a horse. That one is yours, for tonight anyway. Betelgeuse."

She gestured with her head toward a stallion so black Jack had missed it altogether, a nightmarish beast with slender legs that could have been a full story high. The horse, Betelgeuse, gave a distrustful snort. "Beautiful," Jack said.

Hazel swung herself onto Miss Rosalind's back with ease, and unfastened the horse's reins from the post with a single flick of her wrist. She guided the horse into a gentle trot, going around in a circle. "Well, no use standing on ceremony. Come on, hop to it."

Betelgeuse the horse tossed his head back and looked directly at Jack. He seemed no happier about the prospect of Jack riding him than Jack was.

"Wait! Hold on a moment," Jack said to Hazel, barely able to contain his relief. "I have the wheelbarrow. We won't be able to get the body back on horseback. Guess we better walk after all."

Hazel leapt from her saddle to the ground as if the rules of gravity didn't apply to her. "What are you talking about?" She walked around to the side of the stable, where a small cart was leaning up against a bale of hay. Effortlessly, she wheeled the cart around to her horse and affixed its breeching to Miss Rosalind's saddle. "There," Hazel said, pulling a piece of turnip from her pocket and letting Miss Rosalind slurp it from her palm. "Simple. And much easier than carrying a wheelbarrow."

Jack grimaced. "Yeah. Much easier." He sighed, then lifted the sheets and spades from his wheelbarrow and deposited them into Hazel's cart. And then he took a ginger step toward the massive black stallion. "Let's get this over with, mate," he muttered. He said a quick prayer, latched his foot into the stirrup, and pulled himself onto the horse with all the force he could muster. "Not so bad!" It was the first time Jack had ever ridden a horse. He felt strong, secure, as though he and the horse were connected, that they could ford rivers and leap fences.

He gave Betelgeuse a gentle nudge with his heels to get him to move forward. Instead of walking, the horse responded with a malicious little lurch that forced Jack flat onto his stomach. His knuckles turned white from the effort of gripping the reins, and his thighs shook. Hazel and Miss Rosalind were already several yards up the drive. With his

teeth clenched and another prayer (he had done more praying in the last forty seconds than he had in his entire life),
Jack lifted himself back into a seated position and tapped his
heel against the horse's side in the hopes of getting him to
actually move.

Betelgeuse obeyed. As soon as the horse realized he was
freed from his tether to the post, he not only moved but
whipped forward at a full gallop, peeling past Hazel on her
mount and racing toward the distant blackness between the
towering pines that lined the drive.

Hazel shouted something after him, but Jack could hear
only the wind and his heartbeat pounding loudly in his frozen ears. There was another sound, a high-pitched whine like
a teakettle, and it took Jack several seconds to realize it was
his own screaming.

His terrifying ride didn't last long. There was something
dark on the road ahead, something impossible to make out,
a black mass of something horizontal, blocking the way. But
the horse's speed meant that whatever they fast approached
was right in front of Jack before he could react to it: a felled
log, teeming with rot and crawling with insects.

Betelgeuse leapt, and Jack tumbled from the saddle and
onto the hard dirt below. He flipped over once in a somer-
sault and then landed feet-over-head against the rotting log.
The sound of the monstrous horse's hooves diminished into
the distance. Jack moaned. He felt a cold dampness seeping
from the mire through the fabric of his jacket.

Hazel and her horse approached. "I thought you said you
could ride!" she shouted as she dismounted.

Jack groaned again. "I thought I would be able to."

With gentle hands, Hazel helped Jack into a sitting position.

He rubbed the bruised back of his head. "It just looked like it would just be, I dunno, sitting."

"There's a bit more to it than that," she said. "I'm sorry, Jack, I really am."

"Nah, it's not your fault." Betelgeuse trotted close to where Jack and Hazel were seated. The horse flared his nostrils with satisfaction. "It's *his* fault."

"Does anything seem broken? Any bones? Jack, are you dizzy?"

Jack blinked away the fuzziness from his vision and saw the shadowy topography of Hazel's face, just a few fingerwidths away. She was so close that Jack could feel her breath on his forehead while she examined his skull for bumps. The only injury was to his pride. He would have a bruise in the morning, but that wasn't a new experience for a boy who had lived on the streets alone since he was eleven. "I'm fine, really," he said. "It's that beast you should be worried about. A maniac, he is. I'm telling you."

And so, they rode to Saint Dwynwen's on one horse, Jack sitting behind Hazel on Miss Rosalind, with his arms wrapped around Hazel's narrow waist. Hazel had tied Betelgeuse's reins to Miss Rosalind's saddle, and so he walked obediently beside them as they followed a dark forest trail that wove through acres of farmland on one side and the stream on the other. Jack threw Betelgeuse a dirty look. Betelgeuse paid him no mind.

With the exception of Bernard's terrible kiss, Hazel had never been this close to a boy in her life. Most of the time she spent with Bernard had been at teas, where they sat opposite each other on brocade furniture while a handful of servants brought out dishes of fresh biscuits, or else insufferable balls, where they danced with their elbows out, perfectly rigid frames that spun around brightly illuminated rooms like the figurines on mechanical clocks. This was intimate and strange. Hazel could feel Jack's warmth against her back.

With the gentle bouncing of the horse, and his arms around her waist, Jack couldn't help but admit it felt nice, being pressed up against Hazel, smelling her hair and the subtle musk of her sweat.

"Is that . . . ?" Hazel asked without looking backward, trepidation in her voice.

"Oh. Oh!" Jack pulled away the handle of one of his trowels from where it had pressed into her back. He blushed and cursed himself under his breath, and they rode the rest of the way in silence.

Saint Dwynwen's rose from the horizon like smoke, a small iron-colored building with a thin, twisted spire. "We should get off the horses here," Jack whispered. "Go the rest of the way on foot."

Hazel nodded. She slipped gracefully off her horse's back and generously extended a hand to Jack, who took it and still managed to land with a thump next to her. They were surrounded by forest, damp moss and mud beneath their boots. Hazel tied the horses to a nearby branch while Jack gathered the equipment from the cart: two spades, a grimy sheet, and a long rope. "I'm warning you: this isn't a pleasant business."

"Don't worry. I didn't expect pleasant." Jack could see the glint of her sly smile in the shadows.

The two of them set out toward the back of the church,

where the mausoleums and tombs stood in warning like silent sentinels. When they made it to the spiked kirkyard fence, Jack vaulted it immediately, out of habit. Hazel stood on the other side. "It's easier than it looks," Jack whispered, glancing at the little cottage parish house with a single candle lit in the window to make sure no one was coming. "If you can climb onto that beast of a horse, I promise you can jump this fence, truly."

Hazel hesitated, and for half a moment, Jack was convinced this was all a mistake, bringing Hazel here, that she was going to get them caught or cry out—but then she had done it. She had jumped the fence without even catching the hem of her trousers.

"So where's the grave?" she said, catching her breath.

Now Jack was grinning. He tilted his head and led the way toward the southeastern corner of the cemetery, where he had seen the funeral gathering a few days prior. Unfortunately, in the dark, with his head half scrambled with fear and the lingering smell of Hazel's hair, Jack found the fresh grave much harder to locate than he had planned on.

"I swear, it's somewhere around here," Jack whispered. The longer they were here, the riskier it became. The trick to being a good resurrection man was getting in, and getting out, before a mourner half a yard away would even know that you were there.

Hazel walked slowly, trying to make out the names carved onto the gravestones. She stood in front of each one, her mouth silently making out the shapes of their names. "So many children," she said quietly.

And so many deaths in 1815, the year the fever had swept through Edinburgh without mercy, killing rich and poor alike, nobles and their servants. It was a slow illness often, and a brutal one, so contagious in the hours before death that families were known to leave the suffering alone in their homes, weeping and pawing at the windows, begging for someone, anyone, to come and hold them while they died. And it struck children, and young men and women. That was the illness's true cruelty: it often claimed those who had not yet had a chance to live.

"It's here," Jack whispered. He stood before a mound of unsettled earth, damp and recently dug, and a tiny wooden cross.

Hazel joined him and grabbed one of the spades. "So now we dig," she said.

"Now we dig."

They worked in silence for the better part of an hour. Every few minutes, Jack would lift his head to make sure the parish was still quiet, but Hazel, to his surprise, was an astonishingly diligent worker. She scarcely lifted her head, working methodically and creating a hypnotic rhythm: the sound of her spade scraping through the earth, and then the gentle pat of the soil being deposited on the surface. *Scratch. Pat. Scratch. Pat. Scratch. Pat.*

And then a sound broke the rhythm—something distant, in the woods. A crunching of leaves. Maybe the clawing of a small animal against the tree bark. Hazel didn't notice, her spade continuing its task at pace, but Jack lifted his head. The trees were too dark to make anything out. Just the horses, he told himself. Had to be the horses. He'd been doing this long enough not to get spooked by shadows.

A more immediate noise hit them: metal against wood, the sound of Hazel's spade vibrating against the wooden coffin. "All right," Jack said, "I'm going to break it now."

Hazel nodded and shielded her eyes from any errant slivers of wood as Jack lifted his spade aloft and brought it down with a single confident stroke onto the coffin lid. It snapped like a pistol shot. Jack threw his spade over the side of the hole they had dug and back onto the grass, then pulled himself up to follow it. "Throw me the piece from the top of the casket. Then I'm going to lower you down some rope. Wrap it around his legs, then I'll do the heavy lifting."

Hazel nodded her silent assent. She twisted the piece of broken lid free and handed it off, and then assessed what she had revealed: a pair of feet in tattered brown shoes with barely enough material to hold them together, and the vile smell of putrefaction and death. A maggot wriggled between the corpse's toes, and Hazel gagged into her sleeve. "I wish I could say you get used to that," Jack whispered, shielding his own nose.

As he dropped the rope down to Hazel, he glanced back at the woods, where he thought he had seen the shadow. There was movement there. Something impossible to make out. Maybe just an animal, a fox skulking amid the mossy undergrowth. All Jack could do now was finish the job quickly and get out.

Hazel wound the rope around the body's ankles several times, and then tied it off in a tight square knot. "Ready."

Jack pulled, and a spray of soil came down across Hazel's face from where the rope slid up the side of the grave. Hazel tried to help guide the body up and out of the casket, through the splintery gap in the wood, but Jack did most of the physical labor, pulling steadily up and away until the body slithered, feetfirst, back to the living world—six feet up.

Jack lowered a hand then to help Hazel up. "Now we have

to undress him, make sure we don't bring any of his clothes with us. We're not thieves, after all."

They stood over the body when their task was complete, the darkness protecting the dead stranger's modesty. "This is strange," Hazel said. "It feels like we're at a funeral."

"You get used to it," Jack said, already starting the process of wrapping the body in the sheet. He hoisted the body over his shoulder with ease. Hazel had thought Jack was all sharp edges and thin lines, but he was surprisingly strong. He lowered the body into the cart tenderly and then gestured to Hazel and the horse. "After you, m'lady."

Hazel hoisted herself onto Miss Rosalind's saddle, then lowered her hand to help Jack up behind her.

They made it back to Hawthornden just as the sky began to lighten into misty gray. Jack followed Hazel into her dungeon and deposited the body onto her table.

"Would you like to stay for a cup of tea or something?" Hazel said after they had stood in the dim half light for a few seconds. "We can walk up to the castle; I'm sure Cook will be up if you want some breakfast."

Jack shook his head. He pushed his hair away from his face. "Nah, I best be getting back to town," he said. "On foot."

"Oh. All right, then." Hazel looked down at the body, still wrapped in Jack's sheet. "I'll need more than one body, I think," she said. "If there's another one that died of the fever that you hear about."

"No shortage of those," Jack said. Hazel looked up at him, alarmed to see that he was smiling. "Let's say same time next week."

23

To HAZEL'S SURPRISE, JACK ARRIVED BACK at Hawthornden sooner than Sunday night. Just a few days after their successful dig, Hazel saw him standing sheepishly by the stables when she came out after breakfast for her walk.

"I was thinking," he said, "that if you *happened* to be free today, you might show me how to ride. I'm not expecting to be able to learn in one go, especially if you put me on a brute like that Beetle—whatever his name was."

"Betelgeuse," Hazel said, trying to hold back her smile as she approached. "One of the brightest stars in the night sky visible to the naked eye, they say."

"And impossible high up, just like the horse."

Hazel had already entered the stable and brought the tall black Arabian out of his stall. The pair of them approached Jack, who began to look as though he regretted his decision to revisit riding.

If Betelgeuse were capable of smirking, that's exactly what the horse would have done as it gazed down at Jack with a look in his eye that couldn't be construed as anything other than a challenge. Jack raised his arm as if to pet the horse, and then thinking better of it, used his already lifted hand to tidy his hair, pretending that was what he had intended the entire time.

"So," Hazel said, "we're going to want the horse to get to know you."

"I feel like we already had a fairly intimate introduction," Jack said.

"No sudden movements. Move very slowly. Reach out your hand—yes, very good, just like that, and now walk all the way around him, but keep your hand on him the whole time. He needs to know where you are."

Jack obeyed, feeling slightly silly walking around the horse while Hazel watched.

"Now, put your left foot in the stirrup there. Always mount from the left side."

"Why?"

"Actually, I'm not certain. I was just taught that way. I assume it has *something* to do with the aristocracy, but I have no idea what."

"Well, far be it from me to want to disrespect anything to do with the aristocracy," Jack said, his eyes finding Hazel's.

With surprising grace, Jack smoothly pulled himself onto Betelgeuse's back. "Aha!" he cried. "I did it!"

Betelgeuse leaned down to chew on some yellowing grass, and Jack gripped the reins in terror. "It's in your thighs now," Hazel said.

Jack cocked an eyebrow.

"Squeeze from there. And keep your back straight. And try not to be afraid. Horses can sense that sort of thing."

"Right. Yeah. Fearless."

"You dig up dead bodies in the middle of the night in graveyards, and you're afraid of riding a horse?" Hazel asked.

"See, here's the thing," Jack said as Betelgeuse decided to start drifting off to the left. "Dead bodies are never going to bite you. They're never going to do *anything* to you. It's living things that hurt you."

"Yes, I suppose you're right," Hazel said.

Hazel mounted Miss Rosalind, and after a bit of effort, the two of them managed to get their horses walking side by side down the long Hawthornden drive.

"That's probably all we should hope for today," Hazel said when they made it back to the stables. "But if you want, you could come back tomorrow. It could be good for my studying—taking a break, getting some fresh air."

"Yeah," Jack said. "That sounds about right."

THE SECOND TIME THE PAIR WENT riding, they made it all the way to the edge of the farm the next property over, where sheep grazed placidly against the rolling green hills. After that, Hazel took Jack on the narrow path down through the woods to the back of Hawthornden, along the stream.

"Do you believe in ghosts?" Hazel asked as they passed the imposing cypress trees by Hawthornden's back gates. She had always imagined it to be a foolish question, the type children whisper to one another while playing, but the past few weeks fixated on the human body made her more curious about death, and what happened beyond the veil.

"Why do you ask?" Jack said. He rubbed Betelgeuse's neck. The horse wasn't so scary once you got to know him, he found.

"I've never seen any evidence for them myself, but I suppose there has to be something more than electricity animating our flesh. A soul that lives on."

Jack's expression tightened. Death had always been a constant in the Old Town, but over the past few weeks, the streets had become eerie with a new silence, thick as candle wax. No one talked about it, but Jack knew: the disappearances were continuing. It wasn't just resurrection men—the girl who worked at the fishmonger's, who used to wink at Jack whenever he passed the market, was gone, and the man behind the counter had just shrugged when Jack asked about her. No one had seen Rosie, a prostitute who used to smoke cigars with the actors at Le Grand Leon, not for months. Once word got out that the Roman fever might be back, no one asked too many questions when the narrow, crowded rooms of the Old Town contained a few fewer bodies.

"I dunno," Jack said. "I think I do believe in ghosts. But I don't think ghosts would be in kirkyards."

"Why? Something about it being hallowed ground?"

"No," Jack said, plucking a leaf from a passing tree and rolling it in his fingers. "I just don't think ghosts would want to be reminded of death. I figure when they get out of their bodies, they want to get as far away from them as possible. I've dealt with my fair share of corpses, and I can tell you there's no reason anyone would want to hold on to that. We're rotting bags of meat is all, and we start going bad pretty quick. Ghosts can go anywhere, right? No reason to stick around their bodies being eaten by worms."

"That is a rather bleak outlook," Hazel said. "But I suppose it has a sort of poetry to it."

They rode in silence until they reached the point in the

woods where the stream diminished into a thin trickle and then stopped altogether.

"The stream doesn't end here," Hazel said. "Not really. It goes under the earth, I think, or just becomes too thin to really be called a stream anymore. But beyond those trees— see, look, by that ravine there—it starts up again."

"Is it really the same stream, then? Or is it just *two* streams fairly close together?" Jack said.

"It's—" Hazel paused. She was going to answer that *of course* it was the same stream—how could anyone be ridiculous enough to insist that it wasn't?—but she wasn't sure she had a good reason that proved she was right.

"Sometimes things just end," Jack said. "Hey, look there." He pointed toward a small cluster of flowers with small light green petals, so light they were almost pearlescent. Each flower had a pop of white at its center.

Hazel didn't recognize them. Though she had walked this trail hundreds of times, the green flowers were so small and close to the ground that they just disappeared into the underbrush and moss.

"What are they?"

"I don't know their proper name, I suppose, but my mum called them wortflower. She used to make teas from the roots. Said they were good at keeping us strong." Jack hadn't thought about his mother making him tea in years, but as soon as he conjured the recollection, he could smell it: the tea's distinct, tannin bitterness. "I guess now that I think about it, maybe weeds were the only things she could afford to make tea out of."

While Jack was still lost in his reverie, Hazel hopped off her horse and started to dig up a handful of the flowers, being careful to keep the milky white roots intact. "Folk medicine is often far more effective than the bleeding and cupping procedures they do at the hospitals," she said. "Your mother must have learned it from somewhere."

"I suppose so." Jack didn't offer anything else about his mother, or where he had come from, and Hazel didn't pry. Jack was grateful for that. He didn't want Hazel to look at him with pity, which to her credit, she never did. Hazel was one of the few well-to-do people Jack had ever met who didn't act as though she were doing him a great service by deigning to interact with him.

When they got back to the stables, Jack lingered, brushing the horses even though the stable boy always groomed the horses at the end of the day. Betelgeuse tossed his mane in approval. The two had become fast friends after all. "Did you name him?" Jack asked, patting Betelgeuse's neck. "Betelgeuse. Fancy star name."

"My brother George did. He used to love the stars. When I was a child, he would sneak me up through the nursery window onto the roof and teach me the shapes in the stars. He was different than I am. I remember facts and figures. I have memorized all the bones of the body, and the acids I can use to dissolve flesh away. He knew stories. He was . . . kind."

"I'm sorry you lost him," Jack said.

"Thank you."

Jack had run out of clever things to say—he had run through his stable of words, and if he stayed any longer, he would humiliate himself. "I'll see you Sunday night," he said abruptly and a little too loudly. "If you still want to dig, I mean."

"I do," Hazel said.

Sunday night, when Jack arrived at Hawthornden, he found only one horse, Miss Rosalind, already saddled and with the cart attached.

"I figured that with you still being a beginner, we should probably ride just the one horse," Hazel said, looping her foot into the stirrup and hoisting herself onto her horse's back. "The road is a bit more treacherous than the castle property."

"You're sounding pretty smug for a girl who let me do all the digging last time," he said, throwing his equipment into the horse's cart. He reached out his hand to pet Miss Rosalind's back haunches, but thought better of it.

"Someone has to be the brains of the operation, and someone has to be the brawn," Hazel said.

"I assumed I was the good looks," Jack said.

"No," Hazel said, patting the velvety side of her horse's neck. "That's Miss Rosalind."

The ride to the kirkyard seemed to take only a fraction of the time it had the week before. Hazel felt as though they had ridden for mere moments before the trees parted to reveal the spire of Saint Dwynwen's. Jack's hands had been around Hazel's waist the entire ride, warm and comfortable. It was as if the curve of her back had been designed to press up against his chest, and she felt something like regret when she realized they needed to dismount and head toward the graveyard with their spades.

"He died of the fever?" Hazel asked when they had been digging long enough for a thin layer of sweat to have beaded on her forehead.

Jack grunted an affirmation and didn't stop digging. He had seen them bury the coffin, marked with red paint, a sinister, dripping letter R that the hospital had just started using as the number of those killed by the Roman fever continued to swell.

"It's a man, like last time," Jack whispered after he added a hefty pile of dirt to the mound above them and paused to wipe sweat from his eyes. "No family, no funeral. Just a pine box from the charity hospital."

"That's terrible," Hazel said.

Jack lifted his head in surprise. "Yeah," he said. "I suppose it is." It was terrible. He hadn't even thought about that. He had become so numb to the enormity of death in Edinburgh that his first response had been relief: pine boxes were the easiest to break. Standing so close to Hazel in a grave again, Jack felt the magnetic charge of her skin, could smell the salt of her sweat. He wanted to kiss her, but before he could figure out how, the crack of metal on wood came.

There it was, just as Jack remembered it, a pine box with the top of a letter R peeking out from beneath the soil. "For Roman fever," he explained quietly. *This is the moment,* he thought. *Kiss her now.* But instead, he threw his spade out onto the grass and pulled himself up after it.

Hazel knew what to do this time when Jack lowered the rope. She worked quickly, securing it around the body's feet and helping Jack as he hoisted the corpse through the hole in the broken casket by touch so she wouldn't have to look too closely at a face in the process of decomposing.

When the body had made it fully out of the grave, Jack extended his hand down to Hazel. She took it, feeling the calluses beneath her skin, which was raw and blistered from the night's exertion.

"Did your mum ever mention if wortroot helped with

blisters?" she asked, massaging her palms when they were sitting side by side on the inky grass.

"Fraid not."

Hazel made a mental note to try it anyway.

They sat for a few minutes, catching their breath. Jack wondered if he might be brave enough to try to kiss her, but then said, "I suppose we better undress the poor soul now."

When she was in the grave, Hazel hadn't noticed anything unusual about the corpse's face, but now that they were aboveground, she couldn't look away. There was something odd about the face, a strange hollowness that made the skin look like putty. The moonlight wasn't strong enough to allow Hazel to make out the face's features in any detail. "Do you still have that striker and candle?" Hazel asked.

A small flame crackled into life and illuminated both their faces with an orange glow, and for a moment Hazel forgot where she was, that she was fending off the night chill in a graveyard. The glow of the candle transformed Jack Currer's face into something beautiful and strange, angles so sharp Hazel felt the urge to run her finger along the edges of his skin, to print his profile on a coin.

And then Hazel looked down at the body, and her blood turned to ice.

The man's eyes were grotesque sockets, empty caverns stringy with pulp and maggots. But even more horrific: his eyelids had been sewn open. Thin black string in neat Xs that pulled the top lid up to the dead man's eyebrow, and bottom lid down to his cheek. He was a nightmarish marionette. Nothing natural had befallen this man, and whatever did happen, he had been forced to watch it.

Jack made the sign of the cross. "What is this?" he whispered.

"I don't know," Hazel said, "but it's not the Roman fever."

A noise startled them out of their uneasy trance. The sound of leaves crunching. And then a shadow moving between the trees. A human.

"Get down!" Jack hissed at Hazel, and shoved her into the grave they had only moments before finished digging up. He jumped in after her and lowered his head until they were both out of sight, standing side by side in the narrow pit.

Sweat beaded on Hazel's forehead. She had a streak of smut along the right side of her face. "Is someone out there?" she whispered.

"I don't know."

They waited, their chests pounding. There was silence. And then the crunch of boots across the turf. Footsteps. Someone was walking toward the kirkyard. Hazel and Jack jerked their heads to look at each other, their faces so close Jack could make out the dewy glow of sweat clinging to her brow.

"It's probably just a groundskeeper," Jack whispered. "Just a routine inspection." But even as he said it, his heart sank. Groundskeepers didn't usually work after midnight.

"Maybe the priest taking a stroll?"

Jack didn't know. He gestured that they should sit, so the tops of their heads wouldn't be visible to whoever—or whatever—was out there.

The hole in the ground was just wide enough for the two of them to sit side by side, although their knees brushed against the loose dirt on the walls of the grave. A worm wriggled toward Jack's eye, and he instinctively slid away, closer to Hazel. She was hugging her knees, trying to keep her breath quiet.

The footsteps—they were now undeniably footsteps—continued their approach, creeping closer to where Jack and Hazel hid.

Hazel's eyes widened. "The body!" They had left it lying out on the grass, naked. If whoever was out there saw it—

"Leave it," Jack whispered. "It's too dark out there to see it anyway." What Jack didn't say was that if whoever was out there made his way close enough to see the body, he would also be close enough to look down into the open grave and see the two of them, shivering against the chill of the night.

The footsteps were impossibly close now: the creaking sound of boots on wet grass sounded as though they were only a few cemetery rows away, but neither Jack nor Hazel dared to check. And it wasn't just one set of footsteps; Hazel listened intently, and then raised three fingers to Jack. There were at least three men walking together through the rows of tombs side by side.

The footsteps stopped. Again, Jack and Hazel glanced at each other. There was nothing left for them to do. They could run, but climbing out of the hole would take a moment, and by then, they might be ambushed, as well as outnumbered.

"It's fine," Jack whispered. "Whatever it is, it's all right." Without thinking, he lifted an arm and placed it across Hazel's shoulder.

She looked back at him with a small smile. Hazel shifted her weight and heard the sound of her bootheel on wood. They had dug all the way to the coffin. But there was nothing to do about it now. All they could do was wait, and hope whoever was out there wouldn't walk close enough to realize there was a hole in the ground containing two petrified young people.

Hazel pressed her shoulders up against Jack's, partly to

avoid the chill leaching from the moist earth through her jacket, but partly because his warmth—the solidity of his presence—made her less dizzy with fear. It anchored her. They were there, together. Whatever—whoever—was out there, neither of them would have to face it alone.

They remained motionless, listening to footsteps that seemed to approach and retreat for what felt like hours. Hazel's joints ached, but she didn't dare move.

Finally, the footsteps made a full retreat.

The only sounds were the cawing of a night bird and the whistle of the wind through the rows of headstones. Even so, Jack and Hazel kept still, huddled together in the hollow earth above a coffin.

A thin crescent moon had risen in the sky, sharp as a scalpel, and by its light Hazel examined Jack's face: the speckles of silt along his nose, his strange hawklike eyes, the thin line of his lips, and eyelashes darker and longer than hers, curling so that they almost reached his perpetually furrowed brows.

Feeling her gaze on him, Jack turned. "I wonder if—"

Hazel leaned in and kissed him. She hadn't anticipated the moment, hadn't even imagined what it would be like, but when he turned to her, just inches away, she felt pulled toward him like gravity. It was like magnetism, the cold of her lips seeking the warmth of his. Jack's eyes were open in surprise, but then he swallowed the rest of the sentence and kissed her back, hard and urgent.

Jack wrapped his arms around Hazel and kissed her as if she were his only source of oxygen. His hands were in her hair, running up her neck, along her jawline. His fingertips traced the velvet lobes of her perfect ears. Neither had known it could feel like this, that it was supposed to feel like this: effortless. It was as if the other's lips were the only place they'd ever belonged, and fate itself had brought them to this very moment, terrified and aching in a half-dug grave, just so the two of them could come together.

When Hazel pulled away, her face was flushed. "I'm sorry," she said.

"Don't be," Jack said. Hazel curled up against him, the curve of her spine fitting perfectly against his chest. Jack lowered an arm over her, and they watched the moon and listened to the sounds of the night.

THEY WOKE UP TO A LOW gray sky and a priest staring down at them. Jack scrambled to his feet and crawled out of their small trench, which looked even narrower by daylight. The dry earthen walls had crumbled inward while they slept. Jack extended a hand down to Hazel and pulled her onto the grass.

"Morning, Father!" Jack said cheerfully. "Lovely morning. Bit of a fog, though you won't hear any complaining from me."

"I can explain," Hazel said.

The priest's eyes widened in terror. He looked at the mutilated corpse lying naked on the ground, and then back at Hazel and Jack, and then back at the body, and back at them. "Be gone, unholy demons!" he shouted. "Be gone, ye the dead, from this world of the living!" He bent his ancient knees and picked up a clod of dirt. He flung it at Jack and Hazel. "Shoo! Shoo! This be holy and consecrated ground. Flee!"

Hazel lifted her hands to protect her eyes. "Sir—Father, this is all a misunderstanding—"

But Jack interrupted: "Yes! We be the undead woken! And we'll be"—he tugged on Hazel's arm—"going now. *Arghhhh!*"—he wiggled his arms in the air—"Your holiness is just *too powerful for us!*" And then he hissed like a snake.

Before either of them could see the priest's reaction, they turned and raced toward the trees. Mercifully, Miss Rosalind was still waiting for them, cranky and ready for her next meal, but happy enough to take the pair of them back to Hawthornden.

Someone, three someones, had been walking in the graveyard at night, someone was taking resurrection men, and something horrible had happened to a dead man's eyes—but Hazel couldn't think about any of that now. The thoughts swirled in her brain and dissolved in her exhaustion like cream being stirred into weak tea. All she could manage at the moment was staying upright and awake on Miss Rosalind with Jack Currer's hands on her waist, fantasizing about her bed with coals warming the sheets, and Cook's freshly baked fish pie, and the way Jack's lips had felt on hers.

She had kissed Jack Currer in a grave, and he had kissed her back, and even with everything else they had faced, that moment was the hardest Hazel's heart had beaten the entire night.

When Hazel made it back to the main house of Hawthornden Castle, opening the creaking wooden door as silently as she could, she found Charles asleep on the velvet bench in the hall by the library door. Iona was fast asleep right beside him, with her head leaning on his shoulder. Hazel closed the door slowly and took off her boots so she could sneak up to bed without waking them.

24

ITHOUT A FRESH BODY TO STUDY, Hazel devoted all her time and attention to diagramming and preserving the organs of the one body she and Jack *had* successfully retrieved. She pulled samples from every one of its fever sores and submerged the scabs in various solutions: alcohol, tonics, salt, and—on a whim—powdered wortflower root.

But one body wouldn't suffice if she wanted to pass the Royal Physician's Examination. Hazel ordered copies of the latest books on physiology from Paris and Philadelphia and Rome and spent as many hours as she could studying them. She read and reread the edition of *Dr. Beecham's Treatise* that Dr. Beecham had given her so often the pages became soft from the oils of her fingers. She memorized the notes in the margins, mostly small, meaningless annotations. (*Small venous system* written beside a diagram of the gallbladder; *Mercury tonic?* on the page about treating the common cold.)

But still, Hazel was finding it more and more difficult to focus. It seemed with every blink came another nightmarish image of eyes sewn open in blind horror, thick black string pulled through paper-thin eyelids. Hazel read into the small hours to stave off nightmares. When she wasn't thinking of the gruesome body, she was thinking of Jack's lips and the way her heart had flipped in her chest when he was pressed against her. Neither of those things would help her pass the examination. She couldn't let herself dwell on them, not for the time being.

And so Hazel held books while walking and read in bed late at night until the tapers burned themselves to stubs. On more than one occasion, Iona had to replace the book in Hazel's hands at breakfast with a piece of toast to ensure that Hazel was well fed enough. Iona also insisted that Hazel go to Princes Street Gardens on what might be the final reasonably nice day of the year, when the weak sun managed to eke out a bit of warmth in a sleet-gray sky. "Come on, miss," she said, already preparing Hazel's boots. "You can't stay cooped up here all winter. You can take your books down to the gardens! Now, won't that be nice?"

"Iona, my books are heavy. They weigh a ton. I couldn't possibly haul them out to an appropriately pleasant spot on the grass—the horses wouldn't be able to pull me and my books in the carriage to get there."

"Well," Iona said slowly, "perhaps you could take only *one* book with you to read at the gardens. After all, you'll only be there for the afternoon."

Hazel choked on her tea. "One book? *One* book? Now you're being absurd. What if I finish it? Or what if I find it impossibly dull, what then? What am I supposed to read if I either complete the book I brought or I otherwise discover it to be unreadable? Or what if it no longer holds my attention? Someone could spill tea on it. There. Think of that. Someone could spill tea on my *one* book, and then I would be *marooned*. Honestly, Iona, you must use your head."

"Two books then, miss."

Hazel sighed but eventually agreed, and she headed off for the city with three books in the carriage, fully aware that Charles and Iona were probably grateful to have the castle more or less to themselves for a few hours.

EVEN WITH THE SPECTER OF THE Roman fever hanging over Edinburgh, Princes Street Gardens was still bustling with picnickers and strollers, women walking briskly in pairs, carrying parasols—all people celebrating what almost certainly would be the last day before spring that the sun would shine, however faintly, from behind the clouds and the smoky haze. How were they all so content? How did the rich so easily dismiss the chaos and terror within their city?

And yet, Hazel thought, here she was herself, enjoying the unseasonably warm weather, trying to study. *Pass the examination, and then worry about the rest,* she told herself. *Just pass the examination.*

Hazel found an isolated spot on the grass beneath a large leafy elm tree and spread her books out in front of her: *Dr. Beecham's Treatise,* a second anatomy textbook, and a novel called *Sense and Sensibility,* published anonymously and credited only to "A Lady." Hazel liked the author, whoever she was, and had brought the novel along as a reward, should she succeed in completing her review of the pulmonary system.

Hazel settled onto the grass and pulled out *Dr. Beecham's Treatise* to refresh her memory regarding the arteries of the lungs, but before she could even flip to the relevant pages, a shadow came over the book, and Hazel looked up to see Hyacinth Caldwater standing over her and cradling a newly enormous pregnant belly.

Hazel swallowed the lump of bile that made itself known in her throat.

"Oh, Hazel, *darling*!" cooed Mrs. Caldwater. "The social scene has been positively abuzz since your engagement! You left before the dancing! Are you quite well? And more important: Have you set a date? Because I simply must clear my social calendar, I simply must. There's no doubt your wedding will be the event of the season. I imagine the London set will be coming up for it?"

Hazel sighed and folded her book closed. "Mrs. Caldwater. Lovely as always to see you."

"Now, you simply *must* tell me what was going through your mind when Bernard proposed. I confess, we had thought it would be another few seasons before he asked; the two of you are still *young*. You've been so absent this season." Mrs. Caldwater raised one eyebrow conspiratorially and leaned in as if she were sharing a secret with Hazel, but her voice still rang out, shrill as a brass bell. "Half of Charlotte Square is convinced that you've managed to seduce a Polish count, and that Bernard knew he had to strike while he still had a chance. I heard several whispers that your mother was fed up with Bernard's hesitating, and she went down to London to secure you a match with an Englishman and make Bernard jealous! Why else go down so early? Surely she's pleased that the match with Bernard Almont is all squared away now. Is she coming home, now that you're betrothed?"

"My mother is in Bath, with Percy. On holiday. For his delicate constitution. To avoid the fever."

Mrs. Caldwater's heavily rouged face became a mask of sympathy. "Oh yes, of course. Oh, my poor dear. Your poor mother and all she's gone through. Losing her eldest, and your father gone most of the year. Is it hard on her, would you say?"

"Yes," Hazel said, enjoying the conversation less with every passing second. "I imagine it is."

With a herculean obliviousness to Hazel's polite attempts to lower her attention back to her book, Hyacinth Caldwater turned to show off her growing profile, scooping one hand beneath her pregnant belly. Mrs. Caldwater had to be at least forty years old. From the delicate wrinkles lacing their way beyond the outer corners of her eyes, at least fifty, Hazel guessed. And yet it was undeniable: the woman was with child.

Catching Hazel staring, Mrs. Caldwater beamed. "Can you believe it? A miraculous thing. My husband, the colonel, and I have been trying for a child since our wedding, a century ago—ha ha ha—and now finally: *poof!*"

"Poof," Hazel repeated.

"It was an examination from Dr. Beecham himself that did it. Told me all about diets, had me chewing on the most horrendous pastes you could imagine, but, well, see for yourself. The man is a genius. *Horribly* expensive, obviously, but worth every farthing. I have no idea how anyone gets by in this country if they can't afford the best doctors."

"They go to the almshouse hospitals," Hazel said. "Many of them die there."

Mrs. Caldwell laughed as if Hazel had been making a joke. "The almshouse hospitals indeed!" She patted her stomach again. "Well, the two of us need to be properly fed. Please *do* give your mother my best, and feel free to pop by Barton House anytime for tea. Look how skinny you've become! It's an outrage. Scandalous! I'll fatten you up myself if I have to."

"Goodbye, Mrs. Caldwater, and congratulations on your blessing," Hazel said, and then before the woman could turn back with another impertinent question, Hazel opened her book and pulled it up close to her face. Dr. Beecham was a genius, that was certain. Although Hazel had to slightly challenge the judgment of anyone who worked to bring more Caldwaters into the world.

Hazel was flipping through the Beecham volume when something fell out of it: a small piece of parchment, folded so thin that she hadn't noticed it stuck invisibly somewhere between the pages. She unfolded it carefully; the parchment was yellowed and torn at the edges. It seemed as though it was years old, far older than the book that had contained it.

It was a pen-and-ink drawing of a human hand, with its fingers detached. Arrows identified each of the veins that linked the fingers to the palm. To Hazel, it looked like the notes of someone ready to perform intensive surgery.

The parchment was fragile as a butterfly's wing, the ink almost faded. Was it possibly a note from the original Dr. Beecham himself? Saved and preserved by his grandson, who had thrown it in a pile and somehow shuffled it into one of his books? The handwriting was slanted and angular but perfectly precise, each letter even and exact. Had Beecham meant her to find them? Mementos from the most brilliant scientific mind in recent Scottish history, gifted to inspire her, as a gesture of good faith?

Hazel wished she could have met the first Dr. Beecham, the man who had dedicated his life to understanding the human body. This parchment drawing was the work of a man devoted as a monk, a man who had studied joints and muscles and veins with such patience and care that he could reproduce them perfectly on paper. Hazel looked from the paper to her own hand and back again. It was almost enough to make her cry.

Another shadow crossed her work, someone standing above her, who coughed to get her attention, and for a terrible moment, Hazel was convinced Hyacinth Caldwater had returned to inquire about any number of intimate or unpleasant topics. Hazel pulled her book away, ready with a polite dismissal, only to find her fiancé, Bernard Almont.

He coughed again politely. "I'm sorry to disturb your reading. Studying, I take it?"

Hazel nodded.

Her cousin wore a simple navy blue overcoat and gray trousers. The effect, for Bernard at least, was considerably muted and grown up. "May I sit?" Bernard asked.

Again, Hazel nodded.

Bernard laid out a handkerchief and then sat beside her on the grass. "I've meant to come by Hawthornden, or send a letter at least, but I've found it quite difficult to, well, conjure the courage, I suppose. I do regret how I acted at the ball, how I sprang the engagement on you. The way I acted in the servants' passage. I admit I had perhaps more champagne than was advisable, but that's no excuse." He cleared his throat. "I didn't behave as a gentleman should. A proposal shouldn't be a public affair, and should you want to refuse me, Cousin, I would be tremendously saddened, but I would respect your right to do so."

The expanding balloon of shame and embarrassment and relief—of everything that had happened with Bernard—burst in Hazel's chest. "Thank you, Bernard," she said.

Bernard inhaled, pleased. "So . . . will you, then? Marry me, I mean? Please say yes. I know I've been awful, but there's no one I can tolerate half as well as you."

The sense-memory of Jack came back to her, how warm he felt, how kissing him had made her chest clench and head rush. She was back in the grave with him, their hearts racing in parallel. She could feel the soft bristles of hair on the back of his neck where she'd wrapped her arms around him, smell his musk of sweat and elderflower and spearmint, the earthy sweetness that made her wish she could close her eyes and live her entire life on a horse with him behind her, pressed close.

Hazel set aside her book and looked back at Bernard's eager, expectant face. He was asking her a question to which she already knew the answer, had known it her entire life. There was only ever one life for her if she wanted to survive.

"Yes, Bernard," she said softly. "I will marry you."

"Oh, marvelous!" He kissed her, and Hazel leaned in to let him. Her eyes remained open, and she saw his eyelashes fluttering in pleasure. He pulled away with a wet smack. "We'll wait until your mother is back in town to begin preparations in earnest, but my family is going to want quite the fete."

Hazel wasn't sure what to say. She just nodded again and gestured to her book.

"Oh yes, of course," Bernard said. "I promised I would leave you to your reading." He stood and shook the dirt off the handkerchief on which he'd been sitting. He frowned at a small stain, and then folded the handkerchief and returned it to his pocket. He went to leave, but before he fully about-faced, he paused to lift a finger. "Is there—? I'm sorry to even be saying this, I don't know why I'm asking, but—did you have another suitor? I know how ridiculous this is, but the rumors are—well, you know how these things can be."

"No," Hazel said. "There has never been any Russian count or Bavarian duke or whomever else anyone in the New Town has invented in order to amuse themselves while the theater is closed."

Bernard smiled and bowed before taking his leave. Hazel read by the light of the sinking sun until it was too dark to make out the words on the pages, wondering where in the city Jack Currer was at that very moment and why the white lie she had told to her cousin came so readily.

Pray tell, what has happened to the Doctor William Beecham, Baronet? No one would have ever accused him of being a social bon vivant, but in recent months it seems as though he's retired from the social scene completely. I attended the Earl of Tooksbery's annual luncheon at Hampshire last week, and the Countess remarked that she believed the Doctor hasn't been in his right mind since the death of his wife. "And who treats a doctor who has gone mad!" she said to me before flitting off to consult with the Marquis de Fountaine on the latest trends in gardening.

The Countess's estimation is generous. Less kind lips have suggested that the Doctor's madness has to do with an obsession with alchemy and the Philosopher's Stone. Though the Doctor was never a social butterfly, he was at least formerly a fixture in the London social scene. He spent the summer last year on the Isle of Skye and simply never returned to England. Lady Sordell hinted that the Doctor may have fallen out of the good graces of the Royal Family and that his retreat to Scotland was actually an exile at the command of Queen Charlotte. Alas, I don't believe it. Having attended several parties where Beecham stood miserably in the corner, I can personally attest to the fact that Beecham has never enjoyed the company of anyone but his wife and his books and his pet tortoise. There is no doubt in my mind that his retreat from the London set was personal preference of his own unhappy, unsociable volition.

25

WHEN JACK HEARD THE KNOCKING ON the front doors of Le Grand Leon, he was certain it would be creditors, coming to reclaim the property. When the theater closed, Mr. Anthony had given Jack the keys, told him to keep it in fair shape until they could open up again the following season. Thieves Jack could handle. Bankers were the real threat.

In a brief flash of ecstatic hope, he imagined that maybe the knocking was Hazel, that she had come to find him, to run away with him. The memory of their kiss still lingered on his lips, the joy of it, the hidden thrill, and also the terror. That kiss was the night of the nightmarish body, the man with the sewn-open eyes, whom they had left on the grass for the priest. It was easier for Jack just to pretend the entire excursion had been a dream, that none of it had happened.

Dawn had barely broken over the crest of Arthur's Seat, which Jack could make out through the tiny window in the upper gallery if he craned his neck and pulled the curtain aside. But this morning, he pulled his few dingy blankets over his head and hoped the knocking would stop. It didn't.

It continued: clanging, frantic knocks that set the frames on the lobby wall rattling. "Oi, theater's closed! Come back another time!" Jack shouted.

The knocking persisted. Whoever it was would not be deterred. Jack sighed, and rolled off the disused stage curtain he had been using to turn his bed into something that more resembled a velvet nest. "A'right, a'right, whoever ye are! Just shut up for a moment, and I'll be right down."

Mr. Anthony had used heavy chains to keep the doors shut, and Jack was fiddling to get them undone when he heard a voice on the other side of the door. "Jack? Jack Currer? It is you, ain't it? Oh please, be Jacks."

He unlatched the door and opened it to find himself standing face-to-face with Jeanette, his old spy. They hadn't worked together but the once since she got a job as a maid at Almont House—only three months had passed since he last saw her, but she looked as if she'd aged years. She wore her maid's uniform, but it was wrinkled and creased, as if she had slept in it. Her hair was stringy under her bonnet, and her skin was sallow and pale. The shadows beneath her hollowed eyes were almost black. She clutched her stomach. "There's no one I can talk to. If I tell the housekeeper at work, I'll be canned for certain, and I can't afford a doctor. You was always good to me, Jacks. Some of the boys told me you was here, and I—" She clutched at her stomach again, and Jack understood—or thought he did.

"Come on, then," Jack said, ushering her through the front door and closing it behind her. She could use the W.C. to freshen up, and in the meantime he would see if he could scrounge up some biscuits.

AZEL WAS WEARING SPECTACLES WHEN SHE opened the dungeon door and found Jack standing there next to a young woman who was scowling and clutching her stomach.

"You wear spectacles?" Jack blurted to Hazel before he managed a proper greeting.

"Rarely," Hazel said, blushing. "When I have been up late. And the print is small. And I am studying. Shut up. What seems to be the situation here?" Hazel reached past Jack to comfort the woman he was standing with. She shrank away from Hazel.

"It's all right, Jeanie, come on now," Jack said to her, and then to Hazel, "This is Jeanette. I've known her for a long time. She's having some sort of—situation, and neither of us being able to afford a doctor, I figured I'd bring her here. See if you could take a look at her."

"I'm not going to the hospital!" Jeanette cried. "I've been to the poor hospital, and it's bloody awful. I can't take the smells again. The moaning!"

"Hush now. Nobody is going to take you anywhere. We can take a look at you right here," Hazel said.

Mollified, Jeanette followed Jack into the dim dungeon laboratory, although her eyes still cast about with nervous suspicion. Hazel cleared the long table of the books and notes she had been studying and lit a fresh candle, noticing that the one she had been using had melted to a nub. "Sit up here," Hazel said, "and tell me what's wrong." The girl looked familiar, but Hazel couldn't quite place her.

Jeanette complied, and straightened her skirt on her lap. Catching Hazel's glance at her belly, she said, "I'm not with child. I just couldn't be. It just ain't possible. I swear it. Hey! I knows you, don't I, miss? Jacks, I know her. She's—she knows Lord Almont, don't she?"

"He's my uncle," Hazel said. The face came back to Hazel: she was the Almonts' young maid.

Jeanette made an angry scoffing noise and tried to hoist herself off the table. But she got only an inch before the pain caught her again and Jack gently helped her back to sitting. "I can't be here," she said. "If they find out I'm here—if they think I'm with child, I won't be allowed to work no more. Mrs. Poffroy will have me out on the street before I can blink. I know the stories. I know what happens to girls once their reputations is ruined."

"Jeanette," Hazel said calmly. "Jeanette, isn't it? I assure you, I won't tell a soul that you're here today. I swear it, on my honor. Besides, the niece of a viscount is hardly supposed to be running an infirmary out of her home's dungeon, now, is she?"

"Suppose not," Jeanette mumbled.

"Well, then, the solution is quite simple. You keep my secret, and I shall keep yours."

Jack smiled at Hazel then, and warmth radiated from her chest to the tips of her fingers.

Hazel straightened her spectacles and withdrew a notebook from her shelves. She licked the tip of her quill. "So, Jeanette: What seems to be the problem, then?"

Jeanette flicked her tongue across her small dry lips and tugged at her skirt. "I haven't got my monthly. It's been ages. One month I figured I just lost track of the dates, then two months came, and now three. And I'm getting these 'orrible pains, worse than anything I've ever had in my stomach. So bad I can't work without moaning, and Mrs. Poffroy had to let the kitchen maid put me to bed."

Hazel considered her words carefully. "And . . . you're certain you're not . . ."

"I ain't pregnant," Jeanette said. "I swear it. I've never even been with a man before. Few tried to come close back when I was living at Fleshmarket, but I knew what to do with them when they came at me. Just ask Jack, he'll tell ya. So unless they've figured out another way for a girl to get a baby that don't involve no man between her knees, I'm telling you, there's no baby."

"May I?" Hazel asked, gesturing toward Jeanette's belly. Jeanette nodded, and Hazel ran her hand across Jeanette's stomach. She was a slim girl, and her stomach was firm, but there was no bump, nor was there the drum-taut skin of a pregnancy. Jeanette winced at Hazel's touch. "Does that hurt?" Hazel asked.

Jeanette nodded. "I 'ad a weird dream," Jeanette said. "Right when the pain started. I starting 'aving the dreams right then, now I get them almost every night."

"What sorts of dreams?" Hazel asked.

"I'm lying down, under some sort of veil. Almost like a bride, I suppose, but I couldn't tell you what that sort of veil is like. Well, I have it over me, and I'm in a big room with strangers all around me, and then a man comes close, and he's a strange man with a head like a beast. And he holds a knife above me. And he has one eye. Just one big, fat eye in the center of his face. And then as soon as I try to figure out what he's doing with the big knife, I wakes up on my own cot, in the servants' quarters."

One eye. Was it possible that she had interacted with Dr. Straine in some way? That he had hurt her? "Jeanette, when did you go to the poorhouse hospital? What was that for?"

Jeanette wrinkled her brow. "Couldn't'a been more than seven, I suppose. Got my 'pendix out."

"And the doctor—the doctor who operated on you when you were a child, at the poorhouse hospital. Was his name Straine, perhaps? Did he have one eye, and a black silk eye patch?"

Jeanette shook her head. "No. It was some awful French doctor. Don't remember his name, but wasn't no eye patch."

"Do you mind if I examine your stomach?" Hazel asked. "With your shirt up? Jack, would you mind stepping outside?"

Jack gave a small salute and left the laboratory. "I'll be outside if you need me."

"Ay, we never do, you tosser!" Jeanette said, and then she lifted her chemise to reveal a pair of pale, stalky legs and an even paler belly. Several bruises clustered around Jeanette's knees, and an angry scar crusting with green pus ran four inches across, below her belly button.

"Jeanette," Hazel said, "this scar, what's it from?"

"Told you already. 'Pendix coming out when I was a kid."

The scar had been sewn with even stitches, but it was angry and red, inflamed and dripping. "This scar isn't new? You've had it?"

"Practically long as I can remember," Jeanette said.

"Well, new or old, this scar is infected. We'll need to clean it and dress it properly so it can heal again."

"That's the problem, then?" Jeanette said, covering herself. "That's what the problem's been this whole time? My scar?"

"I don't know whether it is the whole problem," Hazel

said. "I would not think an infection would be the cause of you missing your monthly bleedings. But at least we can help to take care of it now."

Hazel cleaned the wound delicately with water and soap, and dabbed a cotton rag soaked in alcohol along its length. Jeanette clenched her teeth together to keep from shouting. "I'm sorry," Hazel said. "I know it stings." When the wound was clean, Hazel made a dressing of honey and turmeric and ground witch hazel flower and bandaged the scar. She gave Jeanette a stack of fresh linen bandages. "Replace the bandage daily," she said, and Jeanette nodded. "And if it doesn't improve in a week, tell Jack to bring you back to me."

Once she was fully clothed again, Jeanette reached into her apron pocket, looking embarrassed. "I don't have much, but to pay you for what you've done—"

Hazel shooed her hand away. "Oh goodness, I wouldn't dream of it. Please don't be ridiculous. I'm still a student. I'm grateful for the chance to learn on a living subject, to be frank."

Jeanette withdrew her hand from her apron gratefully.

"Jack!" Hazel called. "You can come back in."

Jack reentered, shielding his eyes. Hazel swatted his hands down. "Ay, you cure her? Fix her up?"

"I'm not quite sure, but at least we've made a start," Hazel said. "And, Jack: if you have any other friends or acquaintances who need, well, examination. You know I'm not a physician yet, but I do know the basics, and I have to believe Hawthornden Castle is nicer than a poorhouse hospital."

"How do you mean?" Jack said.

"Well, we have a dozen empty rooms, at least. With my mother and father gone, and most of their servants with them—there's plenty of room in the great hall to set up some cots, and mats for those who need rest. We have more than enough food; heaven knows Cook still hasn't become adjusted to ordering for just me and Iona and Charles."

"What about people sick with"—Jack lowered his voice—"the fever?"

"Bring them," Hazel said, hoping her tone conveyed the bravery she wished she possessed. "Anyone who we are afraid might be contagious can go in the solarium."

Jeanette cocked her head up. "I knows a boy hit by a carriage some weeks back. Leg broke and never healed properly. Seen the bone through the skin myself."

"Bring him here," Hazel said. "Hawthornden Castle can become a teaching hospital for one."

THERE WAS NO SHORTAGE OF PATIENTS for Hazel to treat, no shortage of poor men and women and children desperate for medical care that wouldn't require them to descend into the festering stink of the hospital for the poor, where the doctors wore aprons streaked with blood and the destitute slept three to a cot.

A dozen people arrived at the dungeon laboratory for Hazel's help the week after she treated Jeanette. It was thirty the week after that. Between Jeanette and Jack, word had spread rapidly, and soon Hazel found herself treating everything from consumption to constipation. For each person who came to the door of her dungeon laboratory seeking treatment, Hazel took complete notes and detailed their age, occupation, symptoms, and the treatment she was recommending.

Fevers she treated with linseed cordial and orange whey,

keeping the patient warm with blankets and supplied with plenty of tea. Broken bones were set with wooden planks and strips of fabric. Wounds were stitched closed. When a woman arrived clutching her cheek in pain, Hazel pulled a rotten tooth from her jaw and treated the gum with honey and clove oil.

Hazel found herself consulting her well-worn *Dr. Beecham's Treatise* less and less often, becoming more confident in her own abilities and instinct for diagnosis. Most patients Hazel was able to treat in an afternoon and send on their way, but others—like Jeanette's acquaintance, a young boy named Bobby Danderfly, with the broken leg from the carriage accident—Hazel would assist as she could on her table, and then send the patient to a bed in Hawthornden Castle to convalesce.

When the first patient with Roman fever arrived, Hazel gathered the staff in the library.

"None of you need stay in this house," Hazel said. "There's a danger to having the sick here, I know that, especially with the fever." Hazel had set the man up in the solarium with a straw mat, and she had spent the morning doing her best to keep him comfortable, gently washing away the blood and pus from his burst blisters and wiping an ice water–dampened cloth across his feverish forehead. "The gatehouse is more than big enough for anyone who doesn't want to live here." Charles, Iona, and Cook nodded solemnly. Susan the scullery maid scowled in the corner. "And nobody should go in the solarium but me, is that clear?"

"I don't see why we have to leave," Susan scoffed. "I didn't sign up to work in a bloody hospital. I'd like to see what the *lady of the house* would make of all of this."

"Well, while my mother is in England, I think you'll find that I'm the lady of the house, Susan."

Susan mumbled something under her breath.

"And, Cook, I don't suppose you'd mind making a pot of oats? Maybe with the currant jelly? To help our patients keep their strength."

Even as her days became exhausting, filled with tending to patients and mixing poultices and washing sodden rags, Hazel still wasn't able to sleep properly. She had uneasy dreams, nightmares about the horror of the corpse she and Jack had dug up from its grave and its mutilated face. Other times, the face that hovered before her in the spaceless void behind her closed eyelids was Bernard's. Either way, Hazel tossed and turned in her blankets until, with an even mixture of disappointment and relief, she saw the first creeping of pastel-colored dawn through her window.

Sometimes Hazel was so exhausted she found herself staring with her eyes open and unblinking while she stood at her worktable in the dungeon, not sleeping but not entirely conscious either.

"Easy there," Jack said, catching Hazel as she swayed standing up one morning. He was in the dungeon with her, helping Hazel by brewing a fresh batch of wortflower-root tea the way he remembered his mother had done.

"It's the smell of that," Hazel murmured with a small smile after Jack had helped her settle into a chair. "That tea smells like loam and dung."

"Ay, fortunately it only tastes a little bit worse than it smells," Jack said. "Here, I'll brew a pot of black for both of us." Jack stood to leave when they heard a soft knock on the door.

Jack and Hazel looked at each other. Hazel was suddenly entirely awake.

Another soft knock. And then a moan of pain.

Hazel made to rise, but Jack lifted his hand. "I'll get it."

Jack unlatched the door and swung it open, and Hazel leaned forward to see who had arrived in the doorway: a young woman clutching her belly, doubled over in pain, her blond hair hanging lank around her face.

"Is this the place?" she said to her feet. "Please, is this the place where someone can help me?"

"Isabella?" Jack said. The girl lifted her head and revealed eyes wet with tears. "Isabella," he repeated. He took in her pregnant belly.

She moaned.

Hazel walked up behind him. She saw the blood and fluid between the pregnant girl's legs. "For heaven's sake, Jack, step aside. There's a woman giving birth in the doorway."

Jack blinked rapidly and backed into the dungeon. His mouth hadn't closed fully since he had first seen Isabella—here—and pregnant.

Hazel assessed the scene quickly. "Dear Lord. I'm afraid there's no time to get you up to the main house," she said. "Here, sit down quick. Jack, run up to Hawthornden and fetch Iona. Tell her to bring me a basin of water."

Jack nodded and with only one more quick glance at Isabella, he ran outside.

"Was that . . . Jack Currer?" Isabella asked as Hazel gently guided her into the wooden chair.

Hazel was distracted with the mental checklist of everything she would need to do to deliver a baby. "What? Jack

Currer. Yes. Do you know him?" Hazel's eyes widened. "Is he the, uh—?"

Isabella kept her hand on her belly. "The father? No. He enlisted. His regiment moved down to Yorkshire. I was supposed to join him, but—" She gestured down to her stomach. "We were supposed to get married too."

"It'll be two of you joining him in no time at all," Hazel said. "Family together soon enough."

"He wasn't always a soldier. He was a dancer at the theater with me. Jack worked there too. In the rafters. He was always kind to me."

Hazel smiled. "He is kind."

"But then the theater closed with the fever and now my Thomas is away and I just don't know how I'm going to get through this." Isabella's hands shook, and another convulsion took hold of her. "It hurts so bad! They didn't tell me it would hurt this bad." A halo of sweat had appeared along Isabella's hairline. "I just knew I couldn't go down to the poorhouse hospital, with the things I've heard, women crying and lying in their own sick. I just didn't know what I was supposed to do."

Hazel tried to make her voice sound as confident as possible. "Isabella. I need you to listen to me. My name is Hazel Sinnett. This baby is coming, and you and I, we're going to get through this together." Hazel lit the rest of the candles in the laboratory. "Where is Iona with the water?" she muttered.

On cue, Iona burst through the door, bearing a basin. Jack trailed behind with several rags, looking slightly queasy.

"Oh, marvelous. Iona, set the bucket there, and help me. Jack, help me too. We need to get her onto the table."

The three of them gently guided Isabella until she was lying flat on Hazel's workbench. "Uh, Iona, if you could—my copy of *Beecham's*, please?"

Isabella's panicked eyes went from Hazel to Jack to Hazel again. "A book? What's the book for?"

"Nothing! Nothing," Hazel said, frantically flipping through the pages. "Just checking one thing. Yes. Yes, fine. Here." Hazel pulled dried valerian from one of her jars. "Chew on this. To help the pain. Deep breaths, that's very important. You've got to keep breathing. Lie down this way, with your legs up this way. Remember: keep breathing."

"You've done this before, right? Delivered a child?" Isabella asked when Hazel had set up between her legs.

"Not in the *formal* sense," Hazel said. "But I've read a lot about it."

Isabella's response was swallowed by her crying out from the pain of her next contraction.

"Here's what we're going to do," Hazel said. "You are going to look at me, and tell me everything you're going to do with your baby and—and Thomas in Yorkshire. And every time you think of something, you're going to give me a good push. Do you understand?"

Isabella nodded weakly.

"Good."

"We can—we can walk in the park."

"Good. Push."

"We can teach her how to read," Isabella said. "It's going to be a girl. Thomas and I always knew we would have a girl."

"That's a good one. Big push for me."

"We can take a trip to the lake."

"Push! And, Iona—fresh water, please!"

The labor continued as the candles burned themselves

to stumps. Iona had to run back to the main house twice to replace the tapers so that by the time Hazel was reaching between Isabella's legs, she had enough candlelight to make out the bright red infant fighting her way into life, her hair already visible, slick and dark. Sometime during the second hour, Jack had disappeared.

"Oh, goodness. This doesn't look anything like the diagram," Hazel murmured.

"*What?*" Isabella shrieked.

"Nothing! Nothing! Just lie down. It's all going to be fine. We're so close now. I can see her head. Isabella? Isabella, can you hear me? You're going to be a mother."

Isabella nodded her head, but tears continued to stream down her cheeks. "I just wish Thomas was here," she said, almost whispering.

"You're going to be with him so soon. One last push now."

Isabella screamed. And then that scream became two, the sound of a living infant screaming at the cold new world she had just joined.

Hazel wrapped the baby in a clean cloth and gently lowered her onto Isabella's chest.

"You were right," Hazel said. "She's a girl. She's beautiful, just like her mum."

The baby was beautiful—round blue eyes and a cry that merged with Isabella's grateful laughter.

"A baby girl. I have a baby girl."

"You did it."

Isabella looked up from her daughter to Hazel. "You did it too. I don't know what I would've done if it weren't for you, I swear."

Isabella and the child rested then for an hour, while Iona

fetched a few slices of buttered bread for all of them. Hazel graciously accepted and ate her slice. She hadn't realized how hungry she was. It had been hours since she last ate.

Jack returned just as Isabella was beginning to stir again. "Isn't she beautiful?" she said to him. "My baby girl."

Jack pulled something from behind his back. It was a square music box, with bright painted sides. "I wanted to be the first one to give your baby a present."

Isabella reached forward to take it. "Jack, this is too much." She opened the music box, and the thin melody of a waltz filled the laboratory. The dancer in the box's center, a blond ballerina, spun in perfect circles. It was almost impossible to see that the porcelain figure had been broken and stuck together again with adhesive paste.

"Thank you, Jack," Isabella said. "She'll love it."

"Does she have a name yet?"

Isabella looked at her child and then at Hazel. "I think we should name her after you. Baby Hazel. I know Thomas will be pleased."

"Baby Hazel," Jack repeated.

Hazel didn't trust herself to say anything out loud. She just nodded and finished wiping out the basin she had been cleaning, keeping her back to Jack so that he wouldn't see her glistening eyes.

26

THE AFFECTION JACK ONCE FELT FOR Isabella had seemed so real, so immediate and important. And yet the next evening, as he walked down toward the stream where he had seen Hazel sitting by the shore, he realized something: his love for Isabella had been like seeing a candle in a painting, a painting by a master who captures its light and the glow it casts on everything around it, but still a flame made of oil on canvas. When Jack looked at Hazel, the flame was alive and licking at the air around it. He felt its heat and power, heard its crackle. It was seeing fire in person for the first time.

"You were amazing in there," he said. "The things you do, the things you're capable of. It's just—you're amazing."

Hazel looked up but stayed sitting on the shore. "I don't know what I'm doing at all. Jack, I was terrified."

"What? Terrified?"

Hazel nodded. "A whole life in my hands? What if I had messed it up? What if I had hurt the baby, or hurt Isabella? I would—I don't even know what I would do. How would I live with that?"

Jack sat down next to her and looked out at the thin trickling of the water over the rocks. The castle cast a dark shadow over them. The day after the birth, they had managed to bring Isabella and the baby up to the main house, where Isabella could sleep in George's old room. "You did everything perfectly," Jack said. "The baby is perfect."

"This time," Hazel said. She paused, and Jack was wondering whether he had made a mistake in coming down to keep her company when Hazel spoke again. "I used to be so confident. That's the funny thing: I used to think that I knew everything, that I could *do* anything. And then you see it firsthand, and you realize how thin the line is between everything being all right and everything being ruined forever and you just become suddenly aware that you know *nothing*. I'm just a silly little girl playing dress-up and pretending. I haven't even passed the Physician's Examination. What do I think I'm doing?"

Jack took Hazel's hand in his. Hers was cold, almost waxy. White and pale. "Hazel," he said softly. "You are the most brilliant person I've ever met in my life. You're incredible."

"I'm scared," Hazel said.

"Good," Jack said. "That's fine. There's nothing wrong with being scared."

Hazel lowered her head onto Jack's chest, and he extended his arm around her. It began to rain then, a mist that started so softly it almost felt like pinpricks. "Let's get in out of the rain," Jack said, and helped Hazel to her feet. He started guiding her up the path toward the castle, but Hazel pulled away.

"No," she said. "Not quite yet."

Hazel and Jack walked toward the stables, where they were met with air that was warm and dry, smelling pleasantly of straw.

They pulled a pair of horse blankets from the shelves and sat under the barn's roof with its doors open, watching the rain come down as the sky darkened above the outline of Hawthornden Castle's stone parapet. The sun was already setting, the short days of winter having arrived in Edinburgh along with bitterly cold wind.

Hazel pressed her hands inside Jack's jacket to warm them. "I still can't get warm," she whispered.

Jack leaned in to kiss her then, planting his lips so tenderly on hers that they felt more shadow than flesh. And then she kissed him back, and soon they were kissing so deeply that for a moment it didn't feel as though they were two separate people at all. It had begun to rain harder outside the stable's rickety wooden frame, but neither of them cared. Jack pressed Hazel against a beam and pulled the pins from her hair until her curls fell past her shoulders. He pressed his face into her hair and breathed in deeply, and then he ran a finger along the curve of her cheek. "Dear Lord in heaven," he whispered. "You're so beautiful, Hazel Sinnett."

"No one has ever told me that I'm beautiful before," Hazel said. She hadn't even realized it was true until she said it out loud.

Jack stood with his hands on either side of her face and stared at her for a few heartbeats. Then he leaned in and softly kissed both her eyelids.

"Someone should tell you that you're beautiful every time the sun comes up. Someone should tell you you're beautiful on Wednesdays. And at teatime. Someone should tell you you're beautiful on Christmas Day and Christmas Eve and the evening *before* Christmas Eve, and on Easter. He should tell you on Guy Fawkes Night and on New Year's, and on the eighth of August, just because." He kissed her lips once more, gently, and then pulled away and gazed into her eyes. "Hazel Sinnett, you are the most miraculous creature I have ever come across, and I am going to be thinking about how beautiful you are until the day I die."

27

HAZEL'S FIRST DEATH CAME A WEEK later, a Roman fever patient who fell asleep one night after refusing the cool water Hazel had offered him, and never woke up. She did not cry as she wrapped him in sheets and pulled him outside to the cart on the path to the laboratory dungeon.

Jack found Hazel sobbing by the red oak tree, the body still on the cart. Without a word, Jack started to dig a grave.

"I have to study him, Jack," Hazel said when she saw what he was doing. She could barely get the words out for her weeping. "I need every corpse I can."

"Not this one, love," Jack replied quietly. "You knew him. You cared for him. You can bury him, and mourn him. He doesn't have to be parts. Not yet."

Hazel didn't answer. She breathed deeply until the crying stopped, blinked her tears away, and walked back up to the main castle. By the time Jack finished burying the man and made it back to Hawthornden, Hazel was clear-eyed, already treating patients again in the solarium.

There was no medical writing about any sort of treatment,

let alone a cure, for the Roman fever, and so Hazel began with small, harmless remedies. She gave her patients tea with lemon juice and honey. In the afternoon, she insisted they drink powdered cardamom seeds and milk, the way the book advised her to treat consumption. Their bandages were changed three times a day, the fabric almost always sticky with crusted scabs. If they could stand the smell, she offered them the wortflower-root tea that Jack brewed. If he had drunk it in childhood and he never got the Roman fever, maybe there was something about it that could help.

Strangely enough, it seemed to work, at least on some of the patients. An hour after she served wortflower-root tea to four Roman fever patients, one of them knocked gently on the glass and asked Hazel to bring over a deck of cards so they could play whist. The next day, she powdered the wort-flower root and applied it to their boils.

Their scarring didn't heal, but the improvement from the powdered root was undeniable: flesh that had been angry and red with streaks of chartreuse became pink and smooth. The first Roman fever patient who arrived at Hawthornden, a fisherman named Robert Bortlock with white whiskers and a nose shaped like a turnip, had even begun to ask for seconds at breakfast.

The scabs from the Roman fever, which were healing over on the patients' backs, reminded Hazel of the drawings of smallpox she had seen in her books.

She knew the story of Edward Jenner and the smallpox vaccination, of course—how the English physician had noticed that the local milkmaids seemed to be the only ones not succumbing to smallpox, and how he hypothesized that their exposure to cowpox had somehow taught their bodies to fend off its deadlier human cousin. Lord Almont had once even hosted Jenner at one of his salons, and though Hazel had been too young then to absorb what he was saying, she recalled his wispy gray hair and the white handkerchief wound tightly around his thick neck and tied in an elegant square bow below his chin.

But inoculation had existed before then, for decades. Scientists understood it conceptually, that you could train a body to fight a deadly disease by introducing a weakened version of it, and before Jenner and his cows, people were using the healing smallpox scabs, ground into a fine powder needled beneath the skin.

Why had nobody tried it with the Roman fever? It was an illness on a much smaller scale than smallpox, certainly, but surely if the same technique worked, physicians in Edinburgh could save thousands of lives. Was it possible that there were so few healing cases of the Roman fever that inoculation didn't even seem like a possibility? Hazel imagined there should at least have been something in the literature, an essay in the *Scottish Journal of Medicine* or a study published in London. But she found nothing. She decided to write to Dr. Beecham at the Anatomists' Society and ask his opinion.

Dr. William Beecham III
The Royal Anatomists' Society
Edinburgh

Dear Dr. Beecham,

I pray this letter finds you well, and I assure you that I continue to study hard for the Physician's Examination. As part of my education, I have begun rudimentary examinations of several fellow Scotsmen and -women suffering from a variety of medical ailments, including, I am sorry to say, the Roman fever. I hope you'll forgive my impudence, but I wanted to ask your opinion on the matter. Has any experimentation been done with regard to inoculation against the Roman fever? On the advice of a local boy and his memories of a childhood folk remedy, I treated patients with a tea made of wortflower root, and upon seeing positive results, I added a poultice of powdered wortflower root to the dressing when I bandaged their boils. The effect has been encouraging. So encouraging, in fact, that I wondered if the healing scabs could be used in an inoculation. I know that your schedule must be prohibitive, but if you do find the time, please write back.

Yours most sincerely,
Hazel Sinnett
Hawthornden Castle

At the very least, he could point her in the direction of the proper literature from the scientific community. But in the most secret parts of herself, Hazel did fantasize about what his reply might be, the chance that he might write back with his ink splattered in excitement, every sentence punctuated with an exclamation point because *she had solved it, the answer had been there all along!* And no one need ever suffer from the Roman fever again, because her vaccine could be sent all over Scotland. Edward Jenner's namesake society would celebrate her with a dinner and gala event. The King himself would send for her to be presented at court. She would scarcely even need the Physician's Examination; she would instantly be the most famous physician in the kingdom, all before the age of twenty.

When she wasn't in the laboratory examining a new patient or on the first floor of Hawthornden Castle going cot to cot, Hazel found herself lingering in the entrance hall, hoping for Beecham's reply. When she heard a knock at the castle's front door, her stomach tightened into a knot. Outside the window, she could see Jack on the south lawn behind the castle, teaching Charles the basics of sword fighting.

"No, no," she called to Iona. "I'll get the door." Smoothing her skirts, she opened the door to find something even more unexpected than a letter.

"Greetings, miss," said the boy, sinking into a deep bow. His face and hair were streaked with soot. He offered her a grin with several missing teeth as he rose. "I 'eard Jack Currer's been hanging around these parts. Tell 'im Munro is back from the dead."

Dumbfounded, Hazel ushered the boy inside and helped to remove his coat. One of his sleeves flopped loose and empty. This boy, the missing Munro, had returned to the land of the living with only one arm.

28

UNRO DRANK TWO POTS OF TEA and ate a full tray of biscuits before he reclined on the couch, slapped his belly, and smiled out at Hazel and Jack, who had been staring at him with fascination ever since he arrived at Hawthornden Castle.

Munro smacked his lips. "Now, those were some fine biscuits, if I can say, miss. Fine biscuits indeed."

"Thank you," Hazel said.

"Munro," Jack said, unable to help himself any longer. "Where have you been? And how did you lose your arm!"

Munro exhaled with a heaving sigh, fluttering his top lip. "Shame, isn't it?" he said, lifting the empty left sleeve of his shirt. "Still, thank the good Lord it's not my shooting hand, eh? I reckon you get a pistol in my right hand, and I still take out half a dozen grouse before the master of the house knows I'm on his land at all." He turned and gave a saucy wink to Iona, who had been tending to the fire in the grate while pretending she wasn't listening intently to what they were all saying. "I cook up a mean grouse, roasted over a fire with some chestnuts in its belly if I can find 'em. Finest Christmas

I ever had was a stolen grouse and chestnuts, back in the old squat in Fleshmarket Close. Remember that place, Jack-boy? The roof half caved in and the floors bit by termites, but still not a bad place far as those things go."

"Munro," Jack said again. "Your arm. You've been missing. For *weeks*."

"Right, right. The story. 'Fore I start, just supposing it were possible to get more of these biscuits? Oh, thank ye, love, you're an angel, really. From heaven above.

"Before I start, I should tell ye now, I don't remember it all. It comes and goes, like the fog. Like I'm seeing it all through the smoke of some'un's burning dinner. But I at least know where it started, that part is easy enough: I was on a dig in Greyfriars, trying to get the body of a poor bird who died with her baby still in her belly. Killed herself, they said. Boyfriend didn't love her no more. Arsenic, I heard. But o' course the family wouldn't admit it, so they just said it was the Roman sickness. Convenient excuse, having a plague running around the city, that's all I'll say.

"So I went round midnight to the kirkyard by my lonesome. Usually, would have been nice to have a partner in this sort of thing, but you know Bristlwhistle left for Calais and Milstone died last month—tragic thing, tragic—and who else of the crooks am I supposed to trust? Specially when I was looking to make a fortune with that poor pregnant girl. I've been working this game long enough that I don't like to split the profits if I don't have to. When you've been poor as long as I have, greed don't quite seem so bad of a sin, I think.

"So, yeah, I set out alone to Greyfriars in the night—didn't even bother to bring a torch, seein' how I know the grounds there so well. Could walk it blindfolded and not trip on a single stone, I'm telling ye. Not a single rock nor anthill in that place I couldn't sniff out on a moonless night and with both my eyes closed.

"The gate was unlocked. That was the first strange thing I remember. I hopped it out of habit, just in case, but I remember that very clearly. It was closed, mind you, but not locked. So course I assume someone else beat me to it, someone else is going to take my prize pig, so I race over to the grave and no one's there. Dirt tilled from the burial, but no one's dug it up. No one's in the kirkyard at all. No wind either. It was like even the ghosts stopped moving. It was so still I could hear my own heartbeat in my ears. I do remember that part. I don't ken if it's important, or if it means anything at all, but God's honest truth: that last night that I remember the night was as still as I had ever heard her. The lights were even out at George Heriot's. Not even a candle in the window.

"I get to digging, but before I get more'n a few inches into the ground, a man is suddenly standing right in front of me. That's the only way I can explain it, he just *appears* right before my nose. Didn't even hear him coming, couldn't even hear him breathing. He's wearing a hat that blocks his face, and in the dark I can't tell what sort of face is under it at all. But I still have my spade, mind you, and I hold it up at his face and tell him not to come a step closer. This is my body, I says, I found her, and what's more, I was here first. Any resurrection man worth his salt knows not to steal a body from someone who's already stealing it.

"But this man, this ghost or whatever he is, he just smiles something awful, and I see a row of yellow teeth in the shadows. And it's about then that I get the sense that I've seen him before, that he was one of the men that met me and Davey that night—you remember, Jack—and so I think, 'Oh, he's just a copper, then.' I make like I'm about to run, but before I can even tell my legs to get, the gent gets ahold of me and sticks a handkerchief in my face, wet with this sort of sweet-smelling—I don't know. Smelled like flowers, and like death. I tried to hold my breath, tried to struggle against him, but then everything got heavy and dizzy, and next thing I knew, it was sunrise, and he was wheeling me in a chair with a veil over my head.

"We were somewhere in the Old Town, I could tell from the smells and the way the cobblestones moved, and I'm pretty sure we crossed a bridge, but I couldn't tell where. I told ye, I had this heavy, black lace—veil or something—over my head and over me, like I was a widow in mourning or some'un's gran. I tried to run, but it was like my legs were gone and I couldn't move my arms. I could barely see out from beneath the fabric, so alls I could do was wait and hope he would leave me for long enough that I could somehow find a way to get free.

"We made it to a building with a golden plaque on the door, and the man in the hat knocked a few times, and they wheeled me in, through a big room and into another room like a theater. That's like what it was, I remember, a theater with rows of benches and everything, and sawdust on the floor—I could smell that, couldn't mistake it for the world.

"They pulled off my veil then. There was no one in the audience, just two tables on the stage, and a doctor in a coat. There was an old man sleeping on one of the tables. Maybe not old, it was hard to see, but 'e looked old enough to me. And must have been old to be sleeping. The man in the top hat took payment from the doc and left me staring out, hoping they wouldn't notice I was still alive when they had tried to kill me.

"The doctor sharpened a knife, and that was when I couldn't help myself—I called out, I suppose, or maybe just yelped like a dog. And then he got out his own handkerchief and poured some blue potion on it. I tried to move, I tried to run, I swear, but it was like I was strapped in even though my limbs were free. My brain had gone bad. He pushed the handkerchief up to my face and it was that same smell again—a body gone rotten, and some sweet flower like a lady's perfume. And then the room went dizzy and black and I couldn't cry out anymore. It was voodoo or something. It didn't hurt, thought it would, but it didn't. Felt like going to sleep and made the rest of my memories hazy. If I hadn't woken up without ol' lefty here"—he gestured with his head to the space where his left arm had formerly been—"then I might have thought that maybe I *had* dreamed it or maybe I had had too much at the pub the night before.

"Woke up at Saint Anthony hospital feeling like my whole body was on fire. Stuck in a cot with two poor souls, both stonemasons who had their legs crushed beneath a brick the size of Skye. Three of us made a sorry sight, I can tell you that."

"You don't remember anything else?" Jack said, leaning forward on his knees.

Munro shook his head. "They kept me in hospital awhile, trying to figure out how I lost me arm. I told 'em, about the man and the theater and the damp handkerchief and all that, but no one seemed to pay me any mind. Thought I was a common drunk who found himself in trouble, and I suppose I can't say I wasn't. Tried to get out of hospital quick as I could, mind you. Smelled like shit and death in there, and one of the blokes in my bed snored like an elephant who caught cold. Food wasn't too bad, if you were sure you managed to get the bugs out. Maggots are just like the rest of us, trying to get warm, trying to get a bite in their belly, can't fault them for that. Ay, think I can maybe get a swig o' something stronger than tea in here? Seein' as what I've gone through is more or less an ordeal, as they say."

Hazel nodded, and Iona went to get the whisky from the cupboard. "Did the doctors in the hospital say anything about your wound? Anything about why the arm might have been taken?"

"S'matter of fact, they did note that the stitches was particularly neat. Like it was all done by someone who knew what he was doing."

"May I?"

Munro shrugged and pulled his shirt off his left shoulder to reveal all that was left of his arm. It was cut at the joint; nothing below the shoulder remained. And, just as Munro had mentioned, the black stitches were small, and straight, and even. The wound sweated with a small amount of pus, and the skin around it was red and swollen, but the stitches were perfectly in place.

"But why would someone take your arm?" Jack said, dumbfounded. "I just don't understand it."

Munro's whisky arrived, and he thanked Iona with a wink and then took a deep swig. "Beats me," he said, wiping his lips with the sleeve of his remaining arm. "Not gonna be able to dig anymore, that's the shame of it. And how am I supposed to get honest work now? Couldn't get honest work when I had two arms."

"We'll find something for you," Jack said. "You can come work with me at the theater."

"Ay, there's a laugh!" Munro said, croaking. "Haven't been gone long enough not to know what's going on there. Closed from the plague, innit? How's *your* work at the theater going, Jack?"

Jack sank in his chair.

"We can find something for you at Hawthornden," Hazel said. "We always need someone to help tend the grounds. And—and you shoot? I'm certain Cook would be delighted with a few more rabbits."

Munro puffed out his chest. "Even one-handed, there's no one in Scotland who's a better shot, I can promise you that. Thank you, miss. Most sincerely." And he swept off his cap and stood just to bend at the waist in a deep bow. A few playing cards and false coins fell out of his pockets onto the floor, and he blushed as he snatched them up.

"There's nothing else to the story? Nothing else at all you remember? Is it possible that there was a one-eyed man? That the doctor, in the operating theater, was wearing an eye patch?"

Munro took another sip of whisky. "That's the story. Stayed in hospital for a while till they sent me home, went to the pub, then came to find Jack here. As for the doctor . . . I can't say for certain. All of that part goes a bit hazy. I wouldn't even know his face if he had three eyes, if I'm telling the truth."

Hazel sat, thinking. Someone had kidnapped Munro, used ethereum on him—what else could it have been?—and took his arm. That was what she knew. The unknowns were *why* and *who*. The unknown who was worrisome, but not so worrisome as her next unknown: When were they going to strike again? Because it seemed, at least to Hazel, that whoever was kidnapping and maiming the poor in Edinburgh had no intention of stopping.

Hazel sent Charles to summon the police constable, who arrived at Hawthornden at sundown. He had a mustache as thick and straight as broom bristles, and his nostrils were flared in annoyance from the moment his boots crossed the threshold.

"Please, do sit," Hazel said to him. "Iona, fetch a fresh pot of tea."

"Thank you, miss," he said, and stiffly sat on the chair across from Munro, who was lounging on the couch. Hazel winced, seeing Munro through the constable's eyes: streaked with grease and soot, the sleeves of his shirt yellowing, the smell of booze floating around him like perfume.

"So," the constable stated when Munro's story was complete, "you got drunk and had a nightmare, and woke up without your arm."

Hazel stood in anger. "No, that's not it at all! Something is happening at the Anatomists' Society—whether or not someone there is directly involved, they're using the surgical theater. And using their ethereum. At the very least, you need to embark on an investigation!"

Now the constable rose. His mustache shook as he spoke, and clutched the drops of spittle that came out of his mouth with every punctuated *p* sound. "You—*miss*—do not tell me what I 'need' to do. In this or any case. Now, you come from a fine family, and I will assume this—this—this pitiable, pitiful charlatan has fooled you in a scheme for your sympathy and your money, and not that you have willfully summoned me here as part of a crude prank."

"Sir, you've misunderstood," Hazel said. "He's telling the truth. He's not the only one who's had body parts taken. Something—"

The constable interrupted her with a snort. He shook his head. "Your brain is too idle, miss. It runs away with you." He put his hat back on and leaned down close to Hazel to speak to her where Munro couldn't hear. "Between you and me, this sort of thing happens all the time with the riffraff from the Old Town. They find a sympathetic ear, and come up with all sorts of wild stories to arouse your pity."

Hazel twisted away from his grip. "I can assure you, sir, you are not correct."

The constable's upper lip twitched and his mustache vibrated. "I served with your father, in the Royal Navy, some years ago, against the French. I came here to Hawthornden as a courtesy. But I say to you now, miss: I hope your father returns before his daughter becomes a public disruption instead of just a fool."

29

N ONE OF THE ROMAN FEVER PATIENTS Hazel was treating with wortflower root were becoming well, but to Hazel's profound relief and surprise, none of them were dying either. It seemed as though she was able to contain the disease—limit its spread and mitigate its deadliness—even if she wasn't able to defeat it altogether. Yet.

Hazel took careful note of each of her patients and their progress. She had sent a copy of her notes in her letter to Dr. Beecham, to which, to Hazel's dismay, she had still received no reply.

"What could he be *doing*?" she moaned to Iona while removing a splinter from a young boy's shin. "How long does it take to write a letter?"

Iona handed her the cotton wrap and alcohol to disinfect. "It hasn't been very long, miss. He is a quite famous doctor, isn't he? He probably gets lots of correspondence."

"Well, yes, I suppose," Hazel mumbled. The splinter slid out of the boy's leg before he even had a chance to cry out. "There you are. Right as rain. And avoid rickety banisters from now on. You're lucky a splinter was all we had to deal with."

Iona showed the boy out and brought in Hazel's next patient, a young man with red hair and a brown jacket that had seen better days. The boy looked weary and pale. His threadbare shirt was torn at the neck, and someone had attempted a repair.

"Burgess!" Hazel cried in surprise. She had to resist the strange urge to hug him out of sheer shock at seeing him like an apparition in her dungeon laboratory at Hawthornden.

"I—I'm sorry," Burgess said, pale eyebrows knotting in confusion. "I don't believe we've had the pleasure. But—they said that this was a place for treatment?" He looked beyond Hazel, assuming a male doctor was somewhere behind her. From one of the cots in the sunroom came a low moan.

"Gilbert Burgess," Hazel said again. "You don't recognize me. Of course." She pulled her hair up at the nape of her neck. "George Hazleton, at your service."

And then—whether it was shock or his fever or both—Burgess fainted.

J JUST CAN'T BELIEVE IT," HE SAID WHEN HE finally woke up in one of the cots in the castle. The examination hadn't taken long—he had a high fever and fresh sores forming all over his body. It was the Roman fever. Iona had brought him a bowl of oatmeal with jam. He stirred it absentmindedly, unable to bring himself to eat. "A girl, the whole time. Pardon me, a *lady*. And no one ever knew. God, I would kill to see the look on Thrupp's face about now."

"Well, someone knew. Dr. Straine recognized me, and had me banned from lectures."

"We wondered where you went when you disappeared. A few of the boys thought you got sick, or rushed into a marriage or something like that. Thrupp tried to convince us that you were on the run from gambling debts, but I know that was a load of bollocks."

"How are things going there?" Hazel said, trying to keep her voice casual. "At the lectures, I mean. What sort of things have you been learning?"

Burgess looked sheepish and stared into his bowl of oatmeal, which had turned a pastel pink from the raspberry jam. "I dropped out," he admitted. "Few weeks back. I could blame it on the sickness, but really I just was in over my head. My family could barely afford the tuition fees as it was—we borrowed from every relative with half a pulse—and it would have been more than I could bear if I failed the examination after all that."

"So you dropped out? Burgess, no!"

Burgess brushed her off. "Nah, it's for the best. I woulda made a lousy surgeon. Not like you—*you*! You were brilliant. I can't believe they kicked you out of lecture just because you wear a skirt. The nerve of those men, really. Straine, I swear, I wanted to throttle him half the time. Gives me the creeps, the way he just *stands there*, you know? With that look in his eye?" Burgess shivered.

"Well, I might still be a surgeon yet," Hazel said with a small smile. "Or rather, there's a chance." She explained the arrangement she had made with Dr. Beecham, how she would still be allowed to sit for the Physician's Examination to see if she would pass. Success would mean an apprenticeship at the hospital under Dr. Beecham himself and women permitted in the lecture from that point on.

Burgess's spirits lifted as she told him. "That's marvelous, Hazel, it really is! You have to pass. Course you will, you're genius at this stuff."

"Well, you're engaged, aren't you?" Jack said from the corner. Hazel hadn't even noticed him sitting there, reading from one of her paperback books. "Even if you pass, is your new husband going to let you do anything with it at all?"

"I don't think that will be his decision to make," Hazel said stiffly.

"I bet he's going to think it is," Jack said with ice in his voice.

"Uh, belated congratulations!" Burgess said, breaking the tension. "On your engagement! Who's the lucky man?"

"Thank you. And he's the future Viscount Almont, actually."

Burgess's eyes widened. "Hazel, that's—oh, *buttons*! I can't be calling you Hazel! Lady Sinnett, I mean. Lady Almont, rather."

"Hazel is fine," she said. "I've been engaged to him practically since birth. He just wanted to make things more official, is all. We won't even be wed for another year, so it's not as though my life has changed in the meantime in any practical way. The Physician's Examination is a far more pressing concern than my silly marriage."

Jack exhaled hard, snapped the book onto the table, and left the room. Hazel ignored him and turned to face Burgess fully. "Please tell me you remember something Dr. Beecham said about lymphatic system structure, because I am completely hopeless with it."

From that day on, Burgess was her personal tutor and champion. Whenever Hazel finished examining whichever new patients arrived to the laboratory and when she completed her rounds of the patients already in the cots inside Hawthornden Castle, she went to Burgess's bedside, and he helped Hazel study. Burgess was a brilliant quizzer, with a knack for asking exactly the question Hazel was hoping she could slip away with not quite knowing.

By the time the letter from Dr. Beecham arrived with Charles, Hazel was so distracted with naming all the bones of the inner ear for Burgess that she scarcely registered what she was holding in her hands until the parchment was open in front of her.

Dear Miss Sinnett,

What an unexpected pleasure to hear from you. I do hope you recall our wager and that your studies are progressing in time for the Physician's Examination. I must confess a profound hope that you succeed.

Unfortunately, I have no more positive tidings to deliver in this letter. Inoculation was tried in Edinburgh back during the Roman fever's first wave with no positive effects. On the contrary, the few patients who suffered its experimentation succumbed to the illness itself.

I am not familiar with the "wortflower root" you named, and I must assume it is a regional name for a local plant with another, more proper name. Nevertheless, I assure you both I and my esteemed grandfather in his lifetime experimented with a wide variety of the local Scottish flora and found nothing to mitigate the horrible and deadly effects of the sickness.

I must advise that you cease all trials and not continue to treat unfortunate victims with unfounded folk remedies. Do not continue the use of "wortflower root" in any form. Positive effects in the short term may belie deadlier consequences to come. If you are to become a physician, you will learn swiftly that the well-being of the patient must supersede a doctor's overzealous ego.

Fondly,
Dr. William Beecham III

Hazel read the letter, and read it again. She felt as though she had been slapped across the face. She let the paper fall from her hands, and Burgess picked it up, silently mouthing the words as he read.

"Well, I think it was a good idea," Burgess said finally. "And the wortflower root tea has been the only thing since I got this blasted fever that's made me feel like my head wasn't keen to explode, whatever Dr. Beecham says. He's not so all important! You know his grandfather went mad at the end? Alchemy and the like. Maybe the lot of them are mad. Forget it, Hazel."

Hazel nodded absentmindedly. She had been foolish and overambitious. She was just a child, when for years some of the most esteemed physicians in the world had been working on the problem of the Roman fever and it had come to nothing. She hadn't even passed the Physician's Examination yet, and she was arrogant enough to believe that she saw something that Dr. Beecham hadn't. Her cheeks burned, and she tore the letter from Burgess's hands. She ripped it into pieces and tossed them into the fire, not out of anger, but out of a deep humiliation.

"It's no matter," Hazel said, reaching to take the mug of tea Burgess was drinking from his hands. "We'll listen to the experts, at least for now."

Burgess pulled the mug away and took another sip of it in protest. "Not a chance."

"Fine," Hazel said. "Have it your way, but if something goes wrong, let it be on your conscience now."

Burgess took another deep sip. "It's just tea," he said. "And it makes me feel better. I don't know what Dr. Beecham was going on about, but you're the one treating me, not him, and for what it's worth, I trust you, Dr. Sinnett."

It was almost enough to make her smile.

She hadn't smiled much in the past few days. Besides the fact that she was still waiting for Dr. Beecham's reply, Jack had all but disappeared from Hawthornden since Munro's reappearance, trying to find a new job.

"You can stay here," Hazel had whispered to him a few days after Burgess's arrival, while she was still in bed. He pulled on a well-worn shirt and the jacket that he'd left hanging on the back of her chair.

"I can't just stay here," he said, splashing cold water from the basin onto his cheeks. "I need to find work. Who knows how long it will be until the theater's open again. If it's too dangerous to steal bodies now, I need to find something else."

"It *is* too dangerous, Jack," Hazel said. "We don't know who took Munro or why. And the police aren't going to help resurrection men—assuming they're not the ones doing the taking. Please, please promise me you won't go out resurrecting again."

"I promise," Jack mumbled. He laced his boots, kissed Hazel on the forehead, and left Hawthornden on foot. She hadn't seen him since.

20 December 1817
No. 2 Henry Street
Bath

My most darling Hazel,

Word of your engagement has finally reached us in Bath, and I am most positively delighted. What joy to know you will be taken care of and your dear cousin Bernard will finally become your husband. The only recent incident that has brought me as much joy is Percy (finally!) recovering from his cold.

I look forward to seeing you and your husband-to-be in London during the social season. As you know, Percy will be attending Eton next year. I think I might remain in London to be near him in case his cold returns.

I am very proud of you.

—Your adoring mother, Lady Lavinia Sinnett

30

SHE WAS MARRYING A DUKE OR A COUNT OR an earl. One of those. What was the difference? And what difference did it really make? They all lived in big houses and did nothing for a living but order servants about and choose which embroidered handkerchief to keep in their pocket that day. No wonder noblemen had time to invent medicines and maths—they had to, out of sheer boredom.

The theater was still closed, thanks to the sickness. Jack hadn't made a steady wage in months, and without the bonus of new bodies to sell the anatomists, his situation was becoming more and more precarious.

He tried the shipyard first, hoping that being young and relatively fit could secure him a job building ships. But work in Leith had been slow. The foreman laughed in Jack's face when he asked about a job. "Had to dismiss twenty men this year already," he said. He sniffed and spat away from Jack. "Sorry, lad."

It seemed everywhere he tried, there were a dozen other

men, older and more experienced, waiting for their chance to meet with the boss and beg for a decent day's wage.

"There's work in Newcastle, I hear," one man whispered to Jack after they were both turned away from being bricklayers. "If there's nothing keeping you here. And the Americas—there's real money to be made there if you can stand the journey."

Jack nodded politely, but the thought of putting another mile between himself and Hazel felt impossible. Where could he go when she was here? But how could he ask her to give up an earl when he couldn't even make a decent wage? Recently, seeing her face—clean but for the sweat from leaning over bodies and treating new patients—had made Jack feel deeply ashamed of himself, as if the two of them were entirely different species. He was good at selling bodies, that was the God's honest truth—good at digging without being caught, and negotiating with the physicians in their ruffled linen shirts for a few extra quid.

Even with the kidnapper, it couldn't be more dangerous than working in the quarry or the mines. Jack could fight them off; he was smarter than Munro, and a hell of a lot better at fighting. He had made a promise to Hazel, that was true, but she never spent a night hungry the way he had, clenching his fists around his blankets and hoping to fall asleep sooner so he wouldn't have to feel his stomach tightening and contorting any longer. She had never known the isolation of living in a city without a coin in her pocket, knowing that she'd have nothing but her wits to use to fend off cold or exhaustion. She had always been safe.

Poverty made Jack vulnerable, but it also made him reckless.

 AVE YOU HEARD OF THE PARADOX OF THE ship of Theseus?"

The dinner party at Almont House was ostensibly to celebrate Hazel and Bernard's engagement, though the two of them were seated at opposite sides of the banquet table and Hazel was trapped next to Baron Walford, who had been gradually leaning closer and closer to her as he spoke, while Hazel desperately tried to lean as far away as her chair would allow her without toppling over. Four courses in, the baron was so close Hazel could see the spittle on his lips. His acrid breath made her blink back tears.

"Yes, my lord, I actually—"

"It's a complicated philosophical idea, but one I can explain simply enough for a woman by means of a story. Imagine a large ship. Over time, pieces of the ship become rotted. But each rotten wooden plank is swiftly replaced. Over time, every piece of wood that was used to construct the original ship is replaced. Is it still the same ship?"

Lord Almont stood a few seats down. "No!" he said with

delight, pointing at Walford. "Different ship. All different wood."

"Ah," said the baron. "Then *when* would the ship no longer be considered the same ship?"

The lord's outburst had caught the attention of the room. Bernard rose like his father. "Halfway, then. When half the wood is replaced, it stops being the same ship."

"Even if everyone is still calling it the ship of Theseus?" Hazel said quietly.

Everyone turned to look at Hazel. Bernard glared at her. "Yes, darling," he said through gritted teeth. "No matter what people call it. When it's more than halfway, it's not the same ship."

"Some women," Lord Almont said to his son, "have yet to learn that we enjoy looking at them more than *listening* to them."

Baron Walford giggled, and his false eye rolled in its socket. "Aha! But now, return to the ship. Imagine that they've taken all the rotten wood that's been removed, and started to build a second ship, in the British Museum. Which ship would be the real ship of Theseus then? The one still sailing with the original's name, or the one in the museum?"

"The second one," Bernard said immediately. "The second one. The one with the original wood."

"We have a true scholar in our midst!" Lord Almont shouted, clapping Bernard on the back. Bernard beamed.

"Indeed," Baron Walford said, swirling a glass of red wine before emptying it in a single sip.

"Why so philosophically minded, Walford?" Lord Almont asked.

"Well," Baron Walford said. He adjusted his false eye. "I think I might be in the market for a new eye. Scheduled the procedure. Week from Monday at the Anatomists' Society. Going to see for the first time in twenty years, least that's what the doctor says."

"What do you mean?" Hazel said, sitting upright at attention for the first time all evening. "What sort of procedure is going to let you see again? What sort of new eye?"

"Now, now, *darling*," Bernard said.

"Baron Walford, I don't mean to intrude, but please— what sort of surgery could possibly give you back your sight? From a false eye?"

Baron Walford patted Hazel on top of her head. "Nothing a young woman need concern herself about! Not when she has a wedding to prepare!"

"Yes," Hazel said. "A wedding. Of course."

FTER DINNER, THE GENTLEMEN RETIRED TO the library for brandy and cigars, and Bernard stepped out to escort Hazel back to her carriage.

"Hazel," he said after clearing his throat as soon as they were outside. "Your—the fantasy of being a . . . a physician or what have you."

"It's not a fantasy, Bernard," Hazel said. "I'm going to become a physician. I know it's not what *you* or your father want, but I have been studying for weeks now." Once she started talking, she found she couldn't stop.

Bernard looked around nervously.

"I'm good at this, Bernard, I really am. I didn't always believe I was, but I am. I've been treating half a dozen patients—I am *currently* treating half a dozen patients. I delivered a baby!

I am going to pass my examination, Bernard, and I am going to become a physician. I'm actually fairly certain I already am one."

Bernard's mouth gaped and then closed like a beached fish's. "Hazel, calm yourself!"

"I am calm, Bernard. Perfectly calm. But I have to tell you, if you're not going to let me continue this, I'm not certain I can marry you."

Bernard glanced back at the closed door of Almont House, as if he were considering reentering and speaking to his father. He tugged at his waistcoat. "Fine. Well, all right, now. There's no need to say that, Hazel. Let's be rational."

"I'm perfectly rational, Bernard."

Bernard cleared his throat again. "All right. There's an examination, you said? Some sort of examination to be a doctor?"

"The Royal Physician's Examination, yes. In a week's time."

"A week's time," Bernard repeated. "Perfect. You take this—this Royal Examination. And if you pass, we can . . . well, we can at least talk about how this looks as a . . . future."

Hazel brightened slightly. "So you're saying there's a chance? I mean, a chance that you might be willing to let me . . . let us . . ."

Bernard rubbed his temples. "Just . . . Fine. Take your test, and then. And then, we'll figure it out from there. But, Hazel, I swear to God. I swear. If this test doesn't work out, promise me, this is over. And my father can never find out about this."

"Never," Hazel said.

"Do you *promise me*, Hazel?"

"I promise."

"Good." Bernard kissed her on the top of her head and helped her step into her carriage. "Sweet thing. Careful not to jostle on the street!" he shouted up to the driver. "That's my future wife in there!"

32

OR WEEKS, THE DATE OF THE Royal Physician's Examination at the end of the semester had seemed so distant to Hazel, an abstraction that would never actually materialize. And then, all at once, it was upon her. In the end, the information she had learned through endless hours of reading and memorizing her copy of *Dr. Beecham's Treatise* seemed almost comical when compared with what she had learned in the few short weeks she was actually serving as a physician for those who came to Hawthornden. Beecham had been correct in doubting Hazel when they had initially made their wager; if she had studied from books alone, she never would have felt ready. Now she almost did.

The morning of the examination, she read through her notes while spooning oatmeal into her mouth, barely comprehending that she was eating at all, so focused was she on the words in front of her. Pulmonary system? Lymphatic? Organs? She mentally checked off each area she had studied one by one, surprising herself with the realization that maybe she was ready after all.

"Stop that," Burgess said, eating his own porridge with a

vigor that made Hazel smile. He was improving. Though he still sometimes gave a rattling cough, the lesions on his back were shrinking. And his appetite had returned.

"Stop what?" Hazel said without pulling her eyes from her parchment, letting a glob of oatmeal fall into her lap.

"Studying. You know it all forwards and backwards. There's no one in that examination who's going to be half so good as you, and you know it."

"Thank you, Burgess. And thank you for all your help."

Burgess gave a weak laugh. "Feels off that you're the one thanking me, seeing as you've all but saved my life."

"A treatment is good," Hazel said. "A cure is better."

"Well, I have no doubt it'll be here sooner rather than later if Dr. Hazel Sinnett is on the case."

"I'm not a doctor yet."

"Give it a few hours."

She gathered her quills, ink, and knives, and her *Dr. Beecham's Treatise,* more for luck than anything else. "Has Jack come by recently?" Hazel asked Iona as she helped to lace her boots.

Iona shook her head. "Not for a few days, I'm afraid." Then, seeing the nervous look on Hazel's face, Iona continued, "Though there's nothing to worry about with that lad. Could get himself out of any trouble, you know Jack. Slipperier than an adder, and twice as clever."

Hazel could only manage a nod. Jack was fine. She needed to focus on the examination today.

Initially, she had planned on taking the examination dressed as George Hazleton; she had pulled out one of George's best jackets for the occasion, and kept it in her clothing press so it greeted her every morning as a reminder of the task to come. But when the time came to get dressed in the morning, she hesitated. She wasn't taking the examination as George Hazleton; she was taking it as Hazel Sinnett.

And so Iona helped her instead into a dress that had arrived from the seamstress only a few weeks earlier, one Hazel had yet to wear. The skirt was white muslin and lined with ribbon at the hem, before it cascaded into delicate layers at the ankles. The bodice was bloodred silk, with puffs of white linen at her shoulders. The neckline reached her chin, a reminder to keep it high.

"Don't be late now," Iona warned her as she finished lacing. "You've reminded me a dozen times, and I haven't forgotten: it's eight o'clock on the nose."

Hazel straightened the cuffs of her gloves. "I won't be late. Trust me." She still remembered her first morning trying to sneak into Dr. Beecham's surgical demonstration at the Anatomists' Society, and being on the opposite side of a locked door when the bell rang out through the city.

There was still frost on the ground when she set out to the carriage, dew frozen solid in the night and crystallized. Hazel relished the crunch of her shoe on the grass. This was going to be a good day, she thought.

Her confidence lasted until the carriage finished its climb up the slope to Edinburgh's Old Town; through its window, Hazel caught her first glimpse of other prospective physicians marching toward the examination room at the university. They were, as a whole, a serious group, men in dark coats and worn boots, with spectacles and expressions of intense concentration on their faces. They walked across the cobblestones gazing at their feet, brows furrowed. Hazel's stomach clenched and her breakfast turned to bile in her throat. The rocking of the carriage was going to make her sick. "You can stop the carriage," she called out to the driver. "I'll walk from here."

The cold greeted her as she opened the door—her dress was too thin for the December chill, and she had forgotten to bring a fur. Hazel walked at a quick clip to warm herself as she headed over the bridge and toward the university. No one paid her any mind as she whipped along the stone street, past shops smelling like warm meat and day-old ale, beggars curled under blankets under their eaves; past mutts with stiff coats of hair whipping their muscular tails in excitement at whatever scraps had been let out, children playing a game with cups and dice; past a man in a tall hat wheeling a veiled figure in a chair.

Hazel froze. The man and the chair disappeared behind a corner into an alley. How had Jeanette described it to them? Her dream of a veil. And then Munro had told the same story. He had described this, *this exact scene,* being wheeled through the city beneath a heavy black veil. No one on the street but Hazel had stopped or noticed anything unusual. To their eyes, it was an elderly widow in mourning, or an invalid spending a morning out of the house.

Hazel held her breath for a moment and watched as the man and the chair wheeled off the main street and into an alley, the close leading toward the Anatomists' Society. Hazel stepped forward, unable to resist peeking around the corner. She saw the swish of a cape and a closing door to confirm what she already knew: whoever was in the wheelchair was being delivered to the operating theater.

A bell went off in her mind. Today was Monday. Baron Walford was getting his surgery today, at the Anatomists'

Society. Wasn't that what he had said? What was happening behind that closed door?

She had plenty of time before the examination—she had set out so early that she could have walked from Hawthornden to the university and still been settled in her seat when the examination began, with time to fill her inkwell. There was surely no harm in just . . . poking her head in. Seeing what they were doing. It was certainly nothing. Baron Walford had been drunk at the dinner, anyway. He was probably just being fitted for a new glass eye, and the woman in the chair was . . . an elderly widow meeting her grandson, a visiting scholar.

She had time. She had plenty of time. Hazel wished Jack were here, able to talk sense into her, tell her if she was being ridiculous, if she should ignore the baron and the woman and stay focused. Stay focused on getting to the university, on the examination, on her future. But Jack wasn't here; he was somewhere in the city without her, and it was just Hazel standing alone on the busy corner, biting at the flesh of her cuticles while she mentally played out each alternative.

The choice was made for her the moment she saw the wheelchair disappear behind the door, when her heart began pounding in her ears and her excitement and fear made the hair on the back of her neck stand up. Hazel pulled off her hat, looked around to see if anyone was watching her, and disappeared into the small alley to the side of the building, where only a few months before, a boy she didn't yet know as Jack Currer had shown her a secret entrance.

From <u>Dr. Beecham's Treatise on Anatomy:</u>
<u>or, The Prevention and Cure of Modern Diseases</u>
(17th Edition, 1791) by Dr. William R. Beecham:

The purpose of a physician is to protect and serve his fellow man. That is the singular directive of those who commit themselves to this illustrious profession: help those in need. The purpose of study should be the expansion of knowledge, but never for its own sake. Leave knowledge for its own sake to the philosophers. A physician's life is too short to waste it in idle academia—if he uses his mind, he should also be using his hands.

33

THE STONE HALLWAY WAS DARKER THAN Hazel remembered, and narrower. Spiderwebs clutched at her skirts, and she tried to suppress a sneeze from the dust that floated in the air, hovering in the thin rectangles of light that had managed to push through around the edges of the splintering door behind her. It became darker the farther Hazel walked, and colder. Ten steps along the hallway, she deeply regretted her decision; she should be sitting in the examination hall at the university, smirking at Thrupp's taunts because she knew she could handle anything the examination threw at her. Her parchment would have been neat, her handwriting impeccable. Maybe she would have come first in the class. The minutes were ticking by.

She shook her head as if to banish the thoughts. She would still be able to make it. She had plenty of time. The floor began to slope downward slightly, and Hazel heard the quiet lilt of voices from the other side of a door she couldn't see in the gloom.

"—means that you won't feel a thing, I assure you."

"—Gone through the procedure myself—"

"We chose this one because he's young, see? Worth the extra thrippence, I promise ye that."

Hazel turned the heavy metal knob and winced at the squeak. She waited for shouts, for the tempo or temperature of the murmurs on the stage to change, but they hadn't heard her. Hazel opened the door an inch, just enough to let a crack of light through, and then, when there was no reaction from the men on the stage, she opened the door far enough to allow her to turn sideways and slip through.

The smell of straw hit her first—fresh straw had been deposited on the floor of the stage and beneath the risers, presumably to soak up blood. Hazel gave silent thanks for all the etiquette lessons her mother had insisted upon to teach her quiet, ladylike steps, and she crept slow as a sigh through the shadows as far as she dared.

Without the camouflaging benefit of a hundred men's legs hanging off the stands, Hazel was forced to stay far back, close enough to make out the scene on the stage in rough shapes only. There was a man sitting up on a surgical bed, talking jovially. It was his voice that echoed through the hall. The veiled body was still in its chair, with the man in the tall hat standing menacingly over its shoulder. And in the center of the stage of the operating theater, brandishing the blue bottle of ethereum in one hand and a lace handkerchief in the other, was a doctor.

The doctor wore a leather butcher's apron, and a strange contraption covered his face. The contraption looked like goggles, but instead of two pieces of glass, it had only one. One circular magnifying glass in the center of the doctor's face, concealing his identity and turning him into a creature out of Greek mythology. There he was: the one-eyed man Jeanette had dreamed about, a distorted cyclops with a round glass eye set in brass. His magnified iris flashed blue and undulated through the glass like ocean water.

"The ethereum is the key here, my lord. Perhaps you saw my demonstration earlier in the season?"

The figure on the bed rose on its elbows. "I can't say I did, Doctor."

The doctor wet the handkerchief with the iridescent blue liquid. "Well, the effect is quite remarkable. I find that patients have likened it to a good night's sleep. You wake up in a few hours' time feeling quite refreshed. At worst, it's akin to a bad night's sleep. The worst of it will be the soreness in the new eye, but that should abate within a few weeks. You'll find the blurriness improves day to day."

"I much look forward to that, Doctor, I tell you." The figure was Baron Walford, dressed in a plain linen shirt but unmistakable. He smacked his lips audibly and reclined back onto the table. "Do your worst, Doctor," he said. "I look forward to being rid of that dreadful false eye once and for all."

The doctor's expression was invisible behind his glass. He brought the ethereum-soaked handkerchief down on the baron's face, and then he turned to the veiled figure in the chair.

"If you will, sir," the doctor said to the man in the tall hat.

The man whipped the black veil off the figure in the wheelchair and revealed a boy, a boy with blond hair so dirty it looked almost brown, with his hands bound in his lap and a rag tied around his face to prevent him from screaming. The boy wriggled against his constraints, whipping his body back and forth to try to free himself. Even from her distance, Hazel could make out the raw panic in his face, which was turning beet red.

"Now, now," the doctor cooed, and he rewet his handkerchief with the ethereum before pressing it into the hostage's face. The boy struggled against his captors, and then went limp.

"There we are," the doctor said. "Let's get him onto the table. If you will, sir?"

The man in the tall hat helped the doctor lift the boy out of the chair and toward the long table in the center of the stage, directly beside where Baron Walford was lying peacefully as if he were merely asleep. The boy's body dragged lifeless as a rag doll's.

"A nightmare to find the right eye color," the man in the tall hat said, his voice rough as gravel. "Got me a dozen lads before I landed one with the right shade. 'Mahogany,' innit? Tell me them peepers ain't mahogany."

"Yes, yes," the doctor said. "I can imagine the trouble. But for what this fine gentleman on the table is paying, I think it serves us to give him exactly what he wants."

The man in the tall hat cleared his throat. "How much *is* he paying then? This sort of thing?"

"Now, now, Jones, you know I find it uncouth to talk about money. But I assure you, enough that he should be able to request his new eye will match his old." The doctor adjusted the lens of his magnifier and selected a scalpel from the table. "The procedure itself is fairly simple, especially because the client didn't have an eye to begin with. The socket has already been primed. Now all we need—"

He lowered the scalpel with a repulsive squelch onto the

face of the boy, who was unconscious but still bound at the wrists. The boy didn't stir as the doctor's knife dug below his brow bone and carved a thick gash down his nose. "Out we pop," the doctor said, and took the boy's left eye out from its socket. "Jones, please fetch mungroot powder, silver dust, and the poultice I keep in the black jar from the cabinet, if you will."

The man in the tall hat was staring at the open gash in the young boy's face and smiling a terrible, wolfish smile. He nodded and obeyed, bringing the three ingredients the doctor had requested back to the table.

"It's magic is what it is, Doc," the man in the tall hat murmured as the doctor gingerly dabbed a drop of the poultice into the baron's empty eye socket and followed it with the boy's eyeball.

"Not magic at all, Jones," the doctor said with more than a little impatience, continuing to dress the eye socket with the powders. "Nothing more than science. And, of course, an understanding of the human body perfected over decades of practice." He chuckled a little, his focus still on the operation before him.

Hazel was frozen with terror. Her voice was trapped in her throat; her feet were rooted to the floor, heavy as if they were made of molten steel. In her mind she thought of the things she *should* be doing, the actions she should be taking: interrupting with a shout, knocking the knife from the doctor's hands or, at the very least, running away to get help, to get the police constable again, drag him down the passageway in the alley and force him to see what was happening. Somewhere in the back of her mind, she felt the faint tug of the examination. It had probably already started, but maybe if she ran, she would be able to make it. But her body would not obey her mind. The terror inside her had become a living thing, a monster that turned her veins into frozen ice and her muscles to water. She could do nothing but continue to watch as the doctor completed his terrible operation, securing the boy's mahogany eye into Baron Walford's swollen, ruddy face.

When the surgery was complete, the doctor stepped away and examined his handwork, cocking his head. He wiped his knife on his apron and then reached into a pocket and pulled out a tiny vial of something brilliantly golden and glowing. It lit the doctor's face from below, bright as a candle. "There we are. Just a drop to keep the infection away and make sure the new eye takes," he murmured, and delicately tilted the vial so that a single golden drop fell onto the baron's face.

"What should we do with him?" the man in the tall hat said, cocking his head toward the bound boy, whose now-empty eye socket was spilling a river of blood over the table and onto the straw below. "'E's bleeding something fierce."

The doctor was distracted, with all his attention on the baron. "Oh," he said. "Cotton in the wound to stop him bleeding." He tutted and gave the boy a quick glance. "Not sure this one is going to survive, bless him. We'll keep him here for a few hours, see if he recovers. If he dies, send him behind the poorhouse. You know what to do, Jones. It's the Roman fever if anyone asks." He turned back toward the baron, leaning in close to appreciate his own work, the hundreds of tiny veins he had placed and sealed to give the man the new eye he was paying for. "Some of my best work, I think, Jones."

"And some of your fastest too," the man in the tall hat replied. "Done in half the time of some of your other work."

"Well, I did try," the doctor said. His hair was slick with

effort. He pulled off his magnifying lens and wiped the sweat from his forehead with a gloved hand, and then Dr. Beecham turned to the bleachers of the surgical theater and looked directly at where Hazel was standing. "After all, we had an audience today."

34

EFORE HAZEL COULD MOVE, THE MAN in the tall hat had his rough hand around her elbow. He had advanced like a hound in the shadows, so quickly and silently that he was pulling Hazel forward, out toward the stage of the surgical theater by the time she cried out.

"Miss Sinnett," Dr. Beecham said, wiping the blood from his gloves. "Welcome. I confess, I am actually delighted you thought to witness my surgery this morning. I always find my hands steadier when I'm performing for someone. How dull to make art in an empty room, a symphony gone unheard. And you're one of the few who I believe may actually appreciate the gravity of what I do here. The rest of them"—he gestured to the sleeping baron, whose eye was now padded with cotton—"are perfectly content just to get what they want. They pay their fee, and the deed is done. No curiosity. No interest in science beyond their own silly little purposes. It's tragic, in its own way, how small their lives are. How little they care for the world outside their own bodies. But you. You, Hazel Sinnett, you understand. The examination was this morning, wasn't it? I suppose this means you forfeit our little wager. No matter really, no matter at all. I'm so much happier that you're here.

"You understand how miraculous it really is, to take a living part from one man and transpose it into another, to restore the gift of sight via, well, a gift on the part of our generous donor. It took me years to be able to do eyes. Fingers, easy. No time at all. Full limbs, a natural progression from there. Now, the *heart* I haven't quite mastered. Still working on the transposition of a heart. But I'm optimistic yet. The heart will be next for me."

Hazel sputtered, struggling against the viselike grip of the man in the tall hat. All the questions she wanted to ask bubbled up in her chest at once, and the one that escaped her lips was, "What are you doing?"

Beecham stopped wiping his gloves. "What am I doing? My dear, I thought that was obvious?"

Hazel jerked her elbow away from the man in the tall hat, and Beecham raised his hand, indicating that his lackey could stand down. "You're—you're kidnapping people. You're taking poor people, and then operating on them. Using your ethereum, and taking things from them. Limbs, organs, eyes."

"'Taking' is such a crude way of putting it," Beecham said, wincing slightly. "You've lived a very sheltered life, Miss Sinnett, I doubt you know the terrible nature of the way things happen in Edinburgh's Old Town among the truly poor and destitute. These people are thieves and criminals. They lose their limbs and lives in meaningless, terrible ways every single day. This thief here could have died of hunger or consumption, or in a brawl or a thousand other ways. A knife in a pub fight could have taken his eye tomorrow, and no one would care. I simply give order to the chaos. I give meaning to their lives."

"You're a murderer," Hazel spat.

"Perhaps," Dr. Beecham said lightly. "But I also bring life. I save lives with the bodies I kill. Poverty is the real murderer, Miss Sinnett. I didn't create the poor who suffer living twenty to a room in squalor, working twenty hours a day just for a scrap of meat. Is that a life to begin with?"

Hazel looked at the boy with the blond hair and the river of blood pouring from the place where his eye once was. His hair was matted with blood, but his chest still rose and fell faintly with thin breaths.

"He could die! That boy there is dying and you would have killed him because the baron wanted a new eye."

Dr. Beecham chuckled slightly. "Yes, I suppose this instance does seem a bit vain, doesn't it? The wealthy want the best. It started with new teeth—most if not all surgeons are capable of creating false teeth from someone else's mouth. But I'm the only one capable of doing more. And most everyone wants more. And they're willing to pay. Not every transposition I do is for vanity, my dear. This year alone I've done—let me see now—two livers, a uterus, and a lung. All to extend the lives of those who spend their time on art and literature and music and science. Taken from those condemned to suffer lives of misery and toil. Now, tell me, is that wrong?"

Hazel could not tear her eyes away from the boy bleeding on the table with shallow breaths. "Please!" she shouted. "Please, he's dying."

A shadow of disappointment crossed Dr. Beecham's

face, but he carefully replaced it with his pleasant mask. He clicked his tongue. "I so would have wished you could grasp the larger implications here, Miss Sinnett. Really." Anger crept into his voice. "Don't you *see* what I've done? Don't you appreciate it?" He stuck one gloved finger into the bloody socket of the boy on the table, pressed, and twisted. "No, I don't think you do. He's probably going to live, I would say. If the shock were going to kill him, it would have done so already. I think I did him a favor, actually. He was begging on the street when my associate found him, and I hear boys with physical deformities evoke far more sympathy in pass-ersby. He would probably thank me if he could. Humanity is far larger than the sum of its pathetic individuals, and the chosen few are capable of such miraculous achievements. Do you believe God mourns when insects are crushed beneath stones while man is building towers, and cathedrals, and uni-versities?"

Hazel shook her head. "You're not God," she snapped.

Beecham laughed. "If only you knew, Miss Sinnett. The things I have become capable of in my life. The things I have done to the human body. The things I *can do*! But, no—I get ahead of myself."

"What would your grandfather think? Dr. Beecham, in his treatise, the things he writes about protecting mankind, and serving as a—a vessel for the betterment of humanity—"

"My grandfather? What would he—? Oh! Oh, that's rich, that's rich indeed." Beecham laughed again, throatily. He wiped a tear from his eyes. "Those words were written by a fool. A young fool who had yet to live. I promise you, Miss Sinnett, I am far wiser than my *grandfather* who wrote those words so long ago."

Hazel's eyebrows knitted together, but before she could say anything, a knock on the door behind Beecham interrupted them.

"Another delivery," said a muffled voice from the other side.

"Enter," Beecham said.

Two men carried a stretcher between them, with a body hidden beneath a sheet. The men were odd looking, one short and bald, the other half hidden behind a wide walrus mustache. They looked familiar, but Hazel couldn't quite place them.

"Found this one digging for bodies in Greyfriars last night," said the one with a mustache, revealing a row of grotesquely yellow teeth as he spoke. "All alone. Think we scared 'im 'alf to death."

Hazel's stomach knotted. She took a step forward, but the tall man behind her wrapped his beefy arm around her neck, holding her in place. "Oh no you don't, missy," he growled in her ear.

Dr. Beecham sniffed. "Swap out the baron on the stretcher and put the body on the table. The baron can convalesce in the recovery room." The two men carrying the stretcher nodded and set to work. They deposited the sheet-wrapped body on the table next to the bleeding boy. Baron Walford was hoisted onto the stretcher and removed from the operating theater.

"A corpse?" Hazel asked quietly.

"Not yet," Beecham said simply. After the two men had closed the door behind them, Beecham removed the sheet on the second body.

"*No!*" Hazel jerked against the man restraining her. He

tightened his grip. She stomped on his feet and tried to work her elbow into his gut, but he showed no reaction or weakness. Lying there, on the table, calm as if he were sleeping, was Jack. "No!" Hazel shouted. "Please, no! Anyone but him. Please."

Dr. Beecham paused. He looked interested. "You know this boy?"

Hazel thought about what she could say. "I—" Her voice faltered. She shook her head. "Please, just let him go."

"I'm fascinated what a young lady of your social standing would be doing associating with a resurrection man. How you even crossed paths in the first place. Fascinating, truly."

By now, tears were streaming down Hazel's face, messy and wet, catching in her nose and mouth. "Please," she begged, her voice leaving her. "Please."

"Miss Sinnett, I am about to teach you a very important lesson. I have lived a very long life—yes, longer than you might imagine—and attachments, like whatever silly little bond you might have with this boy lying on the table, serve no purpose. Pleasure is fleeting. Science, the information you can gather, the things you can learn—*these* are what last. These are what make a legacy. People like you and me, Miss Sinnett, have the potential to usurp God himself." His face darkened. "Attachments are pain. You may think you understand pain, Miss Sinnett; I'm sure I thought I did, too, when I was your age. But strength comes in the ability to overcome those human impulses. Sentimentality. Treacle."

Hazel couldn't speak. She struggled against her captor even as her muscles seemed to weaken and the room around her began to sway and spin.

"I think I'll take his heart," Dr. Beecham said, a small and wicked smile pulling at the edges of his lips. "I've been meaning to practice a transposition with a heart. It's perfect." He gestured toward the first boy lying on the table. The bleeding in his eye had stopped, and instead become clotted maroon and brown. His breathing had stopped. "Here is a body, ready to take it. Let us see if the resurrection man can resurrect him."

"You can't," Hazel said. "You can't."

Beecham just gave her a sad little smirk and pulled a knife from his table. The knife was eight inches long, mottled with stains from previous surgeries, but still so sharp Hazel could see the glint from its edge.

Jack began to stir on the table.

"Jack!" Hazel shouted. "Jack, please wake up!" The tall man put his other hand over her mouth to muffle her screams.

Beecham lowered the knife into Jack's chest. The blood sprayed, striking the left half of the doctor's face, making him look deranged. He yanked the knife out and had raised it to make his next incision when Jack's eyes twitched and he shuddered against the table.

Dr. Beecham sighed. He put the blade down and picked up the blue bottle of ethereum. Slowly and deliberately, while the blood burbled out of the wound on Jack's chest, Beecham dampened another handkerchief. "So few people know how to do a job well," he said just as Jack's eyes flickered open.

Hazel's fingers found a freshly sharpened quill in the pocket of her cloak, and then everything seemed to happen at once. In a single motion, she whipped it out and stabbed the chest of the man behind her. He stumbled backward, clutching at the place where the quill now stood out from his chest at a perfect ninety degrees. "Jack!" Hazel shouted. "Jack, the handkerchief!"

Jack roused on the table, coming to just as Dr. Beecham turned to see what Hazel had done, watching his henchman fall to the floor. Jack sat up and pulled the handkerchief from Dr. Beecham's slack grip. As if by reflex, he pressed the handkerchief to Dr. Beecham's face with surprising force, and held it there until the doctor fell into the bloodstained hay beneath the table on the stage of the surgical theater.

For a moment, Hazel and Jack just stood, panting and disoriented. And then she ran toward him and wrapped him in an embrace. He collapsed when she pulled away, buckling at the knees. Beecham had made only one incision, to the left of his heart, but it was deep. "Hazel," Jack breathed, his face draining of color.

"We're going to get you help," she whispered back. "Shhhh. Shhhhh. It's all right. You're going to be fine now." Hazel pulled one of Jack's arms over her shoulders and managed to guide him into the abandoned wheelchair at the side of the stage. The front of her dress was slick with his blood, but Hazel barely noticed. Dr. Beecham lay flat on the stage, knocked unconscious by his own ethereum. The man Hazel had stabbed with her pen had fallen to his side. She didn't know whether he was alive or dead; all she could think about was getting Jack out, and getting him safe.

The street arrived in a blur of color and smells, everything spinning, everything too bright, no one stopping to help them. They needed somewhere safe, somewhere quiet. Hawthornden was too far; Jack could be dead by the time they made it to the carriage. Hazel didn't know where the closest hospital was. "Excuse me," she said to a man taking long strides past them. Her voice shook and she sounded crazy. The man gave her a pitying look and continued striding past. From somewhere above them came the splashing sound of a bedpan emptying into the gutter. She needed to get Jack off the street. "It's going to be fine," she murmured to him. Jack moaned in reply. "Keep pressure on the wound if you can."

From South Bridge, she saw a glint of sunlight reflecting off a familiar dove-gray top hat. "Bernard!"

The hat turned. Bernard lifted a hand to block the sunlight and make out who had called his name. "Is that—? Hazel, my word. What are you doing here? What is—?"

"Bernard, I can explain it all later, I swear. Can I bring him to Almont House? He was stabbed, I'm afraid he's going to die."

Bernard hesitated for just a moment. "Yes, of course. Here, let me help you."

The two of them together managed to wheel Jack down Lothian Road, past Saint Cuthbert quicker than Hazel would have managed on her own. "Who's he?" Jack croaked as they turned onto Princes Street, twisting his neck to stare blankly at Bernard.

"Shhhh. Hush now," Hazel said. "We're almost there."

To his credit, each time Bernard looked at Hazel with his mouth agape, as if he were about to ask one of the many questions no doubt on his mind, he shook his head slightly and returned his gaze straight ahead until the pair of them reached the servants' entrance of Almont House.

"There'll be a bedroom on the second floor that's empty," Bernard said. Two footmen came out to assist when they saw the group approaching, and helped Hazel gently lift Jack up the staircase in the servants' corridor to a small room with a bare cot. Though there was a minuscule window above the bed, the room was still deep in shadow. "Could we get a candle, please? And a basin of water? And linen cloth if you have it?" Hazel asked.

Once Jack was lying down, Hazel was able to better see the extent of his injury, the damage that Beecham's knife had done to his chest. Gingerly, she started to peel away Jack's shirt, though some of the cloth was stuck, crusted to the dried blood. The wound was deeper than she had thought; the flesh around it was already hot and bright pink, and the stab wound, several inches long, burbled with fresh purple blood. Bernard winced and retched, then left the room, and Hazel got to work.

Once Jack's skin was cleaned, Hazel could finally exhale, release the breath it felt like she had been holding tight in her chest for hours. The wound was deep, yes, but it also hadn't hit any vital organs, and it being such a clean incision, Hazel was able to stitch it up neatly and keep the skin together to prevent infection.

Sometime in the afternoon, Jeanette entered the room, her hair tucked under a maid's bonnet, with a stack of clean linen clothes and flint to start the fireplace. "When Hamish—that's the footman, I mean—said we had a lady doctor come in, I figured it had to be you, miss." Her eyes landed on Jack's stomach. "That's Jack," she said, her face blank as a confused child's. "That's Jack there. It's Jack."

Hazel nodded.

"Jack," she repeated numbly, seemingly unable to accept it. She took a step forward and handed Hazel the linens. "Jack wouldn't get hurt. Jack never gets hurt. Jack wouldn't die."

"I don't think he's going to die, Jeanette," Hazel said. "I think he's going to be all right."

At that, Jeanette gave a strange barking laugh. "Well, course he is! He has a doctor like you."

Hazel smiled weakly. "I'm not really a doctor yet, Jeanette."

"More of a doctor than plenty of those frauds at the alms-house," Jeanette whispered, newly energized and tending to the fire. "'T'least you listened to me. Anyone else would have said that I was mad."

Once the fire crackled in the grate, the two women sat vigil over Jack for a short while until Jeanette stood. "I'll bring up some dinner for you. Ye must be famished."

Hazel hadn't thought about food all day. She had no idea how long she had been in the room with Jack, only that the small square window, formerly in sunlight, now showed dusk. Jack was sleeping, but his breathing was steady and even. His eyes flickered and Hazel could make out the red blood vessels that traced their way beneath his eyelids. She ran a finger along his cheek, the pale skin darkened by the shadow of his unshaven stubble.

The moment was so quiet and so intimate that Bernard, standing in the doorway, glanced at his feet in discomfort. Instead he exited, and returned a few seconds later with a brief rap of his knuckles on the cracked door.

"I saw a maidservant about to come up with your dinner, so I figured I would bring it myself," Bernard said, depositing a plate of roasted chicken on the small desk pressed against the hall. He sat down in the only other chair in the room. "I hope I'm not disturbing anything, my love?"

"Of course not," she said, looking away.

"Good. And he's— How is he doing?"

"He's going to be fine," Hazel said, looking down at Jack's face. Had he always been that beautiful? Had his lips always curved in a Cupid's bow that way, so that a fingertip would fit perfectly in its arc? Had his ears always been so soft and downy, curled like shells? Had his hair always been so thick and curled? His chest, she could see even through the bandages, was broad but concave at the collarbone. Hazel wanted to rest her head against it forever.

"I suppose now you might be able to tell me what the hell is going on," Bernard said, trying to make his voice sound friendly.

Hazel described it all, the bodies that she had found missing limbs and organs, and then, finally, what she had seen when she sneaked into the Anatomists' Society. "They're taking poor men and women from the streets and selling their bodies, piece by piece. He uses this—this ethereum to cause them to be unconscious while he operates, and then he— Beecham had something else, some vial of something that he used during the surgery to make the parts take. I don't know how, exactly, I don't know what it is, but Jack—I mean, this boy and I barely escaped with our lives."

"And this boy is—?"

"He's a resurrection man. A body snatcher who sold corpses from graveyards to physicians and anatomists to study from. I bought from him. To study for the examination. But he's a respectable man—he is. He works at Le Grand Leon. He's a good man."

Bernard nodded, showing no reaction on his face but never looking away from Hazel. He remained silent for a full minute, and so Hazel began again.

"Bernard," Hazel said, her voice grave. "Something serious is going on. Something real. I don't know how many are dead or how many are going to die or be hurt still by Dr. Beecham. I need you to go to the police constable about it, or tell your father about it, but you need to be the one to do it. They'll believe you; they have to believe you. You're a viscount."

"Son of a viscount."

"It doesn't matter. You know it doesn't matter. I tried to talk to the constable, and he all but ignored me. But now I've seen it with my own eyes, Bernard, I swear it's true. You believe me, don't you? He gave Baron Wolford a new eye today! Next time you see Baron Wolford, he'll have a new eye! Tell me you believe me."

"I believe you, Hazel," Bernard said. "After all, you're my fiancée. You and I are supposed to trust each other." He stood stiffly. "I'll go then, and see you soon." He kissed Hazel dryly on the cheek. "Until then, my love."

Hazel didn't take her eyes off Jack. If she had, she might have seen the thing that raged like smoking coals behind Bernard's eyes.

35

IT WAS TWO DAYS BEFORE JACK felt well enough to travel by carriage to Hawthornden Castle, and another week—of Cook's porridge and Hazel's attentive bandage changes—before he felt well enough to walk. The stab wound scabbed over without infection, and the day after Jack had managed a slow amble around the castle gardens without doubling over in pain, he told Hazel it was time for him to go back to Le Grand Leon.

"Just to check on some of my things," Jack said. He had a few pounds safely hidden in a knothole in the ceiling boards, and two clean shirts—though Hazel had cleaned and scoured the one he'd had on when he was stabbed, it was still stained pink with blood at the breast, and he was never comfortable in the itchy fine fabrics of the shirts he borrowed from Hazel's brother, the one who died. Hazel agreed, so long as he promised to return that evening.

"You need a fresh dressing and bandages if you're going to heal properly. Just what you'd need, to deal with an infection at this stage."

"Ay, fair enough." He hesitated, then leaned as if he were

going to kiss her. But instead he blinked quickly a few times and clenched and released his fist. "Goodbye, then," he said, and turned before Hazel could respond.

Hazel watched from the window as Jack and the carriage disappeared around the bend, where the few brittle leaves that had clung to the trees against the winter frost blocked it from view.

JACK HADN'T THOUGHT HOW DIFFICULT IT would be to climb up to the nest he had built for himself in the rafters of the theater while trying to keep his chest stitches from splitting. Halfway up the ladder, he had to pause and catch his breath. He was just contemplating whether it was worth it to continue up when he heard a knock on the theater's front door.

The knocking was hard and persistent. Strange. The theater had been closed for months. Jack had come in the stage entrance, through the alley, and Mr. Anthony had all the other keys to the place. There was no one knocking at the front door who had any business being at Le Grand Leon.

Jack waited, listening to the sounds of the building shifting in place, wood creaking and cold air whistling through the places in the ceiling where the beams didn't quite come together. The knocking came again, the stern cracking knock of determined knuckles. The knocking didn't stop, and so Jack shuffled through the dust-strewn lobby to reach the front door, pocketing a small knife and keeping his fingers wrapped around the handle just in case.

"Jeanette? That you?" he called. There was no answer.

He pulled open the door to reveal the police constable, two guardsmen, and the magistrate. On instinct, Jack tried to run. The constable pulled Jack into a rough grip with his hands behind his back.

"Hey!" Jack shouted. "Hey! What are you doing?"

"You're under arrest for the murder of Penelope Harkness, Robert Paul, Mary McFadden, and Amelia Yarrow. And no doubt countless others. Sickening." The constable spat on Jack's boots.

"There's some mistake. I'm telling you, there's some mistake."

One of the guardsmen found the knife in Jack's pocket. He brought it out and displayed it for the magistrate, and then put it in his own pocket, shaking his head in disgust.

"Hey, that's mine! Give it here!"

The magistrate cleared his throat and looked down over his nose at Jack, although they were the same height. "We were told we might find you here. Seems some of your little friends at the close on Fleshmarket aren't so trustworthy as you might want to admit. Thieves, murderers, betrayers. God have mercy on all your souls."

"You're lying," Jack said, wriggling against the grip. "You're lying. This is a joke! Why would I murder anyone?"

"Have you been selling bodies to the Anatomists' Society?"

Jack's mouth went dry, and his tongue seemed swollen.

The magistrate smiled. "Stands to reason an industrious young man like you would have wanted to cut out the middle man, so to speak. No need to waste any time waiting around for a funeral when you can just kill someone yourself."

"That's a lie," Jack managed to whisper. "I never killed anybody. I sold bodies, I did, but I dug them up."

The magistrate ignored him. "Very convenient, doing the killing during an outbreak of the Roman fever. Not many people would have been willing to get close enough to check the cause of death."

The police constable nodded. "He even came to me, had convinced a young lady of some elaborate scheme. Covering his tracks. Tried the same thing on the viscount's son." He sneered. "Thank God and King that the young Lord Almont was clever enough to see you for what you are. How many more would you have killed just to line your pockets?"

"Find Hazel Sinnett!" Jack said. "Find her, the lady of the house at Hawthornden Castle. Find her and bring her here, she'll set you right."

The police constable jabbed his elbow into Jack's stomach, knocking the wind out of him. Jack doubled over, but the two guardsmen kept him from falling. He felt his stitches break, and the blood from his old stab wound began leaking onto his shirt. "Don't go telling us what to do, murderer. And how dare you try to blacken the name of one of your social betters."

𝔈𝔡𝔦𝔫𝔟𝔲𝔯𝔤𝔥 𝔈𝔳𝔢𝔫𝔦𝔫𝔤 𝔗𝔬𝔲𝔯𝔞𝔫𝔱

22 December 1817

RESURRECTION MAN TAKEN TO TRIAL FOR MURDER

Yesterday, the Court proceeded to the trial of Jack Ellis Currer, indicted for murder. No trial in recent years has aroused such an intense interest in the general population: In the hour before the prisoner was brought to the bar, the doors of the Court were besieged by a large body of the public trying to get a glimpse of what will surely be an historic proceeding. Lord Maclean and another noble Lord were seated on the bench in the minutes before ten o'clock.

Currer is of tall stature and was dressed in a tattered navy surtout. Nothing in his physiognomy indicates any peculiar harshness of disposition, except perhaps the stern cut of his chin and severe brow. Over the course of the day's proceedings, Currer appeared deeply troubled, although he displayed no expressions of remorse.

Dr. William Beecham III was called to the stand to testify that he had seen Currer hanging around the Royal Edinburgh Anatomists' Society on a regular occasion, looking for clients to purchase his grisly wares. Bernard Almont, of Almont House, son of the Viscount Almont, later testified to the fact that he heard Currer make a full confession when Currer believed he was close to death after a stabbing in a game of cards gone wrong. Currer had been living illegally in the closed Le Grand Leon theater, where the police apprehended him.

Edmund Straine, a doctor at the Anatomists' Society, has also been indicted, for the illegal purchasing of corpses.

36

ON CHRISTMAS DAY, HAZEL WALKED THROUGH the Old Town, her head straight and gaze down. She had decided to walk from Hawthornden, along winding lanes firm with December frost and through miles of empty farmland. Her feet ached, but she barely noticed. There was only the barest awareness that her heel was bleeding, that the wetness was working its way through her stocking and to the leather of her boot's sole. The wind, and the world, had numbed her, and nothing hurt her anymore.

It had been a week since Jack was arrested. Her mother and Percy were still in London and would stay there for the remainder of the year. She was in the city all alone.

The narrow cobblestone streets were quiet, as if all of Edinburgh had found comfort around Christmas hearths, clutching their loved ones close as the threat of the Roman fever continued to loom like fog outside. Hazel had given Iona, Charles, and Cook the day off. There was only one person she needed today.

The classroom was exactly how Hazel remembered it, from months and a lifetime ago. There was no lingering odor of blood or rot—the room had been cleaned after the semester's end, and Hazel entered to the smell of wood varnish and alcohol.

Dr. Beecham was standing at the lectern, organizing some papers. "Just a moment, Miss Sinnett," he said without looking up. "I'm just preparing for my next semester of students after the holidays. You wouldn't believe how much still needs to be done. The paperwork, my god." He shuffled a few scraps of parchment into neater rows and then sighed and looked at Hazel. "Hello, then."

"I came to return your book," Hazel said. She tossed his copy of *Dr. Beecham's Treatise* onto a desk, sending up a small puff of dust. From the pocket of her cloak, she withdrew the small diagram of the hand and fingers that had fallen from its pages. She had kept it safe, a totem of sorts that she had felt linked her to the doctor and writer she once admired so much. She had been staring at it the previous night when the strange pieces of her hypothesis came together. She had examined the evidence. She had determined her conclusion.

"You were welcome to keep the book. I have several copies of my own," said Beecham flatly.

"I finally understand," Hazel said. "I don't know how I didn't before, how I missed it for so long. No, of course I know how. Because it's ludicrous. And I thought it was impossible. But I did always believe the original Dr. Beecham was the greatest physician in the world, so I suppose I should have thought him capable of anything. Thought *you* capable of anything."

Instead of replying, Beecham stepped out from behind the lectern. He flexed his fingers in the black leather gloves he always wore and raised an eyebrow.

"Take off your gloves," Hazel said.

Wordlessly, Beecham obeyed, carefully peeling away the leather from his wrists and then gently tugging each finger until both his hands were naked.

Every single one of Dr. Beecham's fingers was mottled and dead, ten fingers from ten different hands. They ranged in skin tone and size, sewn to Beecham's hand with thick black stitches, neat but visible.

"As you can see," he said, "my handiwork wasn't always so masterly as it is today." He displayed the fingers for Hazel to see, flipping each hand a few times. "May I?" Hazel nodded, and Beecham replaced his gloves. "Fingers were the easiest thing to lose, early on. And before I perfected my tonic for limb transpositions, I'm afraid I just did the best I could. Injuries are so easy when death never comes. So there it is. You discovered my little secret. May I offer you a cup of tea?"

"So it's true, then," Hazel said. "You're the only Beecham. You're the one who wrote the book, the treatise. You—"

"Solved the puzzle of immortality," Beecham said. "The ultimate aim of any physician, I imagine. Turns out the rest of them just weren't as clever as I am."

The thoughts in Hazel's mind fit together with a satisfying click. "There never was a son, let alone a grandson. Only you."

Beecham consulted with the kettle in a small fireplace behind him. "That actually is where you are incorrect, Miss Sinnett. There was a son. Two sons, my boys Jonathan and Philip. And my beautiful daughter, Dorothea. And my wife, Eloise. Early on, I thought that my biggest struggle with immortality would be my limbs and my organs deserting me one by one. And then I realized it would be watching everyone I loved die around me. When Eloise was dying in childbirth, I begged her to take my tonic, pleaded with her on my knees so that she would survive, and live alongside me. She refused. I thought she was a fool. Most days I still do. But on days like today, on Christmas, well, sometimes I think perhaps she was right all along. I wish I could see my children again. She is spending eternity with them, and I am still here." Beecham poured himself a cup of tea. "Do have a cup of tea. It's a marvelous oolong. And I haven't been able to talk to someone as, well, myself since Eloise died. It's surprisingly freeing."

"How did you do it?" Hazel asked, unable to resist.

Beecham smiled like a cat, and from deep within the breast pocket of his jacket, he withdrew a small vial of gold liquid.

Up close, it rolled like magma or liquid mercury, viscous and glistening at its edges with a metallic gleam, but still translucent. It was a universe encased in glass, infinite and eternally changing. "A tonic," he said. "My tonic. If you're asking how I came to discover it, I suppose the only answer is fear. Fear of death. Fear of being forgotten. I knew even from childhood that I was destined for something greater than the tannery where my father worked, where he expected me to work. It wasn't until much later in my life that I actually perfected the tonic. It took nothing short of obsession. If you were hoping to know what the tonic actually contains, well, Miss Sinnett, I decided long ago that the formula would belong only to me. Let's just say the answer is 'sorcery.' Isn't all science magic to those who don't understand it? The burden of knowledge is that it turns the world mechanical. I am immortal in a world in which all the miracles have been explained away." He placed the vial on the table. Hazel, still standing, locked her eyes on it.

"What does immortal mean, then?" asked Hazel. "In a technical sense. Do you age? No, I suppose. Can you be killed?"

"An interesting question! It's been so long since I've had an interesting question. Are you planning on killing me, Miss Sinnett? The simple answer to both your queries is no. Stab wounds, pistol wounds, strangulation. No effect. I imagine that a more systemic approach could do me in—taking apart the pieces, burning me to ash—but as you can imagine, I've been reticent to experiment thoroughly. Please sit. If I can't offer you tea, at the very least, I can offer you a chair."

Hazel organized her thoughts in her head. After a moment, she sat opposite Dr. Beecham and looked him in the eyes. "You're going to kill Jack Currer. They're going to hang him for the deaths of the people you killed."

Steam swirled above Beecham's cup. "You love him," he said simply. It was not a question, merely an observation. "Then I've done you the greatest service of all, Miss Sinnett. Love is nothing but the prolonged agony of waiting for it to end. The fear of losing the ones we love makes us do selfish and foolish and cruel things. The only freedom is freedom from love, and once your love is gone, it can be perfect, crystallized in your memory forever."

"He doesn't deserve to die," Hazel said.

"Every one of us deserves to die," Dr. Beecham said. "It is our only birthright."

"What of Straine?" Hazel said, "They arrested him too."

Beecham cocked an eyebrow. "You defend him? The man who thwarted your medical ambitions?"

"No," Hazel said. "Not him. But he's not guilty of this. I'm defending the truth."

Beecham took a deep sip of tea. "There is no truth, Miss Sinnett. Even the most basic so-called truths of our anatomy can be manipulated to suit new purposes. The only truth is power, and the only power is knowing how to survive."

He picked up the small vial of tonic from the table and stared at it. It had been gold when Hazel first saw it, but from a different angle, it looked almost glistening black.

"I have found a single drop of the tonic," Beecham said, "heavily diluted, is enough to ensure that the limbs and organs I transpose acclimate to their new body properly and without infection—I know you were wondering about that." He rolled the vial in his fingers. "This is the very vial I offered to my wife, Eloise, before she died. I have kept it with me ever since. You know, Miss Sinnett, in a hundred years, the notion of a female surgeon may not seem so absurd. And even less absurd in the hundred after that. You will be far better served in the centuries to come, and by then, you will have learned enough to be more brilliant than anyone can ever hope to be in a single lifetime. Here. Take it."

Hazel extended her hand on instinct, and then paused. In truth, moments before she had contemplated snatching it and running, but now she hesitated. "You give your life's work so freely?"

"Not freely, I assure you. You are only the second person to whom I have ever offered this vial, and the first I am certain could make excellent use of it. No matter what you think of me at this moment, Miss Sinnett, I know you will eventually come to understand the vastness of what I have achieved. Bodies littered the bases of the pyramids, my dear. All progress requires human sacrifice. They were the poor and the destitute. The city had already killed them, and I was just using every piece of the animal."

Hazel's ears rang and her heart pounded in her chest. She took the vial.

"How long will you stay here?" she asked, running her thumb along the vial's glass, which seemed to permanently remain cool. "In Edinburgh, I mean. How long before people notice you haven't grown older?"

Beecham took another sip of his tea. "It'll be quite soon for me, I'm afraid. I think I'll be off to America next. It's a vast country. An easy place for a man to disappear and make himself again. So no tea, then? Or perhaps something stronger! It is Christmas, after all. I think I have some well-aged brandy somewhere around here— Ah yes." From behind the podium, Beecham pulled an amber bottle. He poured a nip into his tea, and then a few fingers into a clean glass for Hazel. "I insist," he said. "It's Christmas."

"Cheers, then," Hazel said. She took a sip that burned her tongue and singed her throat all the way down.

Beecham raised his teacup. "To your engagement," he said, a twinkle in his eye. "I understand you were recently betrothed. Even dons hear the society gossip, I'm afraid."

Hazel shook her head. "It's funny," she said. "I suppose what you said was correct. Losing the one you love is the only freedom."

The morning after Jack was arrested, Hazel woke up with no self-doubt or fear. There was nothing that frightened her about a life without the safety of a title or a castle, about the wrath of her mother or the disappointment of her father. She would live as a witch in a hedge, stitching wounds and delivering newborns, if she had to. She would beg on the streets, work as a maid, sail to the Continent. The change was astonishing—a spark in her brain, a miracle of fluids or electricity, and now her life felt completely different. For the first time in her seventeen years, her life was her own.

She had burned every unopened letter that Bernard had sent by messenger since her refusal. The white lilies he sent she dropped into the stream below Hawthornden.

When Hazel finished her brandy, she stood and thanked Dr. Beecham for the drink. "Good luck in America," she said, and turned her back to leave.

"I do hope you take it," Beecham said. "I meant what I said, about the world not being ready for you yet. I would be delighted to see what you could accomplish in the next century. And I would finally have a scientific mind to keep me company."

Hazel turned. "The only use I have for immortality," she said, "is to discover if it will protect someone against a hanging."

Beecham stood in surprise, his mouth open. He blinked a few times quickly, and then sat again. "Yes," he said quietly.

"As a matter of fact, immortality is stronger than a broken neck and strangulation."

Hazel nodded at the doctor and left, and Beecham was alone in his classroom, the fire illuminating him from behind so he looked less like a man and more like a shadow.

37

THERE WERE NO VISITORS ALLOWED IN THE prison, but Hazel slipped a pound to the guard and he nodded and let her in. "Five minutes," he said, and then turned his back. The verdict had come back quickly. It had taken only four hours for a bench of lords to declare that Jack Currer was guilty and deserved to hang by the neck until dead. For his part in purchasing the bodies, Dr. Straine lost his medical license and he was expelled from the Anatomists' Society, although for days, a mob in the streets had been shouting that Straine should be hanged too.

Hazel had heard them as she walked through the Old Town, but as soon as she entered the prison, the thick stone walls dampened and deadened all sounds from the outside. Only quiet moans of madness and sorrow echoed through the prison hallways, harmonizing with the chittering of rats. They were the whines of those who know there is no one left to listen to them.

Jack had not testified in his own defense at his trial. He offered no excuses or explanations. Better to be thought of as a murderer than a murderer *and* a madman. Hazel had expected tears upon seeing him again, but there were none. They had all left her over the past few days. She was drained of joy and sorrow alike, fully numb and fully hollow.

Jack looked thinner than Hazel had ever seen him, sitting against the wall with his back curved into a C, rolling a die that they had forgotten to take from him after his trial on the floor. His hair hung long and lank, and his eyes were rimmed red with exhaustion.

When he saw her, Jack stood and walked to the bars, and he reached through so he could hold her hands in his. "Hazel," he said. "Hazel, my love." He tucked a strand of her auburn hair behind her ears. He was so close that Hazel could make out the freckles across the bridge of his nose and feel the warmth of his breath.

There was something in Hazel's fist, a small glass vial. Its strange luminescence was visible from between her fingers. Jack stared. He listened attentively while she described exactly what it contained, and the power it would give him. He asked a few quiet questions. Hazel answered.

She extended the vial through the bars, and Jack took it and rolled it around in his palm.

"So it's real, then?" he said simply.

Hazel nodded.

He held the vial toward the dim light of the small window to examine it. A tiny galaxy swirled within the glass. "Would you take it?" he said softly. "If you were me?"

"Jack, you have to take it. Please. Take it and come back to me. Meet me at Hawthornden as soon as you can. This is so we can be together. So we can run away somewhere. To the Continent. To start over."

Jack laughed then, a beautiful, brilliant sound filled with

all the joy and hurt and love he'd felt for Hazel in his brief time knowing her. It was his laughter that finally made Hazel cry. "Why are you laughing?" she said, and then she started to laugh along with him.

Through the gaps of the rusting bars, Jack pressed his lips against hers, and they both tasted the salt of their tears. "No. No, no, no, no, no. Hazel, if I do—decide to take this, I will be a man on the run for my entire life. Or at least for a good long while. My first lifetime and part of my second. You"—he kissed her again—"you"—and again—"beautiful"—and again—"perfect, you"—and again—"deserve a real life. You're going to become a brilliant physician. You're going to help so many people and change so many lives. You're going to light the world on fire, and you can't do that from the shadows. You can't create medicines and cures on the run. None of our greatest minds had to toil for their day's meals before their studying. No, Hazel. No. I can't do that to you."

"That's not your choice to make, Jack. I can choose where to live, and how. That's not a good enough reason."

Jack raised his eyebrows. "Arguing with me? I'm about to be hanged, and I can't get my way?" He smiled. "I suppose you're right. It isn't a good enough reason. Made it seem like I was being a hero when really I'm the one being selfish."

"How do you mean? How are you possibly being selfish?"

"Hazel, there's no hell worse than a world in which I would see you grow old and lose you and then be forced to live another day." The tears continued silently down Hazel's cheeks. "You will always be seventeen to me, Hazel Sinnett. You will always be beautiful and headstrong and brilliant. You will be the last face I see when I close my eyes and the first one I imagine when I wake up."

"Will you take it, then?" Hazel said quietly. "Will you take the tonic?"

"I don't know yet," Jack said. "I'm so scared."

A door clanged somewhere behind Hazel, and the heavy footfalls of a booted guard followed. "That's it, miss. Visit's over."

Hazel leaned forward to kiss Jack again. "I will spend my entire life loving you, Jack Currer," she said. Hazel stuck her hand through the bars to rest her palm on his heart, feeling the stitches she had sewn at the center of his chest.

"My heart is yours, Hazel Sinnett," Jack said. "Forever. Beating or still."

"Beating or still," she said.

THEY HANGED JACK CURRER IN THE GRASS-market the next morning at ten o'clock. They said there had never been a bigger crowd in Edinburgh for a public hanging, but Hazel didn't attend. They said his body was bought and taken to the university teaching hospital.

But they didn't say if it stayed there.

38

WHEN SPRING CAME AND THE FROST melted, and the stream below Hawthornden filled its banks, Iona and Charles were married in the garden. The bride wore a pink dress that Hazel had ordered from a seamstress in the New Town, and her braid was woven with small white flowers and greenery.

"Will you be all right?" Iona asked Hazel after the ceremony and the dancing, while Charles waited by the side of the carriage. The pair were off to Inverness for their honeymoon, and while they would be returning to Hawthornden in a month's time, they would no longer be living in the castle with Hazel. Charles and Iona would live in a small cottage together in the village, as husband and wife. With her father on Saint Helena, and her mother and Percy choosing to remain in London, Hazel would be living alone in Hawthornden Castle for the first time in her life.

Well, not alone. For the entire winter, the first floor of Hawthornden had been serving as a hospital, where Hazel treated patients suffering from Roman fever and worse. Use of wortflower root meant that not a single one of her patients had died, and Hazel was hard at work on an inoculation she believed could prevent the transference of the disease entirely. Dr. Beecham surely would have discovered it himself had the growing pile of bodies from the Roman fever and the fear it elicited not made such a convenient cover for the mutilations and murders he performed.

"I will be more than all right," Hazel said. In truth, she had been looking forward to it, the mornings of solitary walks, and time alone with her books, evenings curled up with a book on the windowsill while the rain fell on the other side of the glass.

"And you're certain you don't mind if Charles and I take the carriage?"

"Of course not, Iona. I have Miss Rosalind if I need to go anywhere. Perhaps I should get another horse for the stables," Hazel said. "In case she gets lonely."

The week after Jack's execution, Betelgeuse had gone missing. It seemed the horse was stolen in the night. Hazel hadn't heard anything from the stables, though—it was almost as if Betelgeuse had wandered away himself.

Iona hugged Hazel. "Please take care of yourself."

"Take care of *yourself*! You're a married woman now. That means no more foolishness," Hazel said, straightening Iona's braid.

Iona beamed. "Me, a married lady! Can ye believe it?"

"Of course I can," said Hazel. "You deserve everything you want in this world—and more."

Iona turned to gaze proudly at Charles, who was slapping dirt from his trousers as he leaned against the carriage door, and then she looked back at Hazel. "And you, miss. You deserve the things you want in this world."

Hazel found that the lump in her throat made it hard for her to speak. All she could do was hug Iona close one last time and watch as the carriage bounced up and away through the garden path and down the main drive.

Jack came to her in her dreams sometimes, his eyes warm and wanting. For the first few months, her pillows would be wet with tears in the morning, but even when the tears stopped, the ache was still there in her heart, heavy as a stone, the sinking feeling that came in the moment before she opened her eyes and had to remember that she lived in a world without him. She sometimes imagined him sailing for France, or the Americas, standing proud on the rigging of a ship somewhere while the sea crashed around him, the boy who would remain young and beautiful forever, the boy she had taught how to ride and whom she'd kissed in a grave. He sometimes spoke to her in her dreams, leaning in close to tell her quiet, tender things she could never recall upon waking. Hazel tried to stay there for as long as she could, in the dim half sleep where the shadows made themselves into Jack's proud profile, the contours of his face. She could see it: the slope of his cheekbones, his long, dark eyelashes, his stern brow—the hundred small places she had touched her lips to his skin.

But then the pale yellow light of morning would press its way into the corners of Hazel's bedroom, and Hazel would rise to begin her day of work, healing the living.

epilogue

THE LETTER ARRIVED AT HAWTHORNDEN Castle with burnt and yellowed edges, bent in odd places. It looked as though it had traveled around the world twice and spent most of its Christmas holidays folded in a child's sticky pocket. It bore a stamp from New York City.

The letter wasn't signed, but the woman who opened the letter knew exactly who it was from. She pinned it above her workstation so that she could read while she brewed wort-root tea and spun bandages and sharpened knives. She read it so often she could see the words in their spindly script when she closed her eyes.

My beating heart is still yours, the letter said, *and I'll be waiting for you.*

acknowledgments

THIS BOOK BEGAN AS A RAMBLING email that I wrote to my agent, Dan Mandel, while I was flying cross-country from New York to Los Angeles. To Dan, thank you so much for having faith in this project and in me, and sending me the encouraging messages I need when I'm close to breakdown. I want to thank Sara Goodman, and the entire team at Wednesday, including Alexis, Vanessa, Rivka, and Mary, for all of their tireless work, and Kerri Resnick and Zachary Meyer for a beautiful book cover beyond my wildest dreams. I'm wildly lucky to have a family that's willing to listen to all of my ranting ideas and celebrate my accomplishments and I'm especially grateful to my sister, Caroline, for reading every draft of this book. Heartfelt thanks to Katie Donahoe for her reading, her ideas, and her encouragement, and thank you to Ian Karmel, who supports me in every way it's possible to support a person.

I used a number of books to help research the early nineteenth century and the history of medicine, including *The*

Butchering Art by Lindsey Fitzharris, *The Royal Art of Poison* by Eleanor Herman, *Dr. Mütter's Marvels* by Cristin O'Keefe Aptowicz, *The Knife Man* by Wendy Moore, and *The Lady and Her Monsters* by Roseanne Montillo.

The story isn't over . . .

Don't miss the eagerly-anticipated sequel to Dana Schwartz's captivating gothic romance . . .

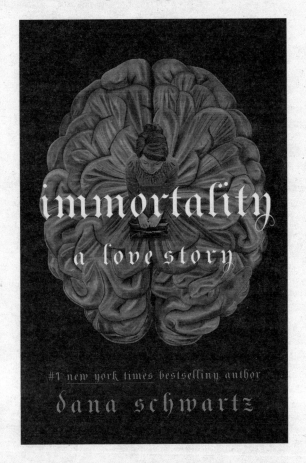